Christine Marion Frase
with world-wide reade
languages. Second you
independence during
Govan district of Glas
rare illness which lan
ended her formal educ
been an avid storyteller, now she began a lone apprenticeship in writing, but it wasn't till 1978 that *Rhanna,* the first novel in the popular series, was published. She went on to write seven more volumes about island life and is also the author of the successful *King's* saga, the *Noble* books, three volumes of autobiography and three romantic novels.

Christine Marion Fraser lives with her husband in an old Scottish manse on the shores of the Kyles of Bute, Argyllshire.

Praise for KINVARA and Christine Marion Fraser

'[*Kinvara*] is a story set in a small, remote Scottish community where the landscape is harsh, the coast is rugged and the inhabitants are colourful and memorable. … [A] lovely book and the author brings the people and the place of Kinvara alive'
Telegraph & Argus

'A rollicking good read … Fraser is Scottish publishing's best-kept secret' Jackie McGlone, *The Scotsman*

'Christine Marion Fraser writes characters so real they almost leap out of the pages … you would swear she must have grown up with them' *Sun*

'Christine Marion Fraser weaves an intriguing story in which the characters are alive against a spellbinding background'
Yorkshire Herald

Also by Christine Marion Fraser

Fiction
Kinvara

Rhanna
Rhanna at War
Children of Rhanna
Return to Rhanna
Song of Rhanna
Storm over Rhanna
Stranger on Rhanna
A Rhanna Mystery

King's Croft
King's Acre
King's Exile
King's Close
King's Farewell

Noble Beginnings
Noble Deeds
Noble Seed

Non-fiction
Blue Above the Chimneys
Roses Round the Door
Green Are My Mountains

Kinvara Wives

Christine Marion Fraser

coronet

CORONET BOOKS
Hodder & Stoughton

First published in Great Britain in 1999
by Hodder and Stoughton
First published in paperback in 2000
by Hodder and Stoughton
A division of Hodder Headline

A Coronet Paperback

10 9 8 7 6 5 4 3

A CIP catalogue record for this title is available
from the British Library.

Printed and bound in Great Britain by
Clays Ltd, St Ives plc

Hodder and Stoughton
A division of Hodder Headline
338 Euston Road
London NW1 3BH

To my niece, Lynn,
who has never forgotten
her Scottish connections.

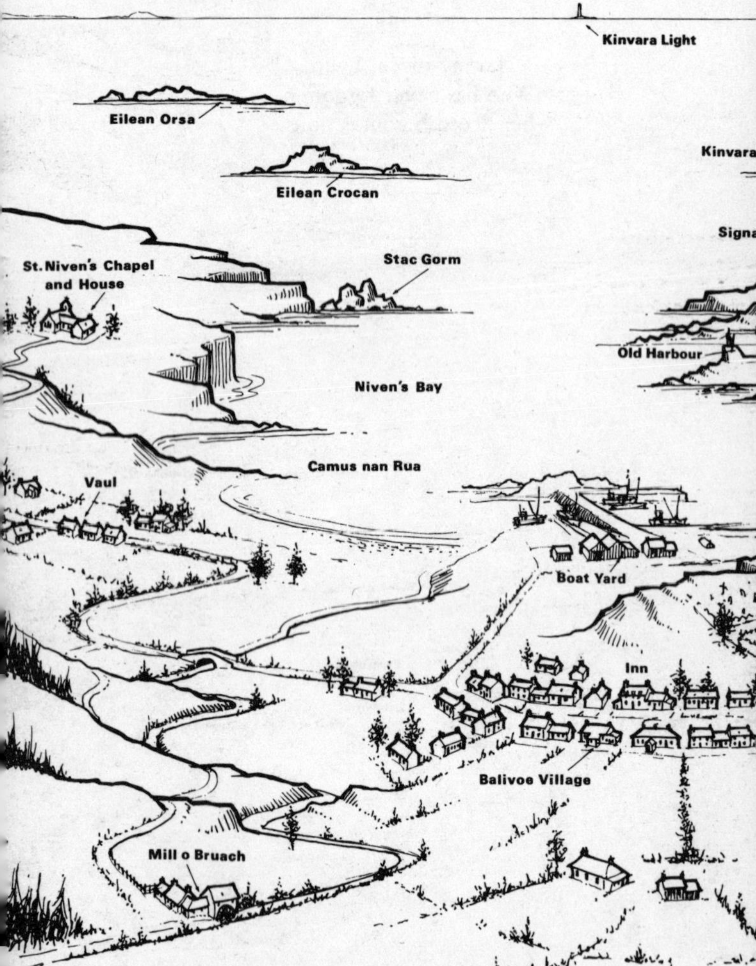
Kinvara Light
Eilean Orsa
Kinvara
Eilean Crocan
Signa
St. Niven's Chapel and House
Stac Gorm
Old Harbour
Niven's Bay
Camus nan Rua
Vaul
Boat Yard
Inn
Balivoe Village
Mill o Bruach

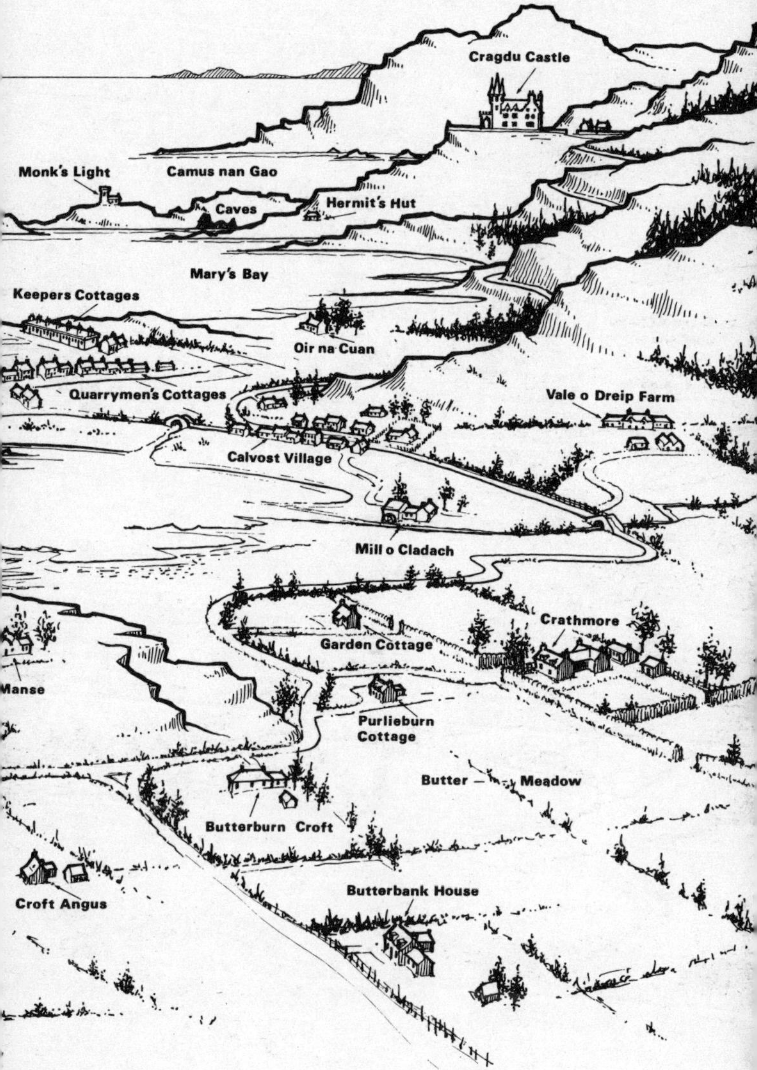

Cragdu Castle
Monk's Light
Camus nan Gao
Caves
Hermit's Hut
Mary's Bay
Keepers Cottages
Oir na Cuan
Quarrymen's Cottages
Vale o Dreip Farm
Calvost Village
Mill o Cladach
Crathmore
Garden Cottage
Manse
Purlieburn
Cottage
Butter — Meadow
Butterburn Croft
Croft Angus
Butterbank House

KINVARA

Autumn 1926

Chapter One

Hannah shivered a little and pulled her shawl closer round her shoulders as she stood for a few minutes on the doorstep of No. 6 Keeper's Row, gazing out over the landscape. It was a cold clear morning in September; night still lay over the slumbering peaks of the hills and on the indigo reaches of the western sea, the flash of the Kinvara Light pricked the darkness. All was silent and still with only the hint of a breeze to ruffle the black calm of Mary's Bay.

But far away to the east, behind the blue-black silhouettes of the inner Hebrides, the day was breaking in a quiet glow that brushed the clouds with a pearly lining and streaked silver across the horizon. The sky grew lighter and brighter and even as Hannah watched the sun burst up over the ocean in a great fiery ball that seemed to vibrate and swell before it climbed higher into the sky to hide its face in a big purple cloud.

Red sky at morning, shepherd's warning. The words of the old adage crept into Hannah's head like a portent of doom. It would just be like the thing if the weather turned nasty after a spell of warm sunshine that had sent farmers and crofters scurrying to gather in their crops while the going was good. Every day for the past week, voices had echoed in the fields, the harvesters had whirred, children and animals had run busily about, and every gloaming had seen the haycarts piled high, trundling along the lanes, the scent of the newly mown hay lingering heavy and sweet in the cool air of evening.

Hannah glanced at the stooks of corn standing in the little patch of croftland at the side of her house, neatly running north to south to make them dry evenly. At sight of them a tear caught in her throat. Only a few days ago she had scythed the field with her husband Rob and to her surprise she had really enjoyed doing it. The sun on her back, the rhythmic swish of the blade, the sight of Rob stripped naked to the waist, strong and muscular, his sun-flushed skin moist with the sweat of his labours, his dark head downbent as he went along.

He was a handsome man was Robert James Sutherland, the kind whose rugged good looks easily attracted the attention of other women. Young, middling, old, it didn't matter what, they laughed and chatted with him and batted their eyes as if they were sharing some secret joke that only he could understand. They were natives, of course, people he had known all his life, who knew him and his ways and who could converse with him on common ground.

There were those in Kinvara who still sighed over him – yet despite them he had married her, Hannah Mabel Houston from Ayr, unaccomplished and plain, not exactly the sort of woman to net a man like Rob, and he most likely never would have married her if the woman he really loved had been available to him at the time . . .

Her eyes travelled to the little white house down there on the shores of Mary's Bay, Oir na Cuan, the house on the edge of the ocean, a simple abode that now lay empty and quiet but had once echoed with the sound of a young woman's laughter. The laughter of Morna Jean Sommero, so fair of face and sweet of nature, comely and bonny, no wonder Rob had loved her as he had – and pined for her yet.

He and Morna had been lovers long before his marriage to Hannah. But a bitter quarrel had sprung up between them and Morna had fled from him back to Shetland where, unknown to him, she had borne his child. By the time she returned to Kinvara he had wed himself to Hannah and had been forced to keep the true identity of his child a secret.

It must have been hard, that, living a double life, longing to declare his daughter to the world yet unable to do so because he already had a wife and a baby son.

There was little doubt in Hannah's mind that he had married her on the rebound and must have regretted it every day of his life. All along someone else had owned his heart and Morna had been lucky, to have known a devotion as deep as that . . . Hannah gave herself a mental shake. This was no way to think of a girl who was dead – that vibrant young woman was gone now and she had probably died with his name on her lips.

Hannah caught her breath. It was hard to bear sometimes, the knowledge that she was second best and probably always would be.

Oh, stop it, she told herself angrily. It's in the past, dead and buried and gone. No use raking it all up, you're here, you're alive, Rob belongs to you now and that's all that matters.

She glanced again at the stooks of corn and a fresh wave of poignancy went through her as she recalled how good it had been working alongside her husband. In the few years they'd been married he had opened her eyes to new discoveries about herself and she had learned not only how to do things but how to enjoy doing them as well.

Rob, such a virile loving man. That was part of the trouble, too virile, too passionate . . . a shaft of apprehension went through her and her hands went to her stomach. With an effort she turned her thoughts away from herself. It was cold out here; with the coming of day a wind had sprung up from the sea, rippling the waves, stealing away the calm of the dawn. Daylight was really here now, touching every corner, glistening on the water, brushing the trees with gold, reaching into the corries of the hills.

When first she had come to this place as the wife of Rob Sutherland she had hated the solitude, despised the emptiness. In time its lonely beauty had touched her heart and now she no longer thought of it as empty but filled with a subtle quality of life and a sense of the past that was so tangible at times it made her stop and gaze around as if expecting to see someone walking towards her.

A movement on the beach caught her eye and made her heart jump. Then she realised it was only Johnny Lonely, the hermit who lived rough in a makeshift hut under the lowering cliffs of Cragdu. He was always combing the beach for anything he could lay his hands on, though what he did with all the bits and pieces was anybody's guess. No doubt it was in his scavenging nature just to hoard rubbish for the sake of it. He lit fires of course, mostly to keep himself warm, but if the notion took him he would move his few belongings up to the Old Chapel Light on Kinvara Point, there to light beacons on the headland as the monks of old had done in ages past to warn off shipping.

Strange lonely man. Hannah felt sorry for him sometimes. But he only had himself to blame. That kind of life was never meant to be lived by any human being. What was he before he became a hermit, she wondered. A poet? An artist? A man of God? He never went to church yet he believed in his Maker.

Ryan Du, who worked to Vale o' Dreip, the big rambling farm on the slopes of Blanket Hill, had said that Johnny always made a point of saying Grace whenever Rita Sutherland took pity on him and gave him meals in return for an occasional job of work. There was undoubtedly something different about him that set him apart. He was apart all right, alone and apart, yet he was good with children; it wasn't unusual to see them gathered about him, avidly listening as he told them stories about shipwrecks and the creatures of the sea . . . perhaps he had been a fisherman, or a sailor. Andy adored him, and while she didn't approve of such an unlikely companion for her son there was nothing much she could do about it, since they were both wanderers, both different, Andy, in his own way, as lonely a soul as Johnny.

She gazed into the distance; the flash of the Kinvara Light was no longer visible on the bright horizon. Rob had left yesterday for his three-month stint of duty as deputy head keeper of the lighthouse and the days stretched ahead of her, empty without him. She should be used to his absences by now but knew she would always find them hard to accept.

Breck, the black and white cross-collie that Rob had given Andy some four Christmases ago, came out of the house to lift his leg and sniff at the grasses. His actions brought some normality back to the scene and she was grateful to him for that. He was missing Rob, there was no doubt about it, and the look he threw at Hannah as she stood there by the door was filled with reproach, as if it was her fault that Rob had gone away.

The dog had never really taken to her, sensing that she didn't like having him in the house. She had always maintained that he ought to be outside in a kennel where he couldn't bring mud and dirt in to her clean floors. The sheepdogs at Dunruddy Farm in Ayrshire where she had been brought up had always been kept in outbuildings and she didn't see why this one should be any different.

'He isn't a sheepdog,' Rob had told her often enough. 'He's Andy's companion and he's as much right to be in the house as any of us.'

The dog's expression had turned to one of expectancy as he sat down and tried to stare her out, the tips of his ears, normally half-folded, erect and listening as if hoping she might say something that would be to his advantage.

Food! That was all he ever wanted from her. Not so much as a wag of his tail or an uplifted paw in return. He reserved all that for Andy and Rob. With them he ran and barked and cooried into their feet at night by the fire and when he looked at them there was comprehension on his face, as if he knew every word they were saying and was glad to be part of everything they did.

All she was good for was providing meals for him and one of these days she would lock him in the shed and see how much he liked that. Then she softened. It was her own fault the creature treated her as he did; she had never shown him any sort of affection and, she had to admit, he was an intelligent beast and had been totally loyal to Andy from the beginning.

It was breakfast time anyway, and she was about to go inside when her attention was caught by a door opening at the end of the Row. Mungo MacGill, head keeper of the Kinvara Light, came out, and even from this distance she could tell he was upset about something. When he banged the door to and went stomping away to disappear round the end of the building she knew that her surmise had been correct.

The next minute the door of No. 1 opened again and Big Bette, Mungo's wife, looked out. Seeing Hannah she gave a brief nod of acknowledgement, glanced to the right and to the left of her, paused for a moment, then withdrawing herself from view she clicked the door to behind her.

During the years that she had lived in Kinvara, Hannah had developed a nose for other folk's business. This she would never have admitted to anybody, least of all herself, and to salve her own conscience she always had to find an excuse for making any move that might in any way be construed as prying.

In this instance however her curiosity was so well and truly aroused she paused only to shut Breck in the house before rushing round the corner of No. 6 to see Mungo walking rapidly across the endrigs of the common grazing. He was making for the shore and she wondered at that. He had returned from lighthouse duty just yesterday and if there was one thing that Mungo liked when he got home it was to take life easy for a few days till he found his 'land feet'.

Hannah had never known him to be up and about as early as this and she wondered if he and Bette had rowed about something. Normally they were like a couple of lovebirds after being separated for so long. 'More like lustbirds,' Mattie MacPhee had said but then, Mattie always did have a coarse tongue in her head, and she should talk, all these bairns at her feet, five at the last count and who knew when there might be another. Secretly though, Hannah was inclined to agree with Mattie. She wasn't all that keen on Big Bette MacGill, who was overbearing and bossy and who had very successfully intimidated her when she had been a newcomer to the Row. She didn't much care for Mungo either, all that fuss he made about being a kirk elder when he was no better than most and a lot worse than some. But at least the pair had restricted their family to three, though God knew how they had managed that as it was a well-known fact they had burst the springs of at least three good beds with all their cavorting and fleering about.

Mungo had topped a rise and was going on down to the shore. Mystified, Hannah made her way furtively over the machair till she came to the marram grasses at the edge of the dunes.

At first she could see no one, only Johnny Lonely wandering about in the bay, then all at once she spied Mungo, making for an overhang of rock. Suddenly he dropped down and to her frustration she could see nothing more. But she remembered the telescope Rob kept on the kitchen windowsill and a short while later she was applying it to her eye and was rewarded for her efforts by the sight of Mungo, his back against a rock, puffing away furiously at his pipe. Now she knew for certain that something had happened to ruffle his feathers.

Because Mungo never smoked a pipe, at least he said he didn't, and took great pains to let everybody know how much he disapproved of both tobacco and alcohol, stressing that one was as bad as the other and anybody who was weak enough to indulge in such evils had been influenced by 'the very de'il himself'.

Hannah was really beginning to enjoy herself and became quite absorbed in what she was doing. It was interesting to watch Mungo's big florid face through the lens and to see him panning the bay to make sure no one was there to observe his actions. He obviously hadn't seen Johnny Lonely because after a while he looked as if he was becoming more confident about himself – and surely that was a flask he was taking from his pocket to hold to his mouth and gulp down the contents. Oh, he was a hypocrite all right! Doing the kind of things he condemned in others and giving every appearance of being familiar with them too!

But wait! That wasn't all he was doing. He had stood up and was unbuttoning his fly and the next thing a huge stream gushed forth. She could see it quite plainly. Like a horse. He must have been saving it up for ages. Oh, the affront! How could he do such a thing with other people watching? Then she remembered. She wasn't supposed to be watching. And she had done the selfsame thing herself when she'd been caught short. Only in a dire emergency of course, when there had been nowhere else to go. And she had always made sure that no one had been watching – but then again, someone might have been – if they'd had field glasses or a telescope!

Hannah was thunderstruck at the idea. Her hands shook slightly but still she kept on looking through the eye-piece, fascinated by her discoveries about the head lighthouse keeper. Not that she could ever reveal them to anyone else. She would give herself away then, give away the fact that she had been spying and that would never do, not when she had always made a point of being disapproving of those who took a delight in poking their noses into other folk's business.

Mungo was finished and was buttoning up his fly, glancing all around him as he did so. Hannah had to duck down several times when his gaze swung in her direction and once or twice she thought he must have seen her when he seemed to stop and stare directly at her.

'Ay, even kirk elders smoke their pipes and drink their drams when they think no one is looking.'

Hannah's heart jumped into her throat. With a gasp she turned to see Johnny Lonely looming above her, his long black hair frisking out from under a greasy deerstalker hat, the collars of his thick duffel coat turned up against the wind. He was standing against the light and she had difficulty seeing the expression on his face, but the tone of his voice was enough, soft and slightly mocking, a note of triumph lifting it a little because he saw he had startled her and Johnny liked nothing better than to creep up on unwary beings and frighten the life out of them.

'Where on earth did you spring from!' she managed to get out in a breathless ragged voice. 'You have no right to sneak up on innocent people the way you do. I thought I saw a seal in the bay and went to get my telescope to watch it,' she finished lamely.

'Ay, the wildlife is very plentiful around here,' he nodded, speaking in that oddly cryptic way that had set many a mind racing as to how much he knew about affairs that were private, how much he had heard that he shouldn't. 'I myself have seen all sorts, and no doubt will see a whole lot more before I'm finished.'

With that he took himself off, never a word of apology for frightening her the way he had; just that curt nod of his and the knack he had of suddenly disappearing from sight so that she was left wondering if he had ever really been there at all or if it had been just a figment of her imagination.

From the side of her eye she saw Mungo retracing his steps along the shore and like a startled hare she took to her heels and ran all the way back to the house, never pausing till she was safely inside the kitchen with the door shut behind her.

Her interest in Mungo's affairs had almost made her forget her own, but her worries came flooding back anew when she went to hook the pan of porridge on the swee and swing it over the glowing embers of the stove. Against her will her eyes were drawn to the calendar hanging at the side of the fireplace. Every month it was the same. The waiting. The wondering. The praying that she could relax and feel safe for a while. So far everything had been fine – but this time it was different, this time she really was late.

A pang of apprehension shot through her. It couldn't be. She was fancying things. She and Rob had certainly been much closer these last few months and it had been so comforting lying in his arms at night, the house still and dark around them, just the two of them, finding one another again, a renewal of the tenderness they had shared at the beginning of their marriage.

She had told him that she wanted no more children, not after Andy, and he had said that he would look after her, that it would be all right. And he had been careful . . . Her mouth twisted. Not careful enough, it seemed. Unless, of course, she was mistaken. It was easy to forget dates, the children, the house, the day to day routine, there were occasions when she even forgot what day of the week it was and was only reminded by looking at the calendar.

Even as she tried to convince herself that she was wrong the sensation of dread at the pit of her stomach grew stronger – and wouldn't go away.

Chapter Two

Big Bette was seated at the kitchen table, sipping a large mug of tea and keeping one eye on the window as she waited for Mungo to come back. He had gone stomping out of the house earlier, without any breakfast, without sustenance of any kind, and as she sat there Bette went over in her mind the events that had led up to this moment.

A few days ago, her seventeen-year-old niece, Maudie, had come from Glasgow to stay with her, sent by her sister who had thought Maudie would have a healthier life in the country and would be better able to find a job.

Work is very hard to come by here in Glasgow, just now, Mags Munro had said in the letter preceeding her daughter's arrival in Kinvara. *Maudie has been hanging around like a spare fart in a paper poke ever since she left her last job as a nanny to some gentry folk in the west end. They treated her like a doormat and made her work like a slave for a pittance and with her being a very sensitive lass she just couldn't take any more.*

On your last visit to Partick I'm sure you noticed what a willing and able girl Maudie is, very good with children and a grand help about the home. She has always thought the world of you, Bette, and if you decide to take her for a while I know she won't let you down. She'll be a great comfort to you and a help with the bairns. I know you work hard in the village store and just think what a relief it will be to have someone like Maudie around the place, looking after everything while you're out and giving you the chance to put your feet up and relax when you come in.

I'm going to miss her sorely in the house as she's been an excellent daughter to me and has never given me a minute's worry from the day she was born. I would never stand in her light, however, and when she said she would like to come to Kinvara to look for work me and Mick somehow scraped up the money for her fares with a little bit extra to help her get started.

Give my regards to Mungo and my love to the bairns.

As always, your loving sister, Mags

Bette hadn't been given any choice in the matter, for on the day the letter arrived Maudie had arrived also, appearing on the doorstep with her bags and her bits, all rosy smiles and breathless greetings and sure of a welcome.

Into the house she had trundled to dump down her luggage and gaze around her with pleasure before flopping into the nearest chair to fan herself with a corner of her shawl and declare that she would love a cuppy as it had been a long journey and she was 'fair wabbit' with all the travelling. There had followed a long and detailed monologue about a broken-down horse pulling a broken-down cart and God knew how she had ever made it to Kinvara from the station but here she was at last and it was just so good to see her Aunt Bette again she could have wept with the relief of it all.

Bette had bustled about, making tea, buttering pancakes and bread, all of which Maudie downed in a few gulps while she went on to speak about her mammy and daddy back home in Partick and how worried she was about leaving them to fend for themselves and the wee ones and 'poor Daddy finding things hard with the General Strike and everything'.

'But, och, it's that nice to get away from the smelly city for a while,' she had beamed, settling herself back in her chair and biting into another pancake with relish. 'And though Daddy's on strike, Mammy has never been idle in her life and keeps herself busy, taking washing to the steamie for the posh folk and scrubbing out closes for the better-off people in Pollockshields – the ones wi' tiles instead o' wally.'

Bette had looked blank at this point and Maudie had gone on to explain indulgently, 'Aunt Bette, a wally close means one wi' plaster walls, the kind I live in, a tile close is more fancy and means the people who bide in them have taken a step up the ladder – but surely to goodness you know that already.'

'Surely to goodness,' Bette had said faintly as she wondered how she was going to keep Maudie for a day, never mind the indefinite period hinted at in the letter. The girl consumed food at a startling rate and still somehow managed to look as if she hadn't eaten at all when she sat gazing regretfully at her empty plate seemingly wondering what had happened to the contents.

There was certainly nothing unhealthy about Maudie if her buxom figure was anything to go by. Her baby smooth cheeks were apple-blossom pink, her large eager breasts spilled unfettered over the top of her frock and bounced about with every move she made, her arms were strong and hefty, her knees deeply dimpled and patterned with scorch marks. Bette knew this for a fact, since Maudie had no sooner sat down than she hoisted up her skirts and exposed her legs to the heat issuing from the grate, giving vent to a blissful sigh of appreciation as she did so.

She was, to put it plainly, 'as fat as she could roll' but somehow it suited her and made her an altogether attractive and appealing sight to behold. Plumpness was not such an unusual feature in Bette's side of the family. She and her three sisters had all developed into sizeable maidens at a tender age and it looked as if Bette's daughter, Babs, just ten and big for her age, was set to follow in her mother's footsteps.

On that first day, it wasn't Maudie's size that worried Bette, however, it was her monopoly of the cosy deep armchair that was, by unspoken law, Mungo's chair, the one his own children referred to as 'Father's chair' and would never have dreamed of using, not even when he was away for weeks on end on lighthouse duty.

From the day she made her entry into the MacGill household, Maudie commandeered the chair for her own and only smiled in her easygoing way when her aunt suggested she should try sitting somewhere else as 'Uncle Mungo might no' be too pleased to come home and find himself ousted from his favourite place by the hearth.'

'Och, Auntie,' Maudie had said placatingly, her hazel brown eyes widening at the very idea of anyone grudging her a comfortable seat at the fire. 'As if Uncle Mungo would think anything o' that sort. In our house in Partick, visitors can sit themselves down anywhere they choose. Mammy and Daddy have aye been mannerly in that respect and would never affront themselves by nit-picking over a wee thing like a chair.'

Bette had wondered then if Maudie was as artless she made out, but the matter of the chair soon faded into insignificance in the days that followed, for over and above all else, Maudie soon proved to be heart lazy. She had shown no inclination to try and find a job and hadn't done a hand's turn in the house since the minute she stepped over the door, staying in her bed in the morning till the lure of breakfast persuaded her to rise and go down to the kitchen in a search for sustenance.

When Mags had written to say she had given her daughter some money to get her started the operative word had been 'little'. It was hardly enough to keep a dog in bones for a week and Maudie had an appetite like a horse. Bette's own three, themselves capable of shifting great mounds of food, were wont to stare mesmerised as their cousin unfailingly and cheerfully polished her plate clean with great hunks of bread before rising from the table to declare that she just had to have a wee rest as she was still fatigued from her long journey.

At first she had slept on her own in a tiny boxroom at the end of the upstairs landing but had soon rebelled against this, saying that all the country noises 'scared the shat out o' her' or 'the loudness o' the silence was so creepy she couldn't get a wink o' sleep because o' it'.

After a night or two of this, Bette had said she could share Babs' room and into this larger and sunnier abode she had moved her belongings and was soon happily settled, much to the delight of Babs who was by this time fascinated by her cousin and positively revelled in all the talk and tales of city life that Maudie was only too ready to share.

Bette had never been a woman to stand any nonsense from anybody and after a few days of Maudie she felt it was high time she voiced her feelings on the matter. But somehow she never did. It was impossible to be angry with the girl since she was the biggest bundle of good nature that Bette had ever known. She seldom grumbled or complained but just went smiling placidly through each day, heaping praise on Bette for her good wholesome cooking, keeping the young MacGills amused with her colourful anecdotes about life up a tenement close and all the people who lived there.

She was an excellent mimic and Bette found herself laughing with the children and wanting to hear more so that it began to be a ritual to sit round the fire at night and listen to Maudie while they drank their bedtime cocoa, Bette whittling away at bits of wood as she did so, expertly carving them into flutes and animals, some of which she gave to Wee Fay to sell in her shop, the rest going to the poorer children in the district and to the Fountainwell Orphanage at Christmas.

Her output was prodigious and the more Maudie talked the faster Bette whittled so that by the end of each evening there was always a pile of wood shavings to sweep up and put in the fire for an extra burst of warmth before the flames were damped for the night.

That happy situation did not last long however; the closer it came to Mungo's return the more his wife began to dread it since Maudie's occupation of the favoured chair had become more noticeable than ever as she really began to relax and feel herself very thoroughly at home.

The day came, the relief boat put into harbour and with it came Mungo, pleased to be home at last and looking forward to his comforts, the fire, the chair, his slippers, his family sitting at his feet, recounting all the little adventures they'd had since he went away.

When he came through the door of No. 1 of the Row the first sight that met him was that of Maudie, sprawled cosily by the hearth in *his* chair, nose buried deep in a book as she munched away at a big rosy apple.

Of Bette there was no sign, for though she had shut up shop early in order to go down to the harbour to meet her husband, she had taken cold feet at the last minute and had gone instead to visit Granny Margaret in Struan Cottage, there to pour her woes into the old woman's sympathetic lugs and partake of a much-needed cuppy laced with a tot of brandy.

'A wee droppy o' that cures a host o' ails,' Granny Margaret had said with the conviction of one who knew what she was talking about. She too had her share of troubles as she was not slow to tell Bette and the pair of them sat, growing more loose-tongued as the minutes slipped by and the brandy slipped down, Granny Margaret prattling on about her leaking roof and a bladder that wasn't much better; the argument she'd had with Kathy MacColl over a knitting pattern, the state her bowels were in after the doctor had prescribed medicine for her throat, how Connie, her eldest granddaughter, had taken the huff over a trivial remark concerning her latest young man.

'I only said he was a poor wee cratur' who wouldny make a good husband for anybody and was probably only looking for a roof over his head,' the old lady had sniffed into her cup. 'Connie took the rue at that and said she had no intention of making a husband out o' him and that it was none o' my business anyway as she had her own life to lead.'

Bette wasn't listening, she was too busy bemoaning the fact that Mungo would be home right now, this very minute, and there in his chair would be Maudie, looking as if she had occupied it for years and not in the least concerned that her presence might be a complete and utter surprise to Mungo, who'd had no warning that she was coming.

Bette didn't need second sight to know any of this; the word picture she painted for Granny Margaret was almost perfect in every detail. Mungo was surprised to see Maudie, though perhaps taken aback might be a more accurate description of his feelings as he stood in the middle of the room gazing at the scene before him, his big florid face growing redder than ever at this most unusual of homecomings.

Maudie gave him no time to think. 'Uncle Mungo!' she cried when she glanced over the top of her book and saw him standing there. She didn't get up but remained where she was, the apple suspended halfway to her mouth as she went on. 'Och, it's that nice to see you again, you do remember me, don't you? Maudie Munro, your niece through marriage. I was only a tiny wee girl the last time you saw me in Partick but now I'm all grown up and Mammy and Daddy thought it would do me good if I came to stay with you and Aunt Bette for a while. It's been a real treat to see her and my cousins and now you're here I just know we're going to be one big happy family.'

Mungo had nothing to say to this; there was nothing he *could* say in the face of such heartfelt enthusiasm. But his heart sank, his heavy jowls dropped; now he knew why Bette hadn't been at the harbour to meet him. She knew only too well the sort of things that upset him and, formidable as she was, she hadn't been able to face his reaction to Maudie's presence in his home.

To her credit, and perhaps sensing his anxiety at finding her here, Maudie had risen from her chair to make him a cup of tea and while he was drinking it she commiserated with him because his wife wasn't in the house to welcome him. 'Something will have kept her at the shop. It isn't like Auntie to be late, especially when she knows you'll be back and wanting a wee glimpse o' her after such a long spell away.'

And a 'wee glimpse' of his wife was all that Mungo got that day for when she at last returned home she was in no fit state to talk to anybody. Up to bed she went, without as much as a by your leave or an apology for anything that had happened, muttering something about a pie in the oven and gravy in the pantry and she didn't want anything because she was full enough already and only wanted to sleep.

'Och, don't worry, Uncle,' Maudie told him comfortingly. 'She's just a wee bit sozzled. When Daddy's like that he conks out for hours but is as right as rain the next day. Mammy swears by the water cure and makes him drink a pint out the tap before he goes to the boozer wi' his pals and is never the worse for wear.'

Babs and Tom came in from school at that moment, Babs pausing only to greet her father briefly before bouncing into his chair to look at him in a way that suggested he was only an occasional visitor in the home, one who had given up all rights of ownership the last time he had said goodbye to his family.

Mungo was terribly upset by this. He was a very orderly sort of man, one who liked to see everything ship-shape and in its place. His years in the Merchant Navy might have had something to do with this but no matter what, he had always believed himself to be master in his own home and now he felt as if it was all crumbling about his ears.

In his absence something terrible had happened here, order had been disrupted, nothing was as he had left it, no word he said would be law from now on . . . It was too much. He had just come back from light duty, Bette hadn't been here to greet him; instead she had gone out and got drunk and he was left with only this very large young woman whom he didn't know at all and had no wish to know – even if she was his niece through marriage as she herself had put it.

How did he know who she was? She could be anybody, and Babs was acting oddly. Normally she came and made a daughterly fuss of him and went to get his slippers from the hearth but now she was regarding him as if he was a stranger. Tom had turned away after a most reserved welcome and when fifteen-year-old Joe came in from his job at the Mill o' Cladach he went straight to the stove to see what was cooking and hardly seemed to notice his father at all.

In those fraught moments Mungo was unable to make any sense of anything and dejectedly he went to the sink to wash his hands and splash cold water over his face, in the hope that it might revive him and help him to better face the remainder of the day.

'Sit down, Uncle,' Maudie instructed kindly. 'I would have made you something myself but Auntie got it ready earlier and all I have to do is lay it on the table.'

Mungo felt that somebody was on his side at last but changed his mind when the pie was withdrawn from the oven and laid down in front of him. The crust was dry and charred, the meat tough and stringy, the potatoes had been cooking too long and were waterlogged and soggy. The gravy was in the pantry as Bette had said, in a jug on the shelf, congealed and greasy and much too late to do anything about it since the meal was halfway through when Maudie suddenly remembered she had forgotten to heat it.

When the meal was over, Babs offered to do the dishes, a most unusual occurrence since she hated chores of any kind and in particular the washing up. The reason for this soon became apparent. She wanted to hear more of Maudie's stories and in no time at all the table was cleared and the dishes done, Tom actually drying them in his hurry to sit himself down, cup his chin in his hands and wait for his cousin to begin.

Even Joe, for all he felt himself to be a man now, was entranced by Maudie and her tales and Mungo knew then that nothing would ever be the same again at No. 1 of the Row. Disgruntled and tired he took himself early to bed, hoping to find some comfort in Bette's willing embrace. But tonight she was dead to the world, her snores filling the room as she lay on her back in a drink-induced stupor.

It was the last straw for Mungo. Normally, the first few days of his return were fulfilling and wonderful. He and Bette were like a honeymoon couple as they rediscovered the earthly joys to be found in one another. He loved it when she smothered him in her huge fluffy bosoms and enveloped him in everything else that was yielding and magnificent and stirring.

But there would be none of that tonight and moodily he lay in his half of the big double bed, frustrated and wakeful. Everything had been spoiled by the arrival of Maudie Munro

– and when Bette wakened in the morning he wouldn't be slow to tell her so. By God and he wouldn't!

When Bette finally opened her eyes it was still dark outside and for this she was mightily glad. Her tongue was sticking to the roof of her mouth, red-hot hammers were pounding away inside her skull and all she wanted was to sink once more into oblivion and not waken up again till she was sure that she was not languishing somewhere in hell but was whole and well and able once more to take her place in the land of the living.

Mungo, however, was not going to let her off so easily. He awoke when she did and began by letting her know in no mean terms just what he thought of her and Maudie and 'the whole jing bang o' them'. His disapproval of her drinking was paramount, his disappointment in her intense; his rather high-pitched voice went on and on until Bette could stand it no longer. She argued back, they went at it hammer and tongs till finally he got up, threw on some clothes, and went blundering away downstairs.

Bette also got dressed, every move she made increasing in her the conviction that she was suffering from some sort of hallucination and that any minute now she would return to normality and all would be fine. But the fangs of pain inside her head kept on biting, the pieces of jelly that were her legs kept on wobbling.

Somehow she made it to the kitchen in time to hear Mungo slamming out of the house. Breath! She had to have that! For a few minutes she stood, drawing air into her lungs, when she at last staggered to the door there was no sign of Mungo, only that Hannah Sutherland gaping at her from No. 6 and looking as if butter wouldn't melt in her mouth.

Now Bette waited, gulping down her second mug of tea, feeling the balm of that blessed brew soothing her nerves. No one else was up yet, just Bette, sitting alone in the quiet kitchen, grateful for a moment of respite from people, noise, worry. She felt sorry for Mungo and really couldn't blame him for taking off as he had. In normal circumstances the first few days of his return were the ones she liked best; after that she grew tired of having him under her feet and was glad to escape to the shop and leave him to his own devices.

Now he would have Maudie for company, and Bette had a notion that he was not going to enjoy that experience in the least . . . yet, the girl was good company, it would be nice to give her a chance to prove herself, she and Mungo just might hit it off . . . and she was his niece through marriage after all.

He was coming back, passing the window, opening the door. She braced herself for further confrontation. But he had calmed down a little, and when she put her face close to his and sniffed she knew the reasons why. Now it was her turn to gloat. 'You've been drinking,' she accused heavily.' And smoking.'

'Ay,' he agreed without a trace of contrition. 'Peeing too, if you must know.'

'Peeing?'

'You heard. I had no time to go to the wee hoosie when I got up so I had my say up against a rock on the seashore.'

'On the shore!' Bette's face was a picture. 'But that Hannah Sutherland might have seen you. She has a nose on her like a ferret and was standing on her doorstep watching when I looked out to see where you had gone.'

'Well, and what if she did?' Mungo's hefty chin jutted. 'The woman would be a hypocrite if she had anything to say about it for she does the selfsame thing herself. I've seen her at it with my very own eyes, behind the whins growing among the dunes.'

'Mungo MacGill!' Bette clapped her hand to her mouth. Mungo also smiled, albeit sourly. Almost shyly, husband and wife looked at one another and for the moment harmony was restored. He accepted a large cup of tea, Bette poured herself a third, they sat on either side of the hearth to drink it – himself ensconced in the big plump cosy chair that he regarded very firmly as his own.

Chapter Three

'When is my mother coming back?'

For the second time that morning Hannah just about jumped out of her skin. She spun round to see Vaila, the love child of Morna and Rob, standing there in the kitchen doorway, her hair a rumple of black curls around her head, her eyes big and dark in her solemn little face as she came further into the room to put her hand to her mouth and suck her thumb.

These last few months had been a strange, sad time for the child, for not only had she lost her mother, she had also been separated from her little half-brother, Aidan, born to Morna after she had married Rob's brother Finlay to give her daughter the Sutherland name.

When all the secrets concerning the little girl's identity had been revealed, and she had turned out to be a true blood Sutherland after all, Hannah had swallowed her pride and had taken Rob's daughter into her home. In truth, she hadn't really been surprised at the turn of events. All along she had suspected that Rob was Vaila's father but she had buried her head in the sand and had let things drift along. Later she'd had to face the fact that she had behaved as she did to ease some of her own personal burdens. Morna had given Rob the kind of things that he needed, and in so doing had relieved his wife of the unwanted intimacies of the marriage bed – because she daren't have another child – not after Andy . . .

It hadn't been so hard having Vaila come to stay. She was a beautiful loving child and she had settled down well into the routine of No. 6 of the Row, only occasionally speaking about her life at Oir na Cuan.

She had talked about her mother certainly, the things they had done together, what they had said, but this was the first time she had voiced such a leading question. Everybody had assumed that she had taken the loss well and had gotten over it with the resilience that children often displayed in the face of tragedy. Now her tremulous mouth and tear-filled eyes proved otherwise and Hannah realised just how much the child had bottled up her feelings.

She was only five years old, after all, and had known many changes in her life of late. A new and strange house, another woman taking her mother's place, the recent bigger world of school, so many different faces and places, and she no longer had the companionship of Aidan who had gone to live with his father and grandparents at Vale o' Dreip.

Vaila hadn't minded being parted from her stepfather. She had never really taken to him and had regarded him as a usurper in her life and a contestant for her mother's affections. Rob was different; she had known and loved him from babyhood. He had come to see her at Oir na Cuan as often as he dared. He had brought her presents and she had called him Robbie, accepting him as someone familiar and special in her young life.

His departure yesterday must have seemed to her like the final desertion and Hannah was afraid because she didn't know how to handle the situation. What could she tell her stepdaughter? That her mother was dead and was never coming back? That she had to get used to living here at Keeper's Row and put up with it as it was, with or without her father? Unless, of course, she would prefer to go and stay with her Aunt Mirren at Burravoe House in Shetland and never see her father or Aidan again.

Hannah's heart fluttered. How could she cope with this along with everything else? She too was grappling with a host of emotions that seemed to be weighing her down like sacks of coal on her back. To make matters worse, and as if to remind her of another burden in her life, her son Andy appeared in the room, walking shakily on his bony little legs, his head looking too big and ungainly on the thin column of his neck, everything about him jerky and unsteady, except for his arms with their bent wrists, held tight and stiff to his chest as if tied there by invisible bonds.

Andy, who was four, had been born with cerebral palsy and it had taken him a long time to learn to walk and talk. Hannah still found difficulty in understanding him. His birth had devastated her. In her torture of mind she had blamed Rob for the boy's disabilities, an attitude which had soured everything that had been good between them and had turned him into a lonely bewildered man.

But he had found his solace in the arms of Morna Jean, and oh how she must have comforted him, that first love of his, such a caring and charismatic young woman, so ready to reach out and soothe the ails of those around her. She had even done it to Hannah, and Hannah had responded and blossomed and had allowed herself to become Morna's friend though deep down she had known that this was the woman Rob really loved . . .

So many regrets, so many heartaches. Time of course was a great healer, as Doctor MacAlistair had so often told her. But time could also magnify past events and make the future seem even more frightening. She looked again at Andy and her memory took her back to the moment of his birth, the terrible shock she had experienced on seeing him for the first time.

So different was he from what she had expected her firstborn to be that she felt no pride in showing him off to the world, only bitter shame that she should have produced such a flawed child. She also remembered the whispers, the pitying glances, the disappointment displayed by her father-in-law when he had discovered the imperfections of his first grandson, all of these combining to make her feel she had done something dreadfully wrong and strengthening her instincts to keep Andy indoors as much as possible in an effort to hide him from view

Yet he had grown to be such an affectionate little boy. The

people of Kinvara loved him and made sure he came to no harm when he was out and about in the little cart that Rob had made for him, pulled by Breck who had learned very quickly just what was required of him. The two were now as much a part of the local scene as anyone else in the place and it was all Hannah could do to keep her son indoors for any length of time.

She never knew half of the adventures he got up to. Often he could be away for hours on end, down there on the shore when Johnny Lonely met him and carried him to some favoured spot to watch the seals playing in the bay and the ships sailing by on their way in and out of the harbour. He loved riding in Dolly Law's cart alongside some of her own brood when she delivered washing to the gentry or collected coal from the puffers at the pier. Or he might be ensconced in a chair in the village store run by Big Bette, revelling in the comings and the goings and all the attention folks gave him when they came into the shop. At other times he enjoyed watching the local lads playing football and he was overjoyed when they let him join them in many of their other activities and often ended up in some house or other to be regaled with a strupak of tea and scones before going on his way.

There was always something for Andy to do, plenty of places for him to go, and quite often Hannah found herself at the door, waiting anxiously for his return should he be later than usual. And lately there had been those other small interludes as they sat round the fire before bedtime, him coming to place himself on her lap and wind those thin little arms of his round her neck, the unexpected ache she had felt in her breast, an ache that was raw and deep, mingling with a small ecstasy when she responded to him by pressing her lips to his dark head and knew the warmth of his face against her own.

He trusted her, and in spite of everything he loved her, yet he must have sensed her rejection of him when he had needed her so much in his very early days. If it hadn't been for Rob she might never have tried with Andy, might never have encouraged him to do any of the things that Rob had always said he could do if he was given the chance. Now here he was, deeply intelligent and sensitive, able to perform numerous small tasks for himself, a thinker, a dreamer, moving towards an independence that allowed him to make fewer and fewer demands on her attention.

And he had powers of his own that went far beyond the concepts of what she had always referred to as 'normal'. At his entry into the room everything seemed to change. With hardly a pause his spindly legs took him over to Vaila. He wrapped his arms around her shoulders. He said things to her in his gruff voice, words that she must have understood because she stopped crying and clung to him tightly, her dark curly head laid against his as they patted and hushed one another there in the inglenook by the grate with the amber glow of firelight brushing their skin so that they seemed locked in a sphere of childhood tenderness that belonged to them alone.

A lump came to Hannah's throat, How easy they made it seem, how simple their affectionate reactions to one another. Had she been like that once, she wondered? Uncomplicated? Able to communicate so easily? Able to give love without question? Perhaps it had never been in her nature to do any of these things. And even if it had been, she had lost the knack now. It was hard for her to show her feelings, she had locked them away for too long.

Vaila glanced up and threw Hannah a soft little smile, including her in the scene, as if she was aware of her stepmother's thoughts and didn't want her to feel shut out. Hannah bit her lip. Here was her chance. It *was* easy. Just a small step across the room to bridge the gap that separated her from that childish world of innocence and acceptance.

Without further hesitation she went over to the ingle and stood looking down at her son and stepdaughter. Then she knelt down and without a word she embraced the two children to her bosom. Andy felt fragile, Vaila soft and yielding.

Hannah took the girl's hands in hers and said softly, 'Vaila, you mustn't worry yourself any more. I'm your mother now, you might never call me that but I don't mind if you just keep calling me Hannah, as you've always done. You came to live here with your father and me and Andy because your own mother died and couldn't take care o' you any more, and though it will be very different for you living here with us I hope you will get to like it because we all want you and love you.'

The words came out, blunt but sincere. Hannah waited; perhaps she had sounded too harsh, too straightforward. She had never been a one for fancy talk and it was difficult, so difficult, to try and explain the harsh realities of life to a five-year-old child.

Vaila's hand came up to softly touch Hannah's cheek. Just a simple gesture but enough to make Hannah feel a sudden rush of true affection for this small being who had lost so much in her young life.

'Hannah.' Vaila spoke the name quietly. 'My mother now.'

'Ay, your mother, and I'll try to be as good a one as you deserve but can't promise more than that. There will be ups and downs, you'll have to abide by my way o' doing things for I'm no the sort o' woman to stand any nonsense from anybody, as well you know already, and that's all I have to say on the subject for now.'

Andy let out a snort that said he knew his mother's nature only too well. Vaila giggled and clapped her hand to her mouth, Breck's wet snuffly nose wormed its way up through Hannah's oxter to make sure that no one had forgotten him. His tongue came out to lick her face and standing up she shooed him off and pointed to his basket into which he slunk with abject shame, though the twitching of the feathery white tip of his tail told that he wasn't taking the scolding all that seriously.

The household was back to normal. Hannah bade the children go upstairs and help one another to get ready. But the surprises weren't over with yet. 'Wait a minute you two,' Hannah said on impulse. 'How would you both like to go in and see Janet for a minute after breakfast? She promised me a recipe for ginger snaps and we might as well get it over before the day is very much older.'

'Janet!' The children's faces showed their delight for they

loved the young woman who was their next-door neighbour and relished any opportunity that took them to her door.

'Ay,' Hannah nodded, carried away with the enthusiasm of the moment. 'Afterwards you and Joss can walk each other to school, Vaila, and might still have time to pop into Wee Fay's on the way. I'll give you a penny or two to buy some o' these sugar-olly twists you all seem to be daft on. Andy, you can go with them, and you could maybe get me a message or two from Big Bette's shop while you're about it.'

'Wee Fay!' Vaila and Andy positively beamed at the idea of visiting the grotto-like sweet shop run by Wee Fay and her husband, Little John, and it was with alacrity that they went off hand in hand, Breck leaving his basket to go bounding upstairs after them.

For once Hannah didn't say anything, her expansive mood allowing her to overlook the kind of things that normally annoyed her. A frown marred her brow. Had she been too anxious to please? Too ingratiating? It would never do to allow herself to become so lenient that nothing she said would be law. The rules of the house had to be adhered to and she didn't want it to seem as if she was bending them too much just for the sake of keeping everyone happy.

The next minute she relented. This was a special day. In soothing Vaila's fears she had somehow allayed her own, no matter how temporary that might be. A feeling of triumph warmed her heart. She felt as if she had achieved something very important that morning and when she went to set the table for breakfast she kept her eyes strictly off the calendar.

All that could wait. It was probably only a false alarm anyway and was most likely caused by the anxiety she'd felt knowing that Rob was going away and she would be left once more with all the responsibilities and worries of running the house alone. She even managed to hum a little tune as she rattled spoons on the table and lifted the singing kettle off the hotplate to make tea.

The sky outside the window was darkening; the rainclouds were piling up over the little islands far out on the grey-bellied sea. The shepherd's warning was coming true after all but skies were vast out here on the Kinvara Peninsula and almost always there was a little glow to be had somewhere among the clouds. Quite often the sun's rays would come spilling through some opening to cast a ripple of silver on the ever-changing moods of the Atlantic Ocean. 'One o' God's wee miracles,' Donald of Balivoe always said of these small cameos of light and Hannah felt some of his optimism seeping into her as she noticed a streak of gold above one of the faraway Hebridean islands. She saw it as a sign that some Greater Being up there was watching over her and would let nothing happen to spoil the new-found contentment of spirit that she had discovered in herself these last few months as she had lain in the strong reassuring arms of Robert James Sutherland.

Chapter Four

Janet Morgan's house was like herself, sunny and warm with vibrant colours that reflected Janet's own happy and carefree personality. The golds and yellows of the curtains that draped the windows found their echoes in the big fat cushions and loose covers that were scattered in gay abandon over the sofa and chairs to successfully hide the scuff marks and dents and the loops of material pulled out by the claws of various cats that Janet had taken into the bosom of her home at some time or another.

The walls of the house were painted yellow and white, 'like the daffodils o' spring', the dark corners were hung with mirrors to reflect the light and 'keep the spooks at bay', vases of russet grasses and bronze chrysanthemums sat on the broad window ledges together with an array of family photos and jars of colourful pebbles that Janet had gathered on the shore while out on the many wanders she enjoyed with Jock, her husband, and Joseph, her son.

Janet's cousin, Kathy MacColl of Vaul, the exact opposite of Janet both in looks and nature, had run up the curtains and loose covers on her little treadle sewing machine, since Janet, as she was the first to admit, 'couldny thread a needle to save herself' and was wont to sigh over her shortcomings as a wife and mother when the holes in the socks of her menfolk were so big she could put her fist through them and they were only fit for the bin.

Cousin Kathy however, in her fond and practical way, was always knitting socks and pullovers for her husband and children, with a mania that Janet sometimes found overwhelming in the extreme since Kathy, silent and purposeful and counting stitches under her breath, knitted wherever and whenever she could: at tea tables throughout the community, on walls and dykes on sunny days, in gardens and fields of friends and neighbours, sometimes even in chapel when she thought the priest wasn't looking and she felt that it was safe to take her knitting from the lapbag that was an essential part of her apparel and had earned her the nickname of Kangaroo Kathy.

Tillie and Tottie Murchison, two spinster sisters who ran the tiny draper's shop in Balivoe and were often referred to as 'the Knicker Elastic Dears', loved it when Kathy came into their shop. It was said she kept them in business with her constant quest for hanks of wool and cotton yarn, not to mention buttons and bows and anything else that she needed to adorn the end results of her labours.

No matter where, and as long as she was provided with the material from those who employed her services outwith the family circle, Kathy's dexterous fingers were forever busy and Big Jock Morgan had become resigned to receiving socks and pullovers, hats and scarves, on birthdays and at Christmas. He often wished that Kathy would surprise him with something different – even if it was just a box of Wee Fay's homemade toffee.

But Kathy, who had been brought up on a Hebridean island and spoke English in the Gaelic, said 'anything o' that sort was bad for the teeths' and a good handcrafted jumper was better than toffee any day of the week. Big Jock could never quite see the connection between the two and consoled himself with the fact that warm feet were better than bad teeth; he could always fall back on Janet's 'boiling jar' when he felt the need for sweeter comforts.

Janet herself, though quite often bewildered at the speed with which Kathy could produce a desired garment with just a few clicks of her needles or a turn or two of her treadle wheel, was nevertheless grateful for everything her cousin had done to make her home into one of great individuality and charm. Janet was always proud to show visitors into her cosy living room, and being a creature possessed of a bottomless fount of hospitality she didn't care what time they came, just as long as they took her as they found her and fitted themselves around whatever she happened to be doing when they arrived.

Hannah Sutherland was not a person who fitted into this last category. In fact, it was always a great amazement to Janet when Hannah deigned to call on her at all, at any hour of the day, and she was therefore all the more surprised to find that same woman standing on her doorstep at such an early hour of the morning, the expression on her face showing her discomfiture at behaving in such an uncharacteristic manner.

'I'm sorry to bother you so early,' Hannah began woodenly, 'It was just – I remembered that recipe you promised me for ginger snaps and as I was going to have a try at making them later I thought you wouldn't mind . . .'

The folk of Kinvara seldom apologised for showing up at anybody's house for whatever reason. Neighbourly visits were part and parcel of Highland life. People knew each other's houses as well as they did their own and were never shy of sitting down for a blether and a cuppy at any homely table that took their fancy.

But Hannah was not of Highland stock, and she was still trying to get used to the free and easy way in which the folks of this airt treated one another. It had taken Janet a long time and much patience to make any sort of headway with her nearest neighbour, who had found it hard going to get herself accepted in the community, mainly due to her own 'queer nature' and the habit she had adopted in the beginning of 'scuttling away into her house like a frightened rabbit' whenever anything resembling a human popped into her line of vision.

'She's afraid o' anything that moves on two legs,' Dolly Law had observed in between puffs of her clay pipe. 'My Shug only has to look at her for her to shrivel up and die and she's a lonely soul because o' it.'

'Ay, that she is,' Connie Simpson had agreed. 'You would think being married to Rob she would consider herself a lucky woman but no, there she sits, gazing up the lum or buried in a book, thinking herself hard done by when she has all she ever needs or wants from life.'

Connie had looked most pained at this point. She and her two sisters had hankered after Rob Sutherland ever since they had discovered there was more to life than just playing doctors behind the school playshed. In the event, Catrina and Cora had managed to get themselves married. Connie however was still single, and with her being the eldest, this state was not at all to her liking, especially as her Granny Margaret was getting older by the minute and relying on Connie more and more as the days went by.

'I'll no' be minding if you get yourself a man and settle down,' the old lady had told her granddaughter, somehow managing to look as if she meant what she said because the last thing she wanted was to be left alone in her dotage. 'When you do, the pair o' you can come and live here at Struan Cottage wi' me for I wouldny like to think o' you struggling to make ends meet when you already have a home you can call your own.'

Granny Margaret could be sly when she liked and knew full well that all three sisters felt they owed her a debt because she had taken them in when they had been orphaned at an early age and she had brought them up with much sacrifice to herself.

Now Connie was the only one of the sisters remaining at home and she felt duty bound to stay there, her job as housekeeper to the Manse, which she had taken over when her sister Cora got married, using up a fair number of her daytime hours. But the nights with just Granny Margaret could be long and lonely and Connie couldn't help but feel that she might be left on the shelf. Not that she wasn't popular with the opposite sex; her bonny smooth face, red hair, and amply rounded figure ensured that she had quite a few admirers, but none of them could match up to Rob Sutherland and she wasn't going to take just any man for the sake of saying she had one.

Hannah Houston from Ayr, as some of the unmarried ladies

liked to refer to Rob's wife when they wanted to diminish her marital status, had stolen a very eligible bachelor from under their noses and that fact had festered quite badly when Hannah had first come among them.

'And her such an uppity besom too,' they had told one another, united in their loss as they had never been in the mating ring.

'Whatever was Rob thinking of, wedding himself to that Plain Jane? He could have gotten anybody he wanted.'

'Ay, somebody o' his own kind would have suited him better. He canny have been in his right mind when he took Miss High and Mighty from Ayr to be his wife and 'tis no wonder he doesny smile near as often as he used to.'

Opinions like these had lessened as the years went by. Hannah had gradually opened up and expanded and was making fairly good headway in the community though it was never easy for her to completely relax in anything that resembled 'a gossiping gathering of cronies'.

When first she had arrived in Kinvara she had rebuffed Janet many times but that young lady's gentle persistence had won through in the end and she was pleased with the progress she had made. Even so, she still found it hard going to win over the older woman's trust and had always to make an extra effort to put her at her ease. And it would be doubly hard this morning because, for once, Janet did not feel like talking to anyone, far less Hannah who was wearing her frightened rabbit look as she stood there on the doorstep uttering her excuses and reasons for being there at all.

A sigh escaped Janet. For the umpteenth time since yesterday she wished her husband was here by her side. With just a word or two he could make anything seem better and there were very few people in Kinvara who didn't respond to his warmth and good nature. But Big Jock Morgan, or Morgan the Magnificent as he was sometimes known because of his marvellous physique and bearing, had gone back to lighthouse duty only yesterday and Janet was already missing him dreadfully. Last night she had lain alone in the big feather bed she shared with him and she had cried into her pillow and found difficulty in getting to sleep without him.

She had woken feeling tired and listless and now here was Hannah, undoubtedly missing her man also, probably worrying herself sick about the house and the bairns and how she would manage to cope with everything on her own. She was most likely looking for a sympathy that Janet didn't feel able to give but being Janet she made an effort. Her voice sounded genuinely warm when she ushered the visitors inside and went immediately to get the jar of boilings from a little alcove in the dresser and allowed the children to dip into it and pick the sweets of their choice.

'It's a good job Cousin Kathy isn't here,' Janet laughed. 'She would have something to say about sugar being bad for your "teeths" and would scold me for putting such temptation in your path.'

Hannah watched, thinking how good her young neighbour was with little ones as she drew Vaila and Andy in close to her and kissed them each on the cheek. They responded to her with laughter and smiles and plied her with tales of the things they had seen and done and how sad they were that their father had gone away again.

'Ay.' Gently Janet touched Vaila's cheek. 'That's how I feel about Jock, but just think, they'll both be back for Christmas, and we'll have a fine time to ourselves telling them all the news.'

Joss made his entrance into the room, a laughing-eyed boy of almost six, with his mother's fair colouring and his father's fine build and stature. Without hesitation he lifted Andy up as if he was a feather and, still able to find a spare hand for Vaila, he took them both up to his room to show them the collection of foreign stamps he had saved from letters and postcards sent to him by his uncle who was in the Merchant Navy.

Hannah settled herself more comfortably in her chair. The room was cheerful and warm with a good fire leaping up the lum. Janet went to fetch the ever-sizzling teapot from the hob to pour herself and Hannah a piping hot brew and the two women sat chatting companionably as they sipped their tea and ate some of the buttered toast left over from breakfast.

Hannah visibly relaxed as the minutes went by. She glanced at Janet and it struck her how nice a person the girl was. At twenty-three she looked little more than a child herself with her long blonde hair and blue eyes and that dreamy thoughtful aura about her that gave the impression of one who never took life's issues very seriously.

Hannah, however, knew better. She had learned quite early on that Janet was a very perceptive young woman who took in more about the world around her than anybody could have guessed. She was soft-hearted, kind and understanding, but she could also be hard-headed and stubborn when she felt reason to be and could get her own way when she set her mind to it. 'A bulldog in lamb's clothing' was how her husband laughingly put it, which neatly summed up his wife and all she stood for.

Hannah had mostly seen Janet's soft side and she had come to truly like and respect her next-door neighbour. The girl even had a canny tongue in her head, a feature most unusual in a place where everyone gossiped as hard as they could and didn't feel complete if they couldn't go home without some juicy titbit of news to recount.

In a less obvious way, Hannah had gradually become like this herself, and almost without thinking she recounted to Janet the 'goings on' she had witnessed earlier concerning Mungo MacGill and his activities on the shore, carefully omitting the part that she considered went against the rules of common decency and easily excusing herself for having watched him breaking these selfsame rules.

Janet looked thoughtful, then she threw back her fair head and burst out laughing. 'Och well, to tell the truth, I'm no' surprised at anything Mungo does. I myself have seen him piddling on the shore. He got such a surprise when he saw me he almost burst his buttons trying to stuff everything back in again and wet his trousers in the process. I never said anything to Jock in case he might think I was a fallen woman and had egged Mungo on to do what he did.'

The two women shrieked with glee and had hardly got their breath back when Hannah added her contribution, speaking hastily as if afraid that her temerity might desert her. 'He did that this morning – as well as the other things. I couldn't help seeing, it just hit me between the eyes before I had a chance to do anything about it – although, of course, I had the protection o' Rob's telescope at the time.'

Janet stared. 'He'll maybe have hidden longings to be noticed by other women,' she decided mischievously.

'But surely Bette is enough for any man.'

'Surely,' Janet agreed and they were off again, holding their hankies to their eyes, unable to make any sort of remark for several minutes.

When Janet finally got up to replenish the teacups Hannah shook her head and said wonderingly, 'Aren't you the dark horse, never saying a word about this till now. Mind you,' she hastened to add, 'I wouldn't have said anything either, only I just wondered to myself if Mungo was all right when I saw him fleering away down to the shore with his face red and banging the door shut behind him.'

'He behaved in much the same way yon time he and Bette had a row about the amount o' hours he spends at kirk meetings,' Janet volunteered. 'Something else must have happened to upset him. It could be something to do with that young girl who arrived on their doorstep a day or two ago, a niece of Bette's, I think.'

'Yes, yes, I saw her too.' Hannah nodded, her face sparkling with an animation that made her look unexpectedly attractive. 'A stout lass, coming up the track, all hot and bothered and looking as if she was ready to drop at any moment.'

'Well, it will be common knowledge before very long. Nothing stays secret in Kinvara and Big Bette tends to say more about her affairs than she should when she's behind the counter of her shop.'

Hannah hadn't enjoyed herself so much in ages and felt a hundred times better than she had on waking that morning. She didn't even mind too much when one of the cats came to rub itself against her legs, though normally she wasn't all that keen on felines of any description and was glad when Breck put them in their place with just a few warning grunts and growls. The laird's Siamese cat, Sheba, was the worst of all, with its airs and graces and disconcerting habit of suddenly plonking itself down on Hannah's knee whenever the laird had reason to visit No. 6 of the Row.

Captain Rory MacPherson was a very easygoing sort of landowner who had always mixed well and quite often took it into his head to pop into a house for a cuppy or a dram. In common with most folk, Hannah liked the laird and enjoyed the informality of his visits but everywhere he went his cat went also and Hannah knew that it deliberately tormented her by seeking her out and making itself agreeable to her in an oddly provocative kind of way, gazing at her with its slanty blue eyes and yowling up into her face as if it was trying to converse with her.

It was a very intelligent beast, she had to admit, with its wiles and wants and habits more suited to a dog than a cat. But it wasn't a dog. Breck was, and he made very sure that Sheba was aware of this fact whenever she entered his domain; he was even more on his guard when the laird's spaniels accompanied their master and tried to dominate the scene by putting on their half-starved look as they sat rigidly to attention at the table waiting for scraps.

It was at such interludes that Hannah really appreciated Breck, who had never stood any nonsense from anyone. She wished she hadn't left him outside since Janet's big tabby had now commandeered her lap and was nuzzling at her hand as it tried to lick the particles of butter that had adhered to her fingers from the toast.

'She's about to have kittens,' Janet smiled indulgently. 'She's hungry all the time and I've a feeling they'll be arriving soon.'

'Oh.' At this, Hannah hastily shooed the animal away, as if afraid that it was about to drop its litter on her knee at any moment, the expression on her face making Janet clap her hand to her mouth and erupt into giggles.

The children came clattering into the room, Joss demanding to know what all the merriment was about.

'School.' Janet jumped up and began bundling him into his coat while he grumbled and protested and said he wasn't a baby and she never told him anything that involved grown-up affairs.

'I know anyway.' He threw her a roguish grin as she wound one of Cousin Kathy's scarves round his neck and made him do up his buttons.

'Oh, do you now, you're getting to have quite long lugs on you for such a nipper. Well, my lad, I want you always to remember this. What goes on inside these four walls is nobody's business but ours. Only doors have letterboxes and if your mouth gets too big, Dougie the Post might easily pop a letter into it and have one o' his panic attacks as he stands there watching while you try to digest the news.'

Joss tried hard not to let her see that this was in any way humorous but Vaila and Andy had no such reservations and shouted with laughter, making Janet and Hannah smile while Joss strove hard to keep a straight face. 'All right.' He held up his hand. 'I give in, you are a very funny mother and I promise I will not tell anybody the things I heard you and Hannah telling each other.'

'You're bluffing, Joss Morgan, off to school with you and don't take all day about it. It's stopped raining for the moment and I want you all to get indoors before it comes on again.'

Joss slung his schoolbag over his shoulder and held out his hand. 'A halfpenny for keeping my mouth shut – and maybe another one later for good behaviour.'

'Joss Morgan!' A swipe with the dishtowel sent him scurrying but at the last moment she relented and dug into her purse to search out the 'silence money'.

Hannah was helping Vaila on with her coat, wrapping Andy up against the rain, telling him not to come back soaked as she didn't want him or his dog trailing mud all over her floors.

Andy was listening with only half an ear. He knew his mother better than anybody. He knew the bite of her tongue, he had heard the same words many times before and had come to realise she only meant half of what she said. She was as yielding as putty underneath all that blethering and barking. She only did it to make herself sound tough but all the time she wasn't . . . Andy smiled and raised one thin arm to pat his mother's cheek as she fussed and scolded and tried not to let him see that she was more concerned about his welfare than about the wet and the dirt he and Breck might bring back when their wanders of the morning were over.

Chapter Five

Breck was waiting beside Andy's cart, looking a bit dejected as he lay with his nose in his paws staring at the door as if willing it to open. When Hannah at last came out he threw her a look of such reproach she felt guilty for having left him outside and only he knew about the piece of toast she smuggled to him from the pocket of her apron. Never would she allow anybody to see that she was 'getting soft', especially with a dog who was 'good for nothing' and only earned his keep when he kept the neighbourhood cats in their place and took Andy to the shops to 'fetch the messages'.

The children came piling out, Andy to climb into his cart, Joss to erect the little pram hood that Willie Whiskers had affixed to keep off the rain. Breck took his place between the shafts; at the last minute Vaila remembered the new schoolbag that was her pride and joy and ran indoors to get it. But at last everyone was ready and they set off down the grassy track to the road, watched by Janet and Hannah from the window of No. 5 of the Row.

'Just look at them.' Janet shook her head. 'It seems only yesterday that they were babies.' A wistfulness crept into her voice. 'Joss is growing so big and independent. I know he would love a brother or sister and I would give anything to have another.'

Hannah said nothing. She had been in two minds about confiding her fears of another pregnancy to her neighbour but now she very firmly decided against it. Janet would go on and on about it and think it was wonderful and Hannah didn't feel able to face that kind of enthusiasm right now. Oh, it was so unfair! Here was she, dreading the thought of another child, and here was Janet, longing to add to her family but unable to do so. She and Jock had been told there would be no more after Joss and it had been a cruel blow to both of them.

'I'm sure Mollie Gillespie's expecting again,' Janet was going on, 'It isn't showing yet but she's got that look about her I've come to know well. Dolly Law's in the same boat, or rather the same pudding club, and I could have told her that before she even knew it herself. Effie says I would have made a good midwife but I don't want to deliver babies, I just want to have them. Everyone else in Kinvara seems able to pop them out like rabbits from a hat and Cousin Kathy is of the opinion that somebody, somewhere, is mixing magic potions and putting them in the water to make sure the population keeps expanding.'

Hannah, desperate to change the subject, burst out irrelevantly, 'To tell the truth, I didn't really come in about the ginger snaps. I suppose I just wanted to commiserate with someone.' Her face had reddened, she wanted to stop talking but instead rushed on, 'Why don't you come in to me later this morning and we'll cook up something together. It's going to be a long first day for us both with our menfolk away and the bairns at school.'

'Ay, why not?' Janet hid her surprise well, since invitations of the casual sort were not characteristic of Hannah's withdrawn nature. Once upon a time she had been known as the Recluse of the Row but Janet had seen a new side to her neighbour of late and most notably in the last half-hour. She had been shy at first, certainly, but had soon blossomed and opened out. There was about her a droll sense of the ridiculous and Janet liked that since she herself was forever giggling her head off over the most silly happenings.

In fact, Janet realised that she had greatly enjoyed Hannah's visit, for not only had she proved to be good company, she was also possessed of a keen sense of observation that allowed her to see the many facets in the characters and personalities of those round about her.

Janet already knew about Hannah's weaknesses. Now she saw her strengths as well and Janet's voice was warm when she went on more enthusiastically, 'Ay, why not? Just let me tidy up here a bit then I'll be in with my flour in about an hour . . .'

She giggled, Hannah smiled, they went to the door and looked out. The rain was lifting, the wind had abated; the mist was rolling back from the hills, gossamer scarves of it drifting into the corries and draping the peaks with mantles of pearly grey. The warm hues of autumn were spreading over the landscape, bright red berries hung on the rowans, the alder leaves were like big golden pennies in air that was laden with the rich ripe smells of mellow fruitfulness.

The sea had quietened again, the horizon was brightening, and clearly visible was the tall lone tower of the Kinvara Light, seeming far away and inaccessible in this weather, so out of reach, so divided from the land and the people who watched and waited and looked forward to the day their menfolk would come back to them again.

Hannah and Janet looked at it and thought their individual thoughts. They glanced at one another in understanding then Hannah went off to her own house, breathing deeply of the dewy fresh air as she went, a spring in her step that hadn't been there earlier. Let tomorrow bring what it would, today had started off well, and she could only hope that nothing would happen to change her mood in the days and the dawnings that stretched ahead of her.

From their window, Babs and Tom spied Joss and the young Sutherlands setting off down the road to school, and with a hasty farewell to their parents and a lingering one to Maudie, they ran to catch up with the other youngsters.

'We've got money to spend at Wee Fay's,' boasted Babs at once. 'Da gave us a whole threepenny bit each even though he was in a bad mood earlier and was fighting in bed with Ma.

Da always gives us money when he gets home from light duty and he said if we're good we'll get more later. At least,' she went on with an air of confidence, 'he'll give *me* more, he spoils me because I'm the only girl in our particular family.'

Tom was used to his sister's high opinion regarding her relationship with her father and merely scowled at this but Vaila and Joss had learned that the only way to keep Babs in her place was to be a step ahead of her and at her words they glanced at one another and began to chant, 'Babs MacGill's a show-off! Show-off! 'Cos she thinks she's a to-off! Money in her pocket and holes in her pants. Up past her stockings crawl beetles and ants!'

Babs stuck her solid little chin in the air at this and said with a sniff, 'I haven't got holes in my pants and you're just jealous because we've got money and you haven't.'

'Oh, yes we do,' Vaila flashed back. 'Me and Andy have it, Joss too, and – and – even Breck's got some.'

'I don't see how Breck could have money,' Babs said disbelievingly. 'Dogs don't get money and even if they did they wouldn't know what to do with it.'

Joss laughed and with a quick sleight of hand he pulled a halfpenny out of Breck's left ear and waved it under Babs' nose.

'I saw you doing that,' Babs said loftily. 'Anyone would think you were a child the way you carry on.'

'He *is* a child,' Tom intervened at this point and with more than a trace of the superior air that was prevalent in his sister. 'You're *all* just children when it comes to the bit, not like me, I'll be leaving school soon and going to work with my brother Joe at the mill – or maybe I'll be helping Ma in the shop. It's still to be decided, but whatever way, I'll be glad to get rid o' you lot and that Mr MacCaskill in particular. He was always clipping me on the ear when I was younger and still does when he feels like it.'

'That's because you can't count,' Joss said bluntly. 'You were always a dunce and won't be much good in your mother's shop. You'd ruin the place in five minutes and

Mattie MacPhee would cuff your lugs as well for giving her the wrong change.'

'Aw, she wouldn't dare hit me.' Tom puffed out his chest. 'My ma would soon put her in her place, my ma can even fight men because she's the biggest strongest person in the whole o' Kinvara. Compared to my mother, Mattie MacPhee's only an ordinary woman and couldny fight her way out a paper poke.'

At that moment he spied that very same woman on the road ahead with two of her younger offspring in tow and he quickly subsided into silence. Despite his derogatory remarks about Mattie he had a very high regard for her, ever since the day she'd lashed him with her razor-sharp tongue when she'd found him trying to wrest a bag of sweets from a child much younger than himself.

But Babs had more than enough to say for both herself and her brother. She was well and truly on her mettle by now and swinging the talk away from Mattie she went on to a subject she had been itching to air for the last few minutes. Glancing at Vaila she said triumphantly, 'My father saw your mother peeing on the shore. I heard him telling Ma this morning when I was coming downstairs for breakfast. Maudie heard too – Maudie's our cousin, you know, and she tells the best stories in the whole wide world.'

'Ay, so you've told us a hundred times already,' Joss said quickly, glancing anxiously at Vaila's face to see how she had taken the first part of Babs' statement. But Vaila had learned a few things since starting school; she was quickly coming to realise that the only way to survive was to give as good as she got and to show that she was able to fight back when the older children thought they could take advantage of her youth and her ignorance.

Babs MacGill was one of those who had seen it as her right to put Vaila in her place and Vaila knew that the only way to win was to beat the older girl at her own game. So Vaila stayed silent for a moment, allowing Babs to think that her words really had bitten home, then to everyone's surprise she burst out laughing, black curls blowing in the breezes, green eyes sparkling, an aura about her of light and air that made Babs stare at her in envy and wish she could look as attractive as that when the wind mussed her clothes and her hair and only ever succeeded in making her look untidy.

'Och, we all do that,' Vaila said at last. 'You do it, only you don't go behind a bush, you dribble in your pants then pretend to fall in a puddle so that you can go home and tell your mother you've had an accident.'

All eyes turned on Babs. There was sometimes a smell off her that was redolent of digestive biscuits and now they all knew why. Her chubby face had crumpled at Vaila's words and that young lady suddenly felt very ashamed that she had spoken as she had. But Babs soon rallied enough to look at Vaila with affected pity and say scathingly, 'Of course, Hannah from Ayr is only your stepmother, so it doesn't really matter all that much what she does as it can't affect you as much as it might Andy.'

Glancing at Andy with a sweet smile she went on wickedly, 'But then, he can't talk properly so we'll never know what he thinks, and your real mother is dead so you really aren't entitled to any opinions and ought to keep them to yourself.'

This did hit home. Rage and hurt danced in Vaila's eyes, Babs' jaw jutted. For a moment it looked as if combat was inevitable between the two, then another surprising thing happened. Andy brought Breck to a halt with a short command and his thin arms shot out to grab both girls and knock their heads together. For such a little lad he was unexpectedly strong, and Joss and Tom could only stare as he held the girls firmly by the scruffs of their collars and ground out, 'Say you're sorry. Say you're sorry.'

Babs wasn't too sure of his meaning but Vaila understood well enough and she gasped, 'I'm sorry, Babs, really truly sorry, and I promise I won't ever laugh at you again.'

'Me too, me too,' babbled Babs, glancing fearfully at Andy in case he might repeat his masterly performence if she didn't come out with something.

Satisfied, Andy subsided back into his cart and bade Breck move on as if nothing out of the way had occurred. Tom looked at him with new respect, Joss with true affection. He had always known that this young Sutherland had many strengths in him; today he had proved that he was as able physically as he was mentally, and Joss rejoiced in that though he felt that Vaila had come off more harshly than she deserved. He was however wise enough to know that her brother had taken the only course open to him in the circumstances.

They went on their way in a rather subdued silence. Andy was regretting taking his feelings out on Vaila. He didn't mind teaching Babs a lesson, her mouth was bigger than her head sometimes and she had a knack of riling people, but Vaila was different. Ever since she had come to live at No. 6 Keeper's Row she had been kind and patient with him and his heart was brimful of love and admiration for her. She had been sad about her mother yet she had borne her loss bravely and strongly and as these thoughts went through his head his fingers reached out to curl into hers.

She threw him a faint smile and he smiled back as he remembered the look on Babs' face when he had grabbed hold of her. She hadn't expected that. Not from him. Helpless little Andrew Sutherland who couldn't do any of the things the rest of them could. Well, maybe she would think differently now. Maybe they would all think differently.

He let out a screech of laughter. Tom snorted. Babs giggled nervously. Joss grinned. A bubble of mirth escaped Vaila. Good humour was restored as they went on their way to Balivoe and the shop known as The Dunny where they spent an enjoyable few minutes gazing into the window before actually going inside.

Children came for miles around to visit this most tempting establishment. The window was filled with homemade sweets of every kind. Humbugs and boilings were crammed into big glass jars; toffee and tablet was laid out on trays; marshmallows and coconut squares were tastefully arranged on frilly lace doyleys; cinnamon and liquorice sticks had been stuck gaily into the clasped fingers of furry little animals together with the sugar-olly twists that were much favoured by the younger customers because they lasted a long time.

On sunny days the black blind of The Dunny was drawn halfway down but today there was no need for that and the contents of the window were shown to full advantage. The children gathered round, pressing their noses against the pane, voicing their preferences according to the amount of money they had to spend. Tom remembered his approaching manhood and said he would get some cinnamon sticks so that he could smoke them later in the playshed, Babs jabbed a confident finger at several coveted items and decided that she would spend all her money in one fell swoop and have a beanfeast at playtime.

The boys went inside. Breck settled down to chew an old bone that Andy had thoughtfully brought with him. Vaila made to go inside also but Babs, anxious to atone for her earlier indiscretions, took hold of the younger girl's arm. 'I'll buy you a sugar-olly twist,' she offered, speaking quickly before she could change her mind.

But Vaila, still smarting over the hurt she had suffered concerning the mother she had loved and lost, said with dignity, 'I can buy my own sweeties, I've got my own money.'

Babs, her conscience pricking badly by now, stamped her sturdy legs impatiently. 'Och, please speak to me properly, Vaila. I'm truly really sorry I said your mother is dead even though she is, and I didn't mean these things I said about your stepmother. Maybe she didn't piddle on the shore. I only said it because I heard Da saying she did after Ma told *him* off for doing it.'

Vaila's face cleared. 'All right, I'm sorry too – for saying you piddled in puddles – even though you do,' she added, just to make sure Babs didn't feel she was getting the upper hand.

'I know, sometimes I can't wait to get to the wee hoosie in the playground,' Babs confided with the utmost seriousness. 'I just tell Ma I fell in a puddle and she believes me – even when it isn't raining and there are no puddles for miles around!'

The girls looked at one another and burst out laughing. In the best of spirits they followed the boys into The Dunny to be given a warm welcome by Wee Fay and Little John, neither of them much taller than the smallest child in Balivoe School but both of them agile and fit and able to look after themselves in no uncertain manner. Cheeky children soon learned their lesson when Little John decanted them bodily from his premises, sly children were seldom sly again when Wee Fay's sharp eyes detected them thieving behind her back.

She told them the walls had eyes when all the time they were simply hung with concealed mirrors angled to catch the mischief-makers in action and it didn't matter if they protested their innocence till they were blue in the face. Wee Fay simply made them turn out their pockets to reveal their ill-gotten gains and with a few well chosen words reduced even the toughest miscreants to tears and let them see that crime in her shop was simply not worth the effort.

By and large, however, children of all ages adored Wee Fay and her husband and liked nothing better then to visit their shop. That morning Babs and Tom had a fine time spending their threepenny pieces and managed not to look too peeved when Little John gave the others more for their halfpennies than he should.

'But they . . .' Babs began then stopped. Little John was winking at Joss as he slipped in a crunchy biscuit for Breck because 'he hadn't come into the shop to spend his coppers himself.'

'But he . . .' Babs began again when a glance at Joss's laughing face stilled her tongue. With a toss of her head she marched from the shop but forgot her mood as she peeked into the enormous paper bag in her hand that contained lots of little bags filled with an assortment of sweets. Her mouth watered. There was everything in here! Everything! What should she have first? A marshmallow or a humbug? Her fat little fingers plundered the rustling depths. Withdrawing a pink marshmallow she popped it into her mouth. It simply melted away. Her eyes rolled ecstatically. She was in seventh heaven, sublimely happy, and she quite generously passed round a bag of humbugs when the others at last emerged from The Dunny.

They walked harmoniously along, cheeks bulging as they sucked and chewed, oblivious to the changing mood of the day as the mist swooped low over the hills once more and a fine drizzle came down to fur their clothing.

'Wish I didn't have to go to school,' Joss said as he watched the tide bringing in great tangles of orange seaweed. 'I could have helped Johnny Lonely look for crabs, or maybe gone out with Charlie Campbell to help him bait his lobster creels.'

Tom's eyes shone. 'Let's play truant,' he suggested eagerly. 'It's a waste o' time going to school anyway. Old MacCaskill couldny teach my granny to suck eggs, never mind anything else he tries to do.'

'Our granny wouldn't want anybody to teach her how to suck eggs,' Babs told her brother scornfully. 'She has her own teeth yet and eats her eggs boiled with a spoon. The only time she eats them raw is when she whips them in milk for her chest.'

Vaila's eyes danced. 'Hannah never boils ours with a spoon. She always does them in a pan with water though sometimes she puts salt in so's they won't burst.'

They giggled, Tom scowled. 'Girls!' he cried, 'I don't know what Ma was thinking of when she had one. Another boy would have been better. At least they don't talk in riddles.'

Joss wasn't listening to any of this. He was sorely tempted by Tom's idea of truancy. Joss hated being cooped up in a classroom when outside all the big wide world was waiting with its thrills and spills and endless small adventures. Because he went to the Catholic school in Vaul it would be easier for him to avoid lessons than it would be for Tom and the girls. Old MacCaskill would smell a rat when half the youngsters of Keeper's Row failed to turn up in the classroom and he wouldn't be slow in telling the respective parents about the sins of their offspring and 'what he had to suffer trying to din learning into their lugs'.

Joss sighed. It wouldn't be much fun anyway. Vaila would be all right but he didn't want Babs trailing along. She would moan and groan about everything and they would all just end up arguing and – he smiled to himself – maybe Andy would knock all their heads together and none of them would be fit for anything!

Chapter Six

They had reached the school gates. Mr Stuart MacCaskill was in the playground, padding restlessly about with his hands clasped behind his back, itching to blow his whistle so that he could marshal his pupils into the lines that had been chalked out at the side of the little whitewashed stone building. One section for girls, the other for boys, and woe betide anyone who shuffled or whispered once they were in position.

Mr MacCaskill loved order in his school. Children on the loose made him nervous and he never felt happy till they were gathered under his wing and he could safely watch their every move and exert discipline if required. But he was never truly at ease till they were inside the school building sitting at their desks, troublemakers at the front where his hawk eyes could observe their every move, beginners in the middle, the rest in the rows behind according to age and rank.

Tom had been in front that week because of lack of attention in class and at sight of his teacher he quickly hid his cinnamon sticks. Mr MacCaskill knew full well that some of his older pupils indulged in certain acts of bravado and tried to impress one another by smoking anything they could get their hands on.

Cinnamon sticks were the latest craze but they were fragile affairs and Tom broke one as he tried to stuff it down the top of his stocking leg.

'Bugger it! Bugger it!' His face grew red as he cursed in his anxiety.

'I'll tell Da you swore,' Babs said piously even while she herself endeavoured to hide her humbugs and liquorice sticks in her satchel and hoped Mr MacCaskill wouldn't notice the bulge in her cheek owing to a toffee that had got stuck in her teeth.

Vaila had none of these things to worry her. She had long ago finished her sugar-olly twist but waited with the others till at last they were ready to face the world of school with innocent, if slightly sticky, faces.

Andy watched a trifle wistfully as they went off, glad that Vaila remembered to turn and wave to him at the last moment. He was still feeling guilty for what he had done to her earlier and slowly he turned Breck's nose in the direction of Calvost, vowing to himself that he would make it up to her, even if it was just to tell her one of his own little stories at bedtime.

She of all the people in his world, with perhaps the exception of his father, understood his difficult mode of speech. As he trundled along he began making up verses and rhymes in his head, his love of words, which seemed always to have been with him, allowing him to forget the feeling of loneliness he'd experienced at the school gates when the others had run away to join their classmates.

Joss had gone on ahead, knowing he would be late this morning, his mind full of the excuses he might give to Father Kelvin MacNeil, the young curate who taught the tiny Catholic school in Vaul alongside Miss Aileen Dinkie, a gentle spinster lady who looked as if butter wouldn't melt in her mouth but who could be quite formidable if she thought anyone was taking advantage of her good nature.

She and the priest worked well together, neither of them believing in the belt but relying on more productive methods of punishment, 'time for crime' being one of their favourites and meaning just that. Anyone stepping out of line could find themselves humping coal for an elderly parishioner or washing the Manse floors, a task of which Minnie MacTaggart, the curate's housekeeper, did not approve since she claimed she had to do them all over again owing to the soapy tidemarks the young domestics left in the wake of their scrubbing brushes.

But being late for the whistle didn't warrant such drastic measures and Joss was soon seated in the classroom, growing a bit red about the ears as Miss Dinkie took him to task in front of his contemporaries and satisfied herself in knowing that she had thoroughly embarrassed him in the process.

Andy made his way along the deserted village street, his little hood offering scant protection against the squally wind and rain that was now driving in from the sea. The only sign of life to be seen was that of Maisie 'Whiskers' MacPhee, briskly sweeping the steps of Anvil Cottage which she was wont to do at any time of the day and in any weather, mainly because she liked to see the world go by and not because she was in any way inclined to hard work.

On warm sunny days Andy liked nothing better than to pause for a while at the Smiddy and watch Willie Whiskers shoeing a horse in the cobbled yard, a big hairy hoof resting on his leather-covered knee, a row of nails sticking out of his mouth, his muscles straining against his damp shirt as he worked, the magnificent ginger-coloured whiskers that had given him his name shining in the sun as he sweated and swore and cursed 'the buggering brutes' that earned him his bread and that he loved like the children he'd never had, despite the choice names he called them.

Today it was far too wet for Willie to be working outside but it was just as good to be inside watching him working the giant bellows or hammering the red-hot horseshoes into shape on the anvil.

Seated outside in his little cart, Andy could hear Willie's hammer beating away in the depths of the forge building, and he hesitated, wondering if he had time to go in and see the blacksmith, remembering what his mother had told him about coming home wet.

'Away you go in, lad,' Maisie called, battering a cobweb with her brush as she spoke. 'Willie's making shoes for that big stallion brute o' the doctor's but you won't be in the way if you leave your cart outside.'

Andy needed no second bidding; in minutes he was ensconced on a kitchen chair inside the warm smoky workshop, fascinated as he always was with his surroundings. On the walls hung a baffling array of tools, some made by Willie himself, others by his forefathers.

Over by the door, supported on a bench, was the tyre bender, used for making iron cart hoops, looking like for all the world like a large clumsy household mangle with its iron rollers and turning handle. Then there was the hearth itself with its canopy and chimney and pear-shaped bellows and as if to complete the picture a cat was sound asleep in a corner, oblivious to the noise and bustle, undisturbed by Breck who regarded it as a tried and tested companion and often curled up beside it to snooze the minutes away while he waited for his young master.

Andy knew and loved it all and this morning it was especially interesting because Willie had recently taken on young Alan Law as his apprentice. Alan was fourteen, the eldest of 'The Outlaws' as his family was known, quick of tongue and fiery of temper, sharp-witted and devious, his shock of red hair having earned him the nickname of Carrots from an early age.

But he was a likeable lad for all that, energetic and eager to learn, cheerful and optimistic, full of ambitions to one day have a forge of his own or to become a travelling farrier so that he could 'see the big wide world'.

In his younger days, Alan had been the leading light in his family, forever on the lookout for anything that would benefit himself and his siblings, able to make use of any opportunity that chanced his way, a boy who could sniff out the weaknesses in human nature and use them to his own advantage. Shug, his father, who detested work, and Dolly, his mother, who was always having children, had taught all their family the art of honest, and sometimes not so honest, survival, and with Alan being the eldest he had soon absorbed the skills that had been handed down to him.

Now he was growing up and wanted more out of life, and though it had hurt Shug to actually have to pay Willie a small weekly fee for the privilege of taking on his son, he had eventually come round to Alan's way of thinking when his glib tongue had outlined all the rosy plans he had in mind for his future.

It said a lot for Willie when he agreed to take on a young fox like Alan but the smith had no son of his own to whom he could teach his craft and so he decided to give Carrots Law a chance. And he was glad now that he had. The boy had the strength and staying power of an ox and willingly fetched and carried, lifted and laid, whistling and singing as he worked, occasionally pinching the odd nut and bolt, helping himself to a coveted tool, simply because it was in his nature to profit from chance and not from a desire to deprive his employer of anything that would harm his business. Willie ignored these minor lapses from grace; the lad more than earned his fly little perks since he had taken many burdens off Willie's shoulders.

He had also learned quickly and well, showing a dexterity and understanding of the craft that met with his master's approval. To show his appreciation, Willie had given his apprentice a handmade shepherd's crook for his birthday and Alan was delighted with himself as he strode along the road, twirling and swinging his crook in a manner that would have befitted Captain Rory MacPherson himself. He felt not in the least dismayed when he chanced upon the man himself one day, swinging *his* crook and glancing askance at Alan as if implying that he should know not to ape his betters.

Andy was exremely fond of the Laws as a whole. They had never showed him anything but kindness, Dolly taking him on her 'washing rounds' or to the harbour whenever it was convenient, Shug humping him around on his back despite the fact that he was supposed to be in a near-perpetual state of pain owing to his lumbar regions 'giving him gyp' and it was 'terrible just' that nobody believed the agony he had to endure in his day-to-day life.

The Law youngsters, conditioned to a lifestyle of anomalies, had never batted an eye when Andy had come among them but accepted him as he was and credited him with normal intellect except for the fact that he 'made funny faces and couldn't speak right but was otherwise much the same as anyone else.'

Alan had always been one of Andy's favourite Laws and he was delighted when he saw the boy's carroty head alongside the fiery one of Willie; he was further enamoured when Alan threw down his tools for a few minutes to take the little visitor on his shoulders and ride him round the smiddy, making noises like a horse as he went, whinnying and neighing and finally galloping full tilt into Donald of Balivoe who had called on Willie to settle an account he owed.

Being short of cash, Donald had come to pay by barter, and in his arms he carried a crate of chickens which dropped to the floor as he and the apprentice made impact. The flimsy spars of the crate sprung apart and the chickens took off, squawking at the tops of their voices and flapping their wings as they went, some making for the shore to hide among the boulders, others to huddle in a nearby culvert, two disappearing into the distance never to be seen again.

'You young bugger, you young bugger!' yelled Donald. 'Get them! Get them! Get them!'

Carrots Law, anxious to make amends, needed no second bidding. Setting Andy down, he also took off and went haring away to collect as many birds as he could manage in one swoop, tucking two under his arms, holding two more by their big clumsy feet so that they clucked and flapped and protested till they were deposited unceremoniously inside the wee hoosie and the blind pulled down to keep them quiet till more suitable living quarters could be arranged.

'There were six!' Donald cried as soon as Alan came back.

'Now there are only four! What's to do, I'd like to know? I have no spare chickens left to pay Willie and it goes wi'out saying I'll no' see a farthing's worth o' compensation from that father o' yours. Getting money out o' him is like trying to poke butter up a hedgehog's arse wi' a red hot needle!'

Donald of Balivoe, a man much respected in the community, hence his title, was normally possessed of an even and placid temperement, but somehow the Laws had always managed to bring out the worst in him. In earlier times there had been Shug and his brothers to contend with, playing tricks, dodging work, committing numerous small unlawful acts yet never getting caught for any of them.

Now there were the present-day young Outlaws to contend with, following in their father's footsteps, riding Donald's horse bareback in the fields so that it was 'buggered' when he wanted it, stealing milk from the udder of his house-cow and drying it out in the process, helping themselves to his dung for their rhubarb patch, the only thing the parent Laws had ever willingly cultivated because they liked to keep the bowels of the little Laws 'regular in the natural way'.

And there was always a baby Law on the way, Dolly and Shug between them seeming hellbent on producing progeny as if the human race was due for extinction at any minute. The prospect of a Law-filled future filled Donald with despair. He was sixty-three years old. If he lived to be a hundred he could easily see in two more generations of Law offspring and maybe even three the way they bred!.

Alan was just turned fourteen but was already more than a mite interested in getting girls' knickers off. Only the other day Donald had spied him behind a shed trying to do just that. For all anybody knew he could be a father several times over! In no time at all the place would be polluted with bastard Laws running wild everywhere. He would never be free of them – never . . .

Donald's imagination ran riot at this point. He broke out in a sweat. He was anything but amused over this business with the chickens. The whole episode had greatly shaken him, and he became further incensed when Willie and Andy went into shrieks of laughter regarding the comments he had made about Shug's meanness. And through it all Alan stood at the door, grinning sheepishly and at the same time striving to look apologetic and downcast.

'Och, come on, man.' Willie wiped his eyes and threw an arm round Donald's shoulders. 'It isn't as bad as all that, accidents happen and Alan didn't mean to barge into you the way he did. Most of the birds have been caught, the rest will turn up when they're good and ready.'

'Ay, in some bugger's soup pot.' Donald sounded calmer now despite his gloomy predictions.

'One o' them's a cockerel anyway.' Alan added his piece. 'Soon there will be lots o'wee chickens running about all over the place.'

'Just like the Laws,' Donald said with a sour attempt at humour. Maisie came in just then with tea and scones. Willie brushed debris from the anvil with the fringed hem of his apron, his wife set down the tray and poured steaming mugs of tea from a big brown earthenware pot.

Outside, the rain hissed, the wind blew, but inside it was warm and cosy. Maisie, a great character in her own right, with her doleful face, whiskery chin, and 'a tongue like a broken milk bottle' to quote her husband, stayed for 'a cleck' and the atmosphere mellowed as gradually Donald thawed in the cheerful company and soon reverted to his good-natured self.

They ate and drank, they talked, the menfolk smoked their pipes and discussed world and village affairs, they swore and blasphemed and Andy thoroughly enjoyed himself despite an occasional twinge of apprehension as he wondered what his mother would say when he arrived home late with 'the messages'.

When he eventually took his leave the morning was halfway through and the rain was drizzling steadily down. Mist was skulking in the hills, the burns were frothing down from hidden summits, Cragdu castle looked like a fairy palace with its turrets poking up through mist-swathed corries to pierce the sky. Masses of dark cloud had banked up over the sea. Andy looked in vain for a sign of the Kinvara Light but it was hidden from view.

Then suddenly a dazzling sunray broke through a hole in the clouds and lit the tip of the tower. It was like a sign from the heavens. A tear pricked Andy's lids. Father, he thought, I see you. I know you're there and I'm thinking of you.

He gave a start. He was dreaming again. Always he was dreaming. Thinking of things that weren't practical, poetic things that didn't get him anywhere – except in his head. In his mind he could go wherever he fancied, he could soar like a bird, fly like a kite, glide over the fields and glens, travel to foreign lands, explore weird and wonderful places . . .

He grinned to himself. He'd better travel all right! Along to Big Bette's shop to get the messages or his mother would have something to say if he went home without them.

Chapter Seven

With all the upsets over Maudie, Bette was late opening up shop that morning. When she did arrive she was puffed and harassed and wasn't in the mood to invite Andy inside out of the rain. Normally she just scooped him up in her big meaty arms and bore him up the steps to wait while she filled his shopping bag. But her mind was too taken up with her own affairs to bother with those of anybody else and the little boy sat outside, getting wetter and wetter, feeling a chill run through him as the rain found its way in under his hood and soaked his clothes.

Bette experienced a pang of guilt when she eventually came outside and saw his white face peeping out at her. 'Go you right home, now,' she directed as she tucked the message bag behind his seat. 'I'm sorry I didn't ask you in but I'm all at sea this morning and can't seem to gather my wits to attend to anything. When I've got a minute I'll make you a flute. You can blow on it to let folks know you're coming and might even learn to play a tune on it if you practise hard enough.'

Andy departed. Bette stood watching him go, feeling ashamed of herself for not having spared him any of her time that morning. She had grown used to his 'wee ways' and didn't mind having him in the shop but his speech was difficult to decipher and she wasn't feeling well enough to be bothered. Besides all that, she kept thinking about Maudie and Mungo, how they were managing to cope with one another, if they'd had words yet about the chair, who would do the unwashed dishes, make the beds, see to lunch.

Bette hadn't felt inclined to do any of these chores before leaving the house. Why should she anyway when there was a perfectly fit young woman in the house to do them for her? Fit and heart lazy! Bette's heart sank. The days stretched ahead of her, filled with Maudie and Mungo, one oblivious to chaos and mess, the other fussy and orderly in the extreme. Someone, sometime, would snap, and Bette took a deep breath of the salt-laden air as she tried to foresee just who that someone would be . . .

The face of Jessie MacDonald hove into view, a drip at the end of her nose and a look on her face that implied trouble. Jessie, although a kindly soul, was never happier than when she was complaining about something and enjoyed situations where she was able to give full rein to her tongue. This was one of them. Jessie liked to be first in line for fresh fruit and vegetables before they were snapped up by 'the vultures'. With this in mind she had been to the shop twice already only to find the door shut and no one there – and in this weather too!

Bette sighed. Her head was still throbbing, she was in no fit state to deal with the likes of Jessie MacDonald who would undoubtedly fill her muzzy brain with moans and complaints and a whole string of trivial worries. Bette couldn't help feeling sorry for herself. It showed on her face and was doubly accentuated when she lifted her eyes skywards and gave an audible groan.

Jessie was not slow to comprehend Bette's frame of mind. The cheek of the woman! Instead of apologising for her lateness here she was, looking as if she was the wronged party and was doing the world a favour by showing up at all. Of course, Jessie sniffed, the MacGills were like that, every last one of them. And now rumour had it that another member of the family had turned up, a young woman by all accounts, as big, if not bigger, than the mighty Bette. No doubt the newcomer would soon be throwing her considerable weight about. As if there weren't enough of them already. Young Babs was getting to be every bit as overbearing as her mother, the boys were a bit better but still too full of themselves for their own good . . .

As for Mungo – well – it stood to reason the children didn't have a chance with a father as bold and as brash as that! Yet there had been a gentler side to him, in the old days, before he had gone and hitched himself to Bette. Who could blame him for changing as he had? He should have stuck with a local lass, someone who would have nurtured the little refinements in his nature. Bette could hardly be described as dainty. And fancy a woman indulging in masculine pastimes, whittling away at bits of wood and generally behaving in a manner that was anything but feminine.

Jessie sniffed again. She herself had been in the running for Mungo's affections and she was not at all pleased that most of the men she had known in her younger days were either married, unavailable, or downright uninterested. Take Charlie Campbell, for instance. She had always had a soft spot for Charlie, despite the name he had on him.

She wondered how it would it have been, a MacDonald marrying a Campbell. Oh, there would have been talk, the place would have rung with it, but it would have died down in the end. Only trouble was, Charlie was quite happy being a bachelor man.

Catching Bette's watchful eye upon her Jessie girded her loins and prepared to do battle. She was about to open her mouth to speak when Effie Maxwell, the district nurse, appeared with her mongrel dog Runt at her heels, a smile on her mobile face with its prominent nose and eyes that were filled with an insatiable curiosity.

Effie was seldom ruffled about anything and was extremely satisfied with her lot, always full of chatter about the latest goings-on in the village, the ploys of her animals, in particular her adored sow, Queen Victoria, who, as well as being a good breeder and therefore a regular source of income, seemed also to be endowed with many human characteristics if everything Effie said about her was true.

Big Bette often felt like throttling Effie who could sometimes be just a little bit overwhelmingly enthusiastic when she was in full flow. But she was just the person Bette needed right then. Jessie would have a hard time getting a word in with Effie around.

As if to complete the picture, Wilma and Rona Henderson of Croft Angus came spanking up in their little pony trap to yell 'Whoa!' at their horse and straighten their hats as they unfolded their large frames from the seat. They were big-boned women of uncertain age, reclusive and eccentric, loud of voice and sober of dress, invariably wearing black to the neck except when clumping about their croft in their big stout boots and striped butcher's aprons.

No one knew very much about 'the Henderson Hens' as they were known because of their passion for keeping poultry. They had only been in the district about twelve years, a mere puff in time by Kinvara standards. Where they had originated was anybody's guess, since they were inclined to be evasive on that count and would mutter something about 'the south' when anybody asked. It was a miracle that they had escaped scrutiny for so long. The people of Kinvara were not slow to find out facts about their neighbours but somehow had never managed it with the sisters.

It was perhaps because of this that everyone was fascinated by them and paid them a good deal of attention whenever they had reason to mingle with the natives. Bette and her cronies were no exception and all eyes turned on the pair as they drew up at the shop.

'We've brought you some fresh produce, Bette,' Rona boomed and, as one, she and Wilma went to the back of the trap and began hauling out boxes of apples and plums, carrots and cabbages, shallots, beetroot and leeks.

The Henderson Hens grew excellent fruit and vegetables. This might have had something to do with the copious amounts of droppings produced by their geese and their ducks, their hens and their turkeys, all of which went into the ground when it was of the correct vintage.

Bette did not mind how the vegetable patch sent forth its results; the quality was so good it was like manna from heaven and she was always grateful when some of it came her way since the sisters quite often carted it further afield when the notion took them as they could get better prices in the larger communities.

Jessie MacDonald was also feeling quite pleased with herself as the boxes of rosy apples and large orange carrots sailed by in front of her nose. This was better than the stuff that came by cargo and was often past its best by the time it reached Bette's shop. Jessie forgot her resentments. She would get in there before the vultures after all and as she followed Effie and the others into the shop she was able to say quite affably to the proprietress, 'It was a long wait but it was worth it, and I was thinking it was maybe just as well you had a hangover today, Bette, otherwise I might have bought some o' that fusty stuff you got yesterday from Shug Law's cart.'

Bette reddened. She glanced round quickly to make sure no one had heard before hissing at Jessie, 'I'll thank you no' to call anything I sell in this shop "fusty". And what do you mean by a hangover? I am as perfectly sober as always and if anyone says anything to the contrary they'll have me to reckon with.'

Jessie was somewhat taken aback by this. She hadn't meant her words to sound offensive but if the MacGill woman wanted battle then so be it. She knew there were those who liked to keep on Bette's right side, as she could be a real terror when she was roused. Jessie herself had to be really on her mettle before she would tackle the likes of such a woman but now she felt quite justified in making a stand and pulling herself up to her full five feet one inch she took a deep breath and went into the fray.

'There is no need to take that tone wi' me, Bette. We all make our wee mistakes and you don't have to get upset over nothing. I was never a body to rile another body, as you yourself very well know, and I wouldn't have said anything about your drinking if it had been just yourself to suffer from it. But I was shocked when I went in to see Granny Margaret earlier. The poor old soul was in quite a state, no teeth in her head, shaking like a leaf, so frail-looking I thought she was going to die on me there and then. Connie and myself between us had quite a job getting some sense out o' her, and it was only after she'd gulped down a pot o' tea nearly to herself that she told us you had been in to see her yesterday and the pair o' you had drunk yourselves silly on brandy. She said you were worried about some niece that had arrived to stay and were so feart to go home and face your husband you just sat where you were and – and got stoned out your skull instead.'

Bette was staring, staring, staring, her eyes looking as if they were getting ready to pop out her head at any minute.

Jessie, determined to show that she had no intention of being intimidated by the bristling bulk in front of her, filled her lungs once more with air before plunging on. 'Legless, she said you were, crying like a bairn one minute, laughing like a hyena the next. It's a wonder to me you ever got home at all, and I'll never know how Granny Margaret made it up to her bed wi' the amount o' liquor she had in her – and with never a body to give her a hand, Connie having gone out wi' her young man after she left the Manse and not knowing what her granny had been up to till she went to try and rouse her this morning.'

Bette was flabbergasted. She could hardly believe the evidence of her own ears. How dare Jessie MacDonald speak to her like that? After all she'd been through that morning with Mungo. If Granny Margaret was ill through drink surely that was her own fault entirely. She was old enough to know better yet there the old bitch was, playing for sympathy, blaming her excesses on Bette, broadcasting confidences to the likes of Jessie who would no doubt have them all over the neighbourhood before the day was halfway through.

Bette was so dumbfounded she lost the use of her tongue. She opened her mouth, shut it, opened it again, but no sound came. Jessie waited, trepidation starting to worm its way into her heart as she began to realise the enormity of what she had taken on when she had dared to bring Bette's activities of yesterday out into the open.

Bette found her tongue. 'You gossiping little fart!' she cried menacingly. 'Who are you to stand there and pretend to be concerned about Granny Margaret when I know fine you often go in there and sup from her bottle yourself! Ay, and not only that, you worry the life out o' her wi' your whines and ails and all the other wee things that fester away in your mind. Oh, I know fine you wanted my Mungo for yourself and canny get over the fact that he wed himself to me instead o' you. It's a man you're needing, Jessie MacDonald, but you'll never manage to get one if you go on as you're doing and it's high time you realised that fact for yourself.'

Jessie had turned white but there was to be no mercy for her. The vitriol continued to flow. In minutes Bette had reduced her opponent to a state of near tears and Jessie was soon bitterly regretting having had the temerity to take on 'the battleaxe of the neighbourhood'.

A few more customers had come into the shop. The initial chatter died away. One and all stared as Bette tore Jessie to ribbons and in the process rid herself of a goodly portion of the bottled-up anxiety she'd felt since Mungo's return.

'Ladies! Ladies!' Wilma's cry of concern resounded round the premises. 'What on earth has gotten into your good selves? Here we all are, gathered together in this excellent establishment, waiting for deliverance of one sort or another that we might return with uplifted spirits to our respective and blessed homes. But instead of goodwill and comradeship we find only dissension and argument and I for one find it upsetting, very upsetting indeed.'

A chuckle ran round the shop. Despite the sincerity of Wilma's words she had made them sound like a sermon. Her face reddened, a supportive 'Hear, hear' from Rona made her feel only fractionally better, and she subsided into the background, overcome with embarrassment.

But her little speech had the desired effect. Bette came

to her senses. Vast chest heaving, she contented herself with a last dark glower at Jessie before thundering over to take her place behind the counter, making the floorboards shake as she did so.

Jessie shuddered. A battleship as well as a battleaxe! A woman entirely without social graces of any sort. Jessie buried her face in her hanky and loudly blew her nose, all the while vowing that she would never demean herself by crossing swords with the MacGill woman again – at least not in front of an audience mostly composed of Bette's cronies, many of whom were as tough as she was and thoroughly lacking in manners.

Jessie gave herself a shake. The vultures were forming a queue, all eager to get their claws into the boxes containing the juicy offerings brought by the Henderson Hens.

Jessie was determined to salvage something from the morning's traumas and without ado she elbowed her way to the front and proclaimed in a loud voice that she had been here before anybody and it was first come first served.

'Ach, don't foul your breeks, Jessie,' Effie advised cheerfully. 'Nobody is going to fight you just for the sake o' a few carrots.' She grinned and added slyly, 'We've seen enough bickering for one morning and will surely be able to bide our time till round two comes along.'

Jessie ignored this. She got the pick of the bunch as it were and with a great show of dignity she paid for her purchases and went to the door. Charlie Campbell of Butterburn Croft, well built and good-looking, had just tagged on at the end of the queue and Jessie was heartily thankful that he hadn't been present when she'd had her confontation with Bette.

'It is yourself, Charlie,' Jessie acknowledged with a flutter of her lashes, keeping her voice low so that none of 'the vultures' would hear what she had to say. 'I am just going home to make a big pot o' soup and will bring you some over when it's ready.'

'No, no, Jessie, there is no need for you to do that,' Charlie said quickly, aware of a few laughing glances cast in his direction. 'As you know, I can make my own soup, and I would never dream of putting you to any bother on my account.'

'Ach, it's no bother, Charlie, no bother at all,' Jessie returned in her best husky tones and with a defiant backward glance at Bette behind the counter she hoisted up her shopping bag, threw back her shoulders, and went out to meet the rain feeling much much better than she'd done less than fifteen minutes ago.

Chapter Eight

'Look at you! Just look at you!' was Hannah's greeting to her son when he finally returned from his wanders of the morning. 'Soaked through and filthy into the bargain! Where have you been, I'd like to know? You'll catch your death if you haven't caught it already. What did I tell you about biding out in that rain? I'm that mad at you, Andy Sutherland, I could wring and wring your neck and never let you go anywhere again!'

If she hadn't been so angry she might have smiled at the ludicrous last part of her statement but she was too carried away to know what she was saying and she hustled the boy and his dog inside, tutting her disapproval at them both, giving Andy no chance to utter a word, leaving his little cart outside in her anxiety to get in out of the wet herself.

Janet had long ago departed. The kitchen was filled with the tempting aroma of spicy buns and biscuits but Andy knew he would not be allowed to sample any of it, not yet, not until his mother had cooled down and was better able to behave rationally.

Breck had slunk into his corner, wet and trembling, not daring to move one whisker for fear of bringing too much attention on himself.

Hannah was in the scullery, rattling the tin tub, taking it from its hook on the wall and bringing it through to the kitchen to dump it in front of the fire. Andy knew the procedure. It was always the same when he had spent too long out of doors in rough weather; the scoldings, the lectures; the hot bath; the banishment to bed.

He knew he shouldn't have stayed out so long but as usual the lure of interesting people and places had been too much for him. Hannah was roughly divesting him of his garments, lifting him into the tub that she had hastily filled from the kettles on the fire, all the while prattling on about his thoughtlessness; the worry he had caused her; what his father would have said if he were here to see for himself just what she had to put up with when he was away.

Again she failed to see the unconscious nonsense of her words. Andy had to smother a gurgle of mirth. He knew his mother. She would go on for a while, get it out of her system, then she would grow calmer, sweeter . . .

He closed his eyes. The water was warm, warm and soothing. He thought about Willie Whiskers and the smiddy, the beat and ring of the hammer; Carrots Law chasing the hens; Donald of Balivoe ranting and raving about hedgehogs and butter; Maisie Whiskers with her scones and her tea and her stories about her life at Durness when she was a girl.

She had said the gales there were often so fierce the washing used to blow off the line and land up miles away; that a wildcat was so desperate for food one winter it had come into the house and had stolen a roast chicken from under their noses and had come back the next day for a leg of lamb! Andy wasn't sure if she had made that last bit up; she was so good at keeping a straight face it was difficult to tell if she was being serious or otherwise. But it didn't matter. Her talk was so entertaining she could have told a pack of lies and he would still have enjoyed it all.

Hannah was clicking her tongue loudly and feeling very hard done by. As if she hadn't enough to do without all this as well. She splashed hot suds over Andy's skinny body as her mind raced on. She could never have any more. Never! Andy and Vaila between them took up enough of her time as it was. Vaila wasn't so bad, at least she was at school all day, but she would be stuck with *him* forever. He would always be under her feet, demanding her attention, needing more and more of it as the years went by.

What was he anyway? Just a rickle of bones with a slack mouth and a big head . . . 'A big head with plenty o' brains inside.' Without warning, Rob's words swam into her mind. Oh, it's all right for you, she argued to herself. You're away half the year. I'm the one who's left to see to your son and daughter and put up with all the bother they cause.

Andy studied her face, trying to assess if it was the right moment for him to have his say. He took a deep breath, his mouth moved. Slowly, awkwardly, the words came out. 'I'm sorry, Mother, I'm sorry.'

She looked at him. His dark hair was plastered over his head, his skinny rib cage was heaving with the effort of speaking; he looked so delicate she felt he might easily break if handled too harshly.

Vulnerable. That's what he was. Easy prey for anyone who wished to cause him harm. Tears pricked her lids. Impatiently she swallowed them back. Then with a sudden swift movement she bent to take the boy's fragile little body to her bosom. He was wet and slippery. His arms came up to wind themselves round her neck. She brushed his hair with her lips and a terrible pang of remorse went through her.

'It's all right, it's all right,' she said huskily. 'It isn't your fault, it's mine for asking you to go for the messages on a day like this.'

Breck was watching from his corner, his nose in his paws, alert to every move in the room. Sensing a lightening of the mood he lifted his head, whined, and looked at Hannah expectantly.

'Not you as well,' she said in exasperation but she got up to seize an old towel from the drying rail. Enclosing his hairy damp body in the warm folds she rubbed him briskly. When he at last emerged from her rough administrations he was tousled and half dry and looking well pleased with himself – and he still had that anticipatory look on his face.

'Oh, all right.' She shook her head at him to indicate that

he was nothing but a nuisance but she went to fetch a biscuit for him just the same and while she was at it she gave Andy a spicy bun, warm from the oven, with bits of crystallised ginger on top and juicy currants embedded in the shiny golden crust.

She was growing soft in the head, she told herself, caused by all the work and worry she had to endure – and in her condition too. No! No! There wasn't any condition. She mustn't think like that. She simply mustn't! Flustered, she went quickly out of the kitchen to the linen kist in the lobby to seek out clean towels for Andy.

A movement in the dark recesses of the kist made her hold her breath. A long spectral wail came floating out to greet her and she sprang back in fright, her heart pumping into her throat. Keeping at a safe distance she craned her neck and peered downwards, her eyes travelling over the neatly stacked sheets and towels. She could see nothing in the dim light filtering in through the tiny window, nothing that could have caused that dreadful hair-raising noise.

'Miaow.' The dainty, almost pleading cry that now reached her ears was like a small voice reaching out for understanding and kindness. It wasn't some nameless creature lurking in there but a cat! And when she looked closer she saw that it was Janet's cat, the large tabby which had commandeered her knee when she'd been in next door. And Janet had said it was going to have kittens at any moment.

Hannah remembered leaving the lid of the kist open in order to air the interior. The cat must have slipped in along with Janet when she'd come through with her baking ingredients. Oh how it must have laughed to itself when it had spied the very nest it needed to give birth! Perhaps the kittens were already here! All nice and cosy in her fresh clean linen!

Hannah gave a little yelp. She wasn't going to put up with it. She simply wasn't going to stand for it. Cats and kittens above all else. Andy in the kitchen waiting to be dried and dressed. The brute tramping all over her floors with his dripping fur and muddy paws.

Like lightning she scuttled back into the kitchen. Lifting

Andy out of the tub she wrapped him in a towel and deposited him into a chair. Warning him to 'bide where he was till she came back' she flew next door and rushed inside without knocking.

The peaceful scene that met her eyes made her feel suddenly like a bull in a china shop. Janet and Cousin Kathy were seated at the fire, drinking tea and eating ginger snaps, Kathy with her knitting as usual, counting stitches under her breath in between bites of biscuit and sips of tea. She was the exact opposite of Janet in every way, a small plump pleasant-looking young woman with dark hair and brown eyes and an easy-going air about her that was very reassuring.

At Hannah's unexpected entry into the scene both women looked up in some astonishment though Kathy still remembered to keep one finger on her stitches so that she would know exactly where she had left off.

'It's your cat, Janet,' Hannah began, feeling suddenly a bit foolish at having reacted so strongly to the situation. 'The one that's expecting kittens.'

'Ay, what about it?' Janet drawled, calmly going on with her midday repast.

'Well, it's made a bed in my linen kist and – and I think it's having its kittens or is about to have them.'

'Really.' A sprite of mischief lit Janet's eyes. 'Well, that's as good a place as any for her to give birth. Trust Tabs to find a cosy wee den, she was always choosy about such matters and must have thought your kist was ideal for the purpose.'

'But – I can't have it,' Hannah faltered. 'I have never been all that fussy on cats and Breck would go daft altogether if he discovered a whole pile o' them lurking in the lobby.'

'Och, a cat is only a cat,' Kathy said without looking up from her needles. 'And Tabs was aye good at keeping the mice down – knit one, purl one, remember to knit two together at the end. She always catches them for her kittens when they get up a bit and just think, Hannah, it will save you the bother o' setting traps. Knit two together change to number ten needles – a job I never liked doing myself and one I aye leave to my Norrie when the wee buggers start coming into the house.'

Kathy's conversation was liberally sprinkled with knitting jargon and Hannah looked at her rather dazedly but had no time to unravel her comments, as it were, since Janet was not slow to add her piece.

'Kathy's right, Hannah, it is not a very nice job for a woman. Jock isn't all that keen on it either, wi' him being a big softie at heart. That is why we have the cats, to keep down the mice and these little shrews that sometimes come in and creep all round the skirting. They have a terrible bite for such tiny wee creatures and I'll never forget being attacked by one when I opened a drawer in the kitchen dresser.'

She was warming to her subject and went on with relish. 'Bats too, the cats keep them away as well, we had one in our bedroom once, crawling across the floor using the hooks on its wings to get it along, making noises like a spook as it came towards us, its mouth wide open as if it was going to gobble us up at any moment.'

Hannah emitted a little shriek at this and Janet relented. 'Och, we're only teasing, Hannah, give me a minute to find something to bring Tabs home in – though it is a shame to disturb her at a time like this,' she couldn't refrain from adding and was rewarded with a small grimace of shame from Hannah who nevertheless stood her ground and waited while Janet went to rummage in cupboards.

'Bugger it, I've dropped a stitch!' Cousin Kathy gave a shout of dismay, then with a resigned smile she temporarily abandoned her needles and arose from her chair to stuff spicy buns and ginger snaps into a paper bag, explaining to Hannah as she did so that 'her Norrie just loved Janet's baking and it was a good job just that he had false teeths or they would have gone bad on him long ago.'

Hannah, trying to digest Kathy's whimsical mode of speech, was silent for a few moments before hazarding, 'But what about you, Kathy? I know you don't like sugar, yet I saw you eating biscuits and buns not five minutes ago and I myself was with Janet when she put a fair amount o' sugar into her baking mixture.'

'Oh, ay, of course I eat sweet things,' Kathy nodded cheerfully. 'I never ever said I didny like them, I just said they were bad for the teeths. I myself have no fears on that score, like my Norrie I was wise enough to get rid o' them a good long whilie ago. What I have now never give me any problems, except when they need changed for new ones every now and again.'

Hannah's brow furrowed, she took a deep breath. 'Kathy, correct me if I'm wrong, but surely at your age you wouldn't have needed false teeth if you had eaten all the right things when you were younger.'

'Ay.' Kathy looked at Hannah as if she was not all there. 'Oh, ay, you're right enough there, Hannah, that is why I'm so against sugar, I know what harm it does, especially in bairns, and I never let my own three eat it unless I am there to supervise the amount they take – they have to keep up their strength, you see,' she finished with a patient gentle smile.

Hannah, looking none the wiser, decided that she had better say no more on the subject and was really quite relieved when Janet appeared back in the kitchen, rumpled and flushed but triumphantly bearing a cosily lined log basket.

Hannah led the way to the kist in the lobby of No. 6. The cat and her four newborn kittens were deposited into the basket, the new mother industriously cleaning them and giving only a cursory mew of reproach at the human intrusion into her chosen nursery.

'I'll wash the sheets,' Janet offered.

But Hannah shook her head. 'No, it's all right, there isn't all that much mess and what there is can wait till later. I'll have to go, I've left Andy in the kitchen. He came home soaked and I had to give him a hot bath.'

Janet laid a hand on her arm. 'It was good fun, wasn't it?'

'What – the cat?'

'No – well that too – I mean the gossip we swapped this morning and the baking lesson.'

'Ay, it was good,' Hannah agreed and had to smile at the look of laughter on Janet's fair face.

The little procession went off, Janet carrying the basket containing her cat and its new family, Kathy with her lapbag holding her knitting and a pile of patterns that just kept on growing and growing and making her more of a Kangaroo Kathy than ever.

Vaila was forbidden to go into Andy's room that night because of the risk of catching the cold off him. He lay in his bed, coughing and spluttering, feeling very sorry for himself indeed and regretting the fact that he wouldn't be able to tell Vaila a story after all.

If only he could put something down on paper. He knew quite a lot of the alphabet. Vaila had printed it out for him in big coloured letters but all he could do was keep it inside his head. With his shaky hands he found it difficult to hold a pencil and even more difficult to keep it steady while he was trying to write.

But he would one day. He would just practise and practise and force himself to do it so that people would understand all the things that were going on in his mind. His father had told him he could do it if he tried hard enough and he knew that anything his father said would come true in the end.

He wished that big dark Rob was here right now. When he was home everything was so much better. He had the knack of making an adventure out of the smallest happening and when he was around there was always a feeling of excitement in the air.

'All things are possible, Andy, always remember that and never give up trying.'

He could hear Rob's voice as if he was standing here in the room with him. His dear father. He must get lonely out there on the lighthouse with the bleak rock and wild seas all around, cut off from his family and the people who knew and cared for him, Yet he had told Andy that it could be exhilarating too, the waves crashing and booming, the vast and wonderful skies that stretched right to eternity, the feeling of being surrounded by mighty forces of nature that made him pause and think of the Great Hand that had created everything.

Andy could picture the scene vividly and he vowed to go out there one day and feel the solitude and grandeur for himself.

Meanwhile, he decided that he would get Vaila to write a letter to their father, saying how much they missed him and wanted him home. Vaila had only been at school a short time but already she could mark down words that made sense and she had been able to count to twenty and recite the alphabet before she had been taught anything in the classroom.

He moved restlessly. He was hot and sticky and he wished that his mother would come in to see him for a moment. But she had gone early to bed, saying that she was tired out with all 'the shenanigans' of the day.

He remembered the look on her face when she'd been telling him about Janet's cat and he chuckled because he had been grateful to Tabs for taking the attention away from him.

Hannah lay on her back thinking over the day's events. There was certainly never a dull moment in this house, what with Andy and Breck and that cat of Janet's having the cheek to land itself in her house and bring forth its young!

It had been a strange mixed day altogether, starting off with that Mungo MacGill and his odd behaviour down on the shore, then her visit to Janet and Janet's visit to her and Kangaroo Kathy with all her garbled talk and her way of mixing everything up so that you began to think that you were the one who was mad.

Still, in the darkness she smiled. It *had* been fun as Janet said, and she was glad that she was finding it easier now to be neighbourly and to feel more relaxed in company. In the old days she would have lain here with no one to think about but herself and Rob out yonder over the sea.

As thoughts of her husband wandered into her head she propped herself on one elbow and tried to see the pinprick of the Kinvara Light on the horizon. But her view was hampered by the curtains and getting out of bed she went to the window. The great blue-black reaches of the Atlantic Ocean lay stretched before her. In the distance the light winked, a spark of life out there in the vast wilderness of time and space and loneliness never-ending. 'Oh, Rob,' she whispered. 'I miss you and I wish you were here to talk to me. I – love you – but sometimes I hate you too for leaving me alone like this.'

She put her cold hands to her mouth. No. No. She hadn't meant that. He was the one person in the world she could never hate, the only person she had ever really loved in the whole of her life.

'I should talk to you more, Rob,' she whispered into the silent heartbeat of the night, 'I should tell you how much you mean to me but it's difficult for me to show my feelings. Maybe in time I'll find it easier, I did it with Vaila today and felt good about it afterwards. So good.'

It was cold here by the window and with a shiver she hopped over the floorboards and back into bed where she drew the quilt about her shoulders and huddled her feet into her nightdress. She was wide awake now and her thoughts turned to Janet's blethers of shrews and mice and bats that went bump in the night. The house was very quiet and still around her; every creak of the timbers, every rustle outside, seemed magnified a thousandfold.

She could hear Andy coughing from his room and she lay for a few minutes longer, wondering if she ought to get up and go to him.

Oh, he was a little devil at times! That wanderlust he had in him, the worry and work he caused her. Yet, she had to admit, she missed him when he wasn't here. In some strange way he brought her a measure of comfort and helped to fill her lonely hours. But he would always be a millstone round her neck, growing heavier and heavier as the years went by. He would never go to school like Vaila, never do any of the things that he would have done if he had been normal.

The racking sound of his coughing was getting louder. She was tired, so tired, it had been a busy day, all she wanted was to relax and go to sleep . . .

Then suddenly it happened. A nerve quivered in her belly. A nerve or a life? Oh, God no, not that! She couldn't be, there was no feeling of heaviness in her body, she hadn't been sick as she had been with Andy. With him she had often felt as if she was dying, all through those long weary nine months hardly a day had gone by without some discomfort of some kind.

The nerve pulsed again. In sheer panic she tossed back the covers, shoved her feet into her slippers, and almost ran through to her son's room. He had thrown off his blankets and was tossing and turning. When she felt his brow it was hot and the rest of his body was bathed in sweat.

At her entry he had lifted his head in some surprise but soon accepted that she was there and even managed to groan an acknowledgement. When she lit the lamp on his dresser it gave off a warm reassuring glow and telling him to 'bide still for a minute' she lit the way downstairs with her own lamp and made her way to the kitchen.

There she poured hot water from the kettle on to a mixture of honey and lemon laced with a drop of whisky. Her own mother had always sworn by this concoction and some of Hannah's best memories involved hot toddy given to her when she was ill in bed with the cold.

Thoughts of her mother gave Hannah food for thought. It had been quite a long while since she'd last seen Harriet Houston from Ayr, as the locals had christened her mother on her visits to Kinvara. She had of course been taken up with sorting out her affairs since the death of her husband some months ago. Hannah had travelled to Ayr for her father's funeral but she hadn't seen her mother since then, though she had written several times. She had received only one reply in return and a sense of guilt had beset her. She really ought to have gone back to help with the aftermath of the funeral. The hotel that her parents had built into a thriving business had been put up for sale; there must have been a lot of paperwork to sift through, together with all the personal bits and pieces her father had gathered in his lifetime.

But there were lawyers to see to such things, and Harriet had always been a very capable sort of person. Even so, Hannah's conscience had been bothering her lately, and she told herself she would go and visit her mother at Christmas when Rob was home to look after the children.

From his corner, Breck was regarding her with interest, as if waiting for her to speak or show some indication that she was aware of his presence. His tail flicked and she knew he was getting ready to get up and come to her. She felt oddly gratified by this. For a moment she couldn't think why this should be the case. Then it struck her. In years gone by Breck had rarely responded to her as a person worthy of his attention. But more and more of late he was beginning to display a certain affection towards her and she found herself thinking how strange it would be without this big cross-collie of a dog in the home, guarding Andy with love and devotion, protecting everything and everyone in his fiercely loyal way.

Hannah felt safe with him nearby and she knew she wouldn't want to be in here now in the dead of night without Breck in his corner, alert to every noise and movement around him.

She gave herself a little shake and was about to turn away but could feel his eyes on her, willing her to take notice of him. With an impatient tut she turned back and gave him a morsel of biscuit from the tin before going on upstairs with the hot toddy.

Andy spluttered as he drank it down but she made him take it all and then she bathed him with the cool water from the ewer and waited with him till he fell asleep. Now she didn't want to go back to her own lonely bed with her fears and imaginings. The thought of it made her shiver. She looked down at her sleeping son and without more ado she removed her dressing gown and got in beside him. The narrow bed wasn't meant to hold two people. She felt as if she was going to drop off the edge at any moment. She moved closer to him and wrapped her arms around him. He was hot but she was cold and she felt oddly comforted just holding him like this. His breathing was easier than it had been and soon her own became deeper and more even as she drifted into slumber beside the little son she had once so vehemently rejected.

Chapter Nine

Hannah was dismayed when she beheld the row of people waiting in the entrance hall of Butterbank House to see the doctor. She had imagined the morning surgery would be less busy than that of the evening but here they all were, the half of Kinvara it seemed, some rowed on a bench under the window, others on straight-backed occasional chairs with scuffed tapestry padding and scratched wooden legs that told of much usage.

'It is yourself, Hannah,' Dokie Joe greeted, sliding along the bench to make room for her. 'Sit you down and take the weight off your legs.'

'Ay, it's me right enough,' Hannah returned rather stiffly, in her heightened state of awareness reading more meaning into his words than he had intended. 'And I will remain standing if you don't mind, I always get sore when I sit on a hard seat o' any sort.'

'It isn't often we see you at the doctor's,' Minnie MacTaggart remarked off-handedly, though a glitter of curiosity lit her eyes.

'That's because I very seldom have reason to visit the doctor.' Hannah's voice was tighter than ever.

'Are you not feeling too well, Hannah?' Dolly Law probed gently, chewing the stem of her unlit clay pipe as she spoke.

'I'm well enough.'

'It is just a social visit then,' Mollie Gillespie stated with a touch of sarcasm.

'Ay,' Dolly nodded sagely. 'Sometimes it does a body good to have a wee chat wi' the doctor when there is something worrying them.'

'There is nothing worrying me,' Hannah insisted with more assurance than she was feeling, wondering if she should go away and come back later. 'It – it's about Andy,' she added, annoyed for feeling she had to justify herself.

'Och, the poor wee mite.' Dolly spoke with some concern as she scrabbled in the pocket of her smock for her matches. 'I was thinking I hadny seen him about for a whilie and hope there is nothing serious wrong with him.'

Hannah felt herself smarting under all the cross-examinations. 'No, he just has a cold, that's all, and I thought the doctor might give him something for his cough.'

Minnie looked at her pityingly. 'But I am sure the doctor, being the good kind soul that he is, would have dropped by to see Andy personally. You only had to mention it to him.'

Connie Simpson, who, as well as 'working to the Manse' also did some cleaning for the MacAlistairs, came into the hall just then with her feather duster and proceeded to look busy as she flicked it over the seashells that decorated the windowsills. But the duster was only a prop. Connie liked nothing better than a chat with the doctor's patients and she had no sooner appeared than everyone was agog to know how her Granny Margaret was faring after her 'wee brush wi' the bottle'.

Talk had got round about Big Bette's part in the affair and it was generally agreed that Granny Margaret couldn't very well be blamed at her age and Bette should have known better than to encourage such excesses in a harmless old woman.

Minnie folded her lips. She was not one of those on Granny Margaret's side. She knew very well that the old besom was more than fond of a tipple and always kept a bottle in her medicine cupboard with the pretence that she needed it for her heart. Harmless indeed! She could down raw spirits with the best of them and Minnie had never forgiven her for making Father MacNeil merry last Christmas when he'd called in at Struan Cottage on a goodwill visit. And her a Protestant too!

Minnie did not therefore add her voice to those of the old lady's supporters but veered more to Bette's side though she did not approve of that lady either and called her Bossy Boots behind her back.

The doctor's wife, Long John Jeannie, named so because she was always 'mending the arse' of her husband's combinations, came through pushing a tea trolley containing bottles of mixture and pills. She was joined by Effie who shouted out the names on the labels and ticked off each one as they came up to receive their medicine.

'The colds and chills have started early this year,' she remarked cheerfully as Donald of Balivoe came up to her, his horny fingers closing over the bottle she handed him.

'It is just a wee drop liniment for my rheumatics,' he explained quietly and with dignity. But Dokie's Joe's long ears heard every word and shaking his head he said knowingly, 'It has all to do with the climate, Donald, it changes like the weather.'

'The climate *is* the weather,' Donald returned loftily, glad to get one over Dokie, who, in his opinion, was far too nosy for his own or anyone else's good.

'Ay.' Dokie Joe was unperturbed. 'One is as bad as the other and I was saying to Mattie only the other day it's no wonder we're all half dead with colds and flu the way it can be warm and sunny one minute and blowing stink the next.'

Donald did not deign to acknowledge such banal observations. Turning his back on Dokie he delved into his commodious pocket and handed Effie a brown paper parcel tied carefully with string. 'Be giving these to the doctor,' he hissed, tapping the side of his nose and bringing his eyelid down in a conspiratorial wink. 'And tell him I'll make it up to him when I'm better able to see my way.'

Effie took the parcel of eggs and laid them on a table beside a small mound of other barter payments. It was nothing new for

Doctor MacAlistair's patients to pay for their medical expenses in this way. Some brought pots of homemade jam; others bags of flour for Jeannie or oats for the doctor's 'big stallion brute'. Fish; rabbits; ducks; chickens; Christmas turkeys; freshly caught salmon; once even a fatted calf all ready smoked so that it would last for a good part of the winter.

The doctor said he would never grow rich but would never starve either and it didn't matter to him if the salmon was poached from The MacKernon's river. He told Jeannie it tasted all the better for it and only laughed when she threw up her hands in mock horror and told him he was as bad as the rascals who had caught the spoils in the first place.

The arrival of the mobile dispensary had taken the attention away from Hannah and she began to feel more at ease – until Effie suddenly turned her attention on Mollie and Dolly to beam at them and say, 'And how are our young mothers this morning?'

Both women were sitting beside Hannah and for one wild moment she imagined that Effie had included her in the question. She was not the only one to be startled. Mollie, too, was somewhat taken aback and stared at Effie wordlessly.

Mollie was a fresh-faced attractive young woman in her late twenties, quiet and well spoken, with something cool and self-contained about her that set her apart from the other wives in Keeper's Row. She and her husband, Donnie Hic, had one daughter, beautiful little dark-haired Runa whom Donnie suspected had sprung from his wife's former liaison with Ryan Du, a black-bearded giant of a man who worked at Vale o' Dreip.

But Ryan Du was now respectably married to Cora Simpson and neither of them was prepared to listen to Donnie's talk concerning Runa, Cora being of the opinion that Donnie was too drunk half the time to know what he was saying and he had better watch out or he'd have her to deal with.

Gradually, Donnie quietened down about Ryan Du, telling himself that he was all the man Mollie needed and he was going to prove that fact to her if it was the last thing he did. But his efforts to increase the Gillespie line had been in vain. His wife had seemed content with just Runa and was quite frank about not wanting more children.

Now, here she was, her cheeks flushing red at Effie's unthinking words, saying quickly that she was here for just a check-up and all the while looking at the nurse as if she would like personally to throttle her.

Dolly, on the other hand, was not in the least put about by all this. Effie might be a lot of things she shouldn't be but by God! She had a nose for a pregnancy! Often before the mothers-to-be knew it for themselves. A smile touched Dolly's mouth as her thoughts took her back to the morning, lying in bed sucking her clay pipe as she wondered if this next one would be a boy or a girl. It had only just struck her that she was 'away wi' it again' and she quite philosophically accepted the fact. If you lay with a man you had children by them. It was natural. It was normal. Although she was small and skinny she was wiry and fit and never seemed to be up nor down whether she was expecting or not.

A boy would be good, she had decided, boys were always handy with their strength and their ability to do the more manual tasks around the place. On the other hand, girls were better when it came to domestic matters, and very often their wits could be sharper when dealing with awkward situations.

There was however one drawback to having children and that was money. There was never enough of it in the Law household. Alan's apprenticeship to Willie Whiskers was costing a bob or two and while Mary had gone into domestic service and was good at handing over most of her pay packet there were still a lot of young mouths to feed and now there was going to be another.

Dolly's husband, Shug, had been snoring peacefully by her side but that pleasant state had not lasted for long. Removing her pipe from her mouth Dolly had bawled out his name and he had emerged hastily from the blankets, hair on end, mouth agape as he yawned and scratched himself and demanded to know what the hell was going on.

'You'll have to get a job,' Dolly had stated baldly. 'We have another on the way.'

Shug had taken this last piece of news far less seriously than the first. 'A job!' he had said, aghast. 'What brought that on at this ungodly hour o' the morning?'

'It's half past eight,' she had calmly returned. 'High time you were up seeing to the household.'

'The bairns will do it, they always do it before leaving for school, and anyway, only Sammy's going this morning, it's his turn for the shoes.'

'That's just it,' Dolly had told him severely. 'There's going to be another mouth to feed and I'd like this one to have shoes all the time. You could try dykes. I know Jim Coulson's looking for labourers.'

'Dykes!' Shug almost had apoplexy. 'You're havering, woman, I know nothing about building dykes and even if I did my back would never stand up to it.'

'It stood up to it well enough last night,' Dolly had snorted.

'Aw, come on now, Dolly.' A grin had spread over his face. 'You know you enjoyed it, and though I'm suffering for it this morning I'd do it all over again just to please you.'

At that she had swiped him with a slipless pillow and had told him, 'Jim Coulson, this very day, and I mean it this time, Shug Law.'

An hour later, suddenly and inexplicably, Shug had tripped on his way to fetch his mare, Sorry, from her shed, and now Dolly was at the doctor's, not to have her pregnancy confirmed, she didn't need anybody to tell her that, but to ask Doctor MacAlistair if he could possibly give her husband something that would help his ankle as well as his back, and in this way get it through to her spouse that she really had meant business when she'd told him he had to get a job.

Hannah looked at both Dolly and Mollie and sucked in her breath. So Janet had been right about these two after all, and if she knew about them how much had she guessed about Hannah herself? This place! Everybody knowing everybody else's business almost before they knew it themselves. All these questions! That Effie, opening her big mouth and thinking she was so smart voicing the things she did.

Of course, she might not have meant to imply that anyone was pregnant, they *were* all young mothers after all – except – Hannah glanced again at Dolly. A young mother indeed! Never by any stretch of the imagination could Hannah think of her as such. In all the time Hannah had known her she had always looked the same, smoke-begrimed skin, lips stained with nicotine, that filthy hat sitting on her head looking for all the world like an ancient cowpat.

Nothing ever seemed to ruffle Dolly and she had merely grinned at Effie's words. Mollie on the other hand had looked positively murderous and Hannah found herself wondering why the young woman should be so flustered at the suggestion that she was having another baby. She was healthy, strong, she'd had no bother giving birth to perfect little Runa, Donnie wanted more children . . . unless it wasn't his and Mollie was still seeing Ryan Du . . . Hannah pulled herself up. She was getting to be like all the rest, surmising, speculating, making up things in her head that had no foundation whatsoever.

Dolly had lit up. Clouds of pipe smoke rose in the air. 'Really, Dolly,' Jeannie coughed as the fumes wafted to her nostrils. 'I don't know what pleasure you get from that nasty thing.'

'But the doctor smokes a pipe,' Dolly pointed out.

'Yes, I know that, but he's a man, Dolly.'

'Oh, ay, he is that,' Dolly agreed. 'I have often shared a fill o' baccy with him and he once told me I was as good as him any day wi' my beer and my pipe.'

'Oh, did he now? Well, I'll have a word with him about that, for while I know he likes his pipe and his dram I had no idea he drank beer as well.'

Dolly looked surprised. 'Och ay, Jeannie, he wouldny be a man if he didny drink beer, would he now? And there's no call to take him to task about it since it would only get me in trouble as well.'

Jeannie's rosy face grew determined. 'Put it out, Dolly, whatever you and my husband enjoy in private is strictly for outside the surgery. Alistair might enjoy his tobacco and I myself don't mind that in the least, but he never does it here in my hall. Never.'

This was not exactly true, since the doctor, believing that a man's home was there to be lived in, puffed his way merrily throughout the rooms of his house and to hell with etiquette.

Jeannie did not care very much for etiquette either, but she hated housework, and even though she had Connie there to help she had quite a job keeping the busy entrance hall in order and wasn't going to have dirty ashtrays adding to her burdens.

Dolly tapped out her pipe, folded her hands over her stomach, and looked pained. Having won this round, a satisfied Jeannie took herself off to the kitchen regions and with a lull in the proceedings Dolly glanced around as if seeking a new diversion. Hannah hoped fervently that she was not going to be it, as a bored Dolly meant a curious one and Hannah had had enough of questions for one day.

Rescue came in the form of Ivy MacNulty of Quarrymen's Cottages. She too smoked a clay pipe and had a ream of children at her feet as well as a man who was as work-shy as Shug Law. Ivy and Dolly therefore had much in common and were great friends, swapping stories about their menfolk, sharing plugs of tobacco, moaning to one another about the cost of living and how difficult it was to make ends meet 'wi' all the hardships they had to endure'.

In view of all this, Dolly was only too willing to let Hannah go in front of her, and that lady accepted the offer with alacrity. But before she departed the scene she noticed Connie Simpson looking at Mollie rather strangely and she couldn't help wondering about Mollie all over again as she opened the door of the surgery and went quickly inside.

Chapter Ten

Doctor MacAlistair looked at Hannah over the top of his specs and in his straightforward way said, 'Well, and what ails you, lass?'

This habit he had of coming directly to the point never failed to unnerve Hannah, more than ever this morning when her stomach fluttered with nerves and she could feel her tongue sticking to the roof of her mouth. For while she *had* come for a cough bottle for Andy, her main reason for being here was to ask the doctor to give her a pregnancy test in order to settle her mind one way or another.

But now, with the doctor's searching gaze upon her, she found her courage deserting her. 'It isn't about me – it's about Andy.' The words were out before she could stop them.

'The wee lad, eh?' There was something in the way he spoke that made her think he knew she was evading the issue, for despite his amiable manner the doctor was a very astute man with years of experience in human nature behind him. Of jovial appearance, portly and pink-faced with a purple-veined nose that showed his liking for a good dram, he was a very distinctive figure, one who was respected and trusted throughout the community and who seldom turned up his nose at any hospitality offered him while out on his rounds.

He had always called a spade a spade, and though he was perhaps just a little too blunt for comfort, people knew where they stood with him and recognised that he was nobody's fool.

Hannah was aware of all this and was unable to meet his eyes as he lowered his head and scrutinised her from under his bushy white brows.

'Ay, Andy,' she confirmed. 'He's had a bad dose o' the cold and I thought you could maybe give him something for his cough,'

'Ay, ay, as you say, and I'll certainly see to it right away. But I would have called in to see him if you had asked. You only had to leave word with Jeannie. Andy's a wiry wee chap for all he's handicapped but a bairn like him can be more prone to infection than most and shouldn't be left too long without proper attention.'

Hannah squirmed at the reproach in his tone. Proper attention indeed! Didn't she give the boy that in full measure? What did anybody know of the anxiety he caused, the care she lavished on him? The doctor didn't have any children, healthy or otherwise, and was not qualified to lecture her in this way, man of medicine or no.

Unconsciously her chin went up. The doctor saw the action but said nothing, knowing how aggrieved she had been by Andy's birth, the difficult years that followed, the progress she was making in accepting him as he was. She was a deep one was Hannah Sutherland, shy, withdrawn, afraid of many of life's twists and turns and always worried about the cares and woes of her daily existence. Anything new or strange seemed to frighten her a good deal and he had always tried to handle her with kid gloves.

He smiled to himself. Kid gloves indeed! As if he could ever do that. He had always been outspoken in the extreme, his tongue leaping so far ahead of his thoughts he had often felt like biting it off.

Still, he would have to be careful with Hannah. She had something else on her mind but he could see she wasn't going to tell him about it; best to wait and let it come naturally. If he asked outright he would just scare her off and God alone knew how long she would bottle it up. With this in mind he began to talk of everyday affairs, asking if she'd heard from Rob, how Vaila was coping, how she was getting on at school.

He really was a nice man. Hannah felt her tension easing as they chatted. Even so, she wasn't going to let on about her condition. Her hands tightened on her bag. Why did she keep saying that to herself? There was no foundation for it, none whatsoever . . .

'As a matter of fact, I was coming to see Andy anyway.' The doctor's voice broke into her thoughts. 'I think it's time he was fitted with callipers.'

Hannah blinked. 'Callipers?'

'Ay, they would help to support the muscles in his legs and allow him to get along better. It would mean a visit to the Fountainwell Orphanage. A doctor goes there once a month from Inverness to assess some of the youngsters with walking difficulties. Would you agree to that, Hannah?'

Hannah nodded, in her confusion trying to take in everything he was saying.

'Very well.' He reached for his pen and a piece of paper and scribbled a few words. 'There, that's done, might as well strike while the iron's hot. When the hospital gets this they'll be in touch and let you have a suitable date for Andy.'

So saying he licked a stamp and thumped it down on the envelope. 'I'll get Jeannie to post this first thing, and I'll be along later to see Andy and explain to him what I have in mind.'

Feeling dismissed, Hannah stood up. He smiled and nodded and ran a hand through his white thatch which always looked in need of a good trimming.

She let herself out. The surgery had grown in her absence. 'What was he doing in there?' Maisie Whiskers said by way of greeting. 'Performing a major operation?'

Hannah's face reddened. She glared at the grinning countenance of the blacksmith's wife and turning on her heel she fled out into the windy autumn day as if all the hounds of hell were snapping at her ankles.

* * *

Johnny Lonely was waiting outside No. 6 of the Row when Hannah arrived back from the doctor's. He was just standing there, in the biting cold wind driving in from the sea, looking as if he didn't mean to be there at all and that it was purely a chance happening that had brought him to this spot in the first place.

When Hannah came up, he transferred his gaze from the bay and brought it to rest on a clump of grass at his feet, and Hannah found herself looking down also, trying to see what he was staring at in such fascination. But there was nothing, just a tuft of dried sedge, windburned and sorry looking, and impatiently she shook her head. She certainly wasn't in the mood for the hermit's eccentricities at that particular moment in time; with a tut of annoyance she turned away and was making to open her door when his voice suddenly came out, rumbling from the very depths of his throat like a growling dog.

'I heard the wee lad was ill,' he intoned, still staring at the ground. 'I've got some books he might like to look at.'

Hannah regarded him coldly, still smarting as she was from the fright he had given her a few days ago on the shore. She didn't feel like speaking to anyone just then, far less someone as strange as Johnny Lonely, and she was about to turn away once more when her eye was caught by the stoop of his shoulders and the sad impression of desolation that surrounded him. A sudden twinge of compassion seized her. He looked cold, she thought, his nose was red, his weatherbeaten face haggard under its coating of grime. His coat collars were turned up against the wind, his hands dug into his pockets, but she saw how blue they were when he withdrew one to rasp it across his nose with a watery sniff.

Johnny had been one of those who had loved Morna Jean Sommero. He had trusted and confided in her and had spent some of his happiest hours down there at Oir na Cuan. No one had been able to get as close to Johnny as Morna had. She more than anybody had possessed the ability to talk to him and listen to him and inspire him with a hope that had put a spring in his step whenever he was in her company. It was Johnny who had found Morna, lying on the shore where she had died; after that Johnny had become more of a recluse than ever, avoiding human contact as much as he could, shrinking away when anybody approached and seeming to dissolve into thin air as if he were a ghost.

Both Father MacNeil and the Reverend Thomas MacIntosh had tried to speak to him on separate occasions but to no avail. He had simply shut the door of his ramshackle hut and wouldn't open it for anybody and when he had to go out he did so early in the morning and at night when he thought no one would be around.

As the weeks slipped by he had started to be seen again, but Morna's passing had left a great gap in his life and now he was lonelier than he had ever been. He had no one he wanted to talk to, except for the children; only they could get near him and bring some meaning into his solitary existence.

With them he seemed able to open up and expand and allow himself to relax and even to smile as he told them his tales and listened to their chatter and animated questions about the wonders and mysteries of the universe.

Hannah thought of all this as she and he stood outside the portals of No. 6 of the Row and she straightened her shoulders as she came to a decision. 'All right,' she conceded abruptly. 'You can come in, but only for a wee while, I have things to do.'

She hadn't noticed the bulge under the lapels of his coat till he delved inside and took out some books, not dog-eared as she might have imagined, but well-preserved volumes with gold tooling on their spines and gold leaf around the edges.

Hannah herself had always loved books and had carefully looked after her own collection of novels, poems and some of the classics she had been given as a young girl. She therefore nodded her approval of Johnny and had just opened the door to usher him inside when Janet, who had been sitting with Andy, appeared in the aperture.

'I heard the voices,' she explained, her glance taking in

Johnny, managing to hide her surprise at seeing him with Hannah whose tolerance of the hermit was of a limited nature and who only put up with him at all for Andy's sake.

'Johnny,' Janet acknowledged with genuine warmth since it wasn't in her nature to reject anybody who had strayed from the concept of what was regarded as normal. 'Have you been here long?' she continued. 'I never heard anybody knocking.'

'I met him at the door,' Hannah said hurriedly, wanting only to get indoors away from the wind. Janet made to depart, saying over her shoulder that she had left a fresh pot of tea on the hob and some pancakes to heat in the lower oven.

Hannah showed Johnny the stairs and told him where to find Andy's room. He went quickly upwards, as if glad to escape her watchful gaze, and she moved thankfully into the warm kitchen to divest herself of her outer garments.

As good as her word, Janet had left a large pot of tea simmering on the stove. Hannah was about to pour herself a cup when she remembered Johnny, how pathetic he had looked standing outside in the rain and the wind, how embarrassed he had been having to talk to her, explain his reasons for being there outside her house.

She paused with the teapot in her hand as a thought struck her. Johnny rarely permitted himself to visit anyone unless it was strictly necessary, usually when he was forced to seek a job of work in order to provide the basic requirements for his spartan existence. Even that had stopped when he was mourning the loss of Morna.

Now he was beginning to pop up again, often at the most unexpected and awkward moments, catching people out in compromising situations, seeing things he wasn't meant to see, unnerving saints and sinners alike and keeping them on their toes lest he should take it into his head to shame them publicly.

Hannah's lips tightened. She knew all about the hermit and his unhealthy prying habits but thankfully he seemed to keep what he knew to himself; no one had yet pointed the finger at him as the perpetrator of unsavoury gossip.

It must have taken a lot of courage for him to come to her door that day, and he hadn't been motivated by necessity but by caring and affection for a little spastic boy who had always been special to him.

In his turn, Andy loved Johnny Lonely and fiercely defended him if anyone dared to demean him behind his back. They were soulmates, the boy and the man. Hannah had to admit Johnny took great care of her son and was always vigilant of his welfare, never allowing him to stay out later than he should or let him do anything that would endanger him in any way. Andy had found something in the hermit that no one else had bothered to look for; when they were seen together, absorbed in some simple pursuit, communicating in a manner that often needed no words, laughing at little jokes, people would shake their heads pityingly and tell one another only oddities behaved like that even while they wished they could discover the secret of Andy's and Johnny's enjoyment.

Johnny Lonely – not so lonely sometimes. There was an indefinable air of dignity about him, an intelligence that showed in those dark glittering eyes of his, a cultured quality in his voice, a strength that oozed from every self-contained pore in his make-up and an aura of mystery about his past that was the source of much enjoyable speculation at fireside gatherings everywhere.

The folk of Kinvara didn't understand Johnny and often resented his intrusion into their most private lives, but for all that he was part of the landscape part of the scene of things

'Oh!' Impatiently Hannah shook her head. Why did she allow herself to think like this when she had enough of her own affairs to occupy her mind? That boy! That man!

'That dog!' she exploded aloud when she saw that Breck wasn't in his place in the corner but was most likely upstairs snuggled in bed with Andy, spreading his fleas and his dirt and his hairs everywhere. Sometimes she could take the two of them and knock their heads together. All they ever did was take advantage of her good nature, see how many rules they could break before – before she was driven to chastise them with painful tongue-lashings.

Even while she was thinking these things she had put cups on to a tray together with a plate of steamy pancakes topped with a coating of homemade blackcurrant jam. Before she could change her mind she went upstairs to Andy's room where she had lit a fire. It was warm and cosy. Andy was in his element with Johnny, laughing, animated as Hannah had seldom seen him. He was talking and Johnny was writing things down, apparently able to understand everything the boy had to say. The books that Johnny had brought were lying on the bed, their musty odour permeating the room; pointedly Hannah gathered them up and placed them on the bedside table.

Neither of them noticed, so engrossed were they in what they were doing, though when Hannah laid down the tea tray Johnny suddenly scraped back his chair, shot to his feet and clawed his hat from his head in a gesture that was as oddly touching as it was respectful,

'Sorry, missus,' he said dourly. 'I forgot.'

'That's all right,' Hannah said gruffly, thinking how contrary he was, to show manners in some respects yet be so completely unrepentant when it came to spying on his fellow men – and women. 'Take your tea before it gets cold.' She glanced at the books, at the pencils and jotters on the bed, saw the sparkling eyes of Andy, who looked better than he had done for days. 'Is that what you were, Johnny?' she said softly. 'Before you ran away? A teacher of young children? A man who feels easy in their company and knows how to get the best out o' them because it's the sort o' thing that comes naturally?'

Johnny's face showed nothing. 'I am what I am now,' he said succinctly as he bit into a jammy pancake.

'I often feel like doing that myself,' she went on musingly. 'Running away, I mean. Sometimes it all gets too much.'

'But you have everything!' The words erupted out of him, loud and passionate. 'It's all there under your nose, Hannah Sutherland, only you can't see it for looking!'

It was difficult to know who was the most surprised by

this outburst, Hannah or Johnny himself. He said nothing more and turned away, though she noticed his hands clenching and unclenching at his sides. She knew that somewhere deep in the heart of Johnny Lonely a chord had been touched and something inside of herself was moved by the realisation that he wasn't as tough as he made out.

'You don't know anything, Johnny,' she said flatly. 'Or you wouldn't talk like that. Men can't know what women feel, the kind o' things that torment them.'

His eyes glittered strangely. 'Oh, ay, but I do,' he answered with such conviction she stared at him till she felt her own eyes growing dry and sore and was the first to turn away.

He said his goodbyes to Andy and made his way downstairs, soft as a cat, padding rather than walking. She could see why he was able to sneak up on people and frighten them the way he did, never a rustle to herald his approach, never the snap of a twig or a crackle of leaves to let them know he was coming. Oh, ay, he was a creepy creature and no mistake and the less she had to do with him the better. But that day she liked him more than she had ever done before and even went so far as to convince herself that she would never feel threatened by him again – not after he had sat in her house, drinking her tea and eating her food and enjoying the companionship of her son.

Janet's appearance at her door coincided with Johnny's departure from No. 6. It was obvious that she had been waiting for him to come out. Going forward she pushed a paper bag into his hand. 'Take this,' she told him kindly, 'I've been baking so much I don't know what to do with it all, even with Joss eating me out of house and home.'

Johnny's fingers closed over the bag. He had a great liking and respect for Janet and Jock, who never made their charitable acts seem anything more than neighbourly goodwill. With a nod and a curt word of thanks he went off, his coat flapping in the wind, his steps taking him back to that lonely place under the cliffs where the gulls wheeled all day and the sea battered the rocky inlets on the western side of Mary's Bay.

'Poor Johnny,' sighed Janet. 'He's so alone, yet there's something about him that makes me think he was once very much to someone.'

'He's just a hermit,' Hannah said rather brusquely. 'And must like living the way he does. His moods are as changeable as the weather. Today he was fine, tomorrow he'll be dour and silent and back to those queer ways he has about him.'

Janet was quiet for a moment, thinking to herself that Hannah's description of Johnny could easily apply to herself, blowing hot one minute, cold the next. Janet knew her neighbour all right, and she smiled a little as she wondered how Johnny had fared in Hannah's company, how she had managed to handle his gruffness and shyness when she herself was burdened with much the same complexities.

'He isn't as bad as he makes out,' Hannah said suddenly, as if reading the younger woman's thoughts. 'I even got him to talk about himself which amazed me as much as it did him.'

'A bit like yourself, Hannah,' Janet was unable to refrain from saying.

'And just what is that supposed to mean?' Hannah's face took on a closed look and her voice was tight as she asked the question.

'Och, come on now, Hannah,' Janet went on doggedly, knowing even as she spoke that she would have fared better if she had kept her opinions to herself. 'You know you never give much away about how you're feeling – thinking. Did you, for instance, tell the doctor that you were expecting again?'

Hannah was immediately on the defensive. Her face flared, she glared at her neighbour as if she would like to kill her. 'It isn't true!' she rasped in a rigidly controlled voice. 'It just isn't true and I'll thank you no' to go spreading such talk around the place. I thought you were different but you're just like all the rest, saying things you shouldn't, sticking your nose in where it isn't wanted.' Her nostrils flared as she went on relentlessly. 'Kinvara is a hotbed o' gossip and scandal and it's people like you who make it that way! Oh, I know you think you're smart, sitting there in your house, rhyming it all off, but just because you're so desperate to have another bairn doesn't mean to say we're all tarred with the same brush so don't speak to me again about things you know nothing about!'

Janet's young face had also coloured. For a long moment she looked at Hannah before saying quietly, 'Time will tell all, Hannah Sutherland, and when it does I'll be here if you feel you need a friend to lean on. I never would have believed that anyone could behave the way you do, denying something that you should be glad to shout from the rooftops, instead o' burying it away as if it was an evil thing to be avoided at all costs.'

With that she turned back into her house without another word and softly closed the door behind her.

Hannah stood on her step, feeling the mellow air of the October day cooling her flushed cheeks. The wind was abating, the mist was lifting off the hills revealing the slumbering blue peaks, draping pearly scarves of mist across the shoulders of the russet slopes and drifting languidly in and out of the corries. Against the sombre browns and greens of the foothills the red leaves of autumn made vivid splashes of colour; blond grasses and golden bracken swayed in the breezes; a ray of sunlight shivered over the water, casting silver on the wavelets that rippled to the shore in Mary's Bay.

Hannah felt something of the lonely beauty seeping into her troubled soul and dismay touched her heart as she thought about the words she'd had with Janet. Of all the folk in Kinvara, Janet was the one she liked and trusted most, and as the last remnants of her anger faded Hannah was genuinely sorry that she had spoken as she had to her nearest – and perhaps dearest – neighbour.

Her gaze travelled to the pinnacle of the Kinvara Light in the distance and she whispered, 'Oh, Rob, why do I always say the wrong things to the people I like best? You know all about that and I wonder you put up with me the way you do.'

Perhaps it's because he loves you, a small voice whispered.

'Ay,' she said softly, 'it might be that or it might be Andy and Vaila that keep him bound to me.'

She sighed. If only he had never known Morna, if only the past could be blotted out and they could start all over again with just one another, if only she wasn't so afraid all the time and could face up to life as bravely as other folk seemed to do for all the ails and worries that beset them. She put her hands on her belly and shuddered. If only . . .

KINVARA

Late Autumn 1926

Chapter Eleven

Big Bette was at her wits' end. Maudie had been staying with her for several weeks now and in all that time had shown no inclination to try and find a job.

This state of affairs did not please Mungo in the least. 'The girl is eating us out o' house and home,' he had complained. 'I work my fingers to the bone in order to keep my family clothed and fed and Maudie does not come into that category. She'll have to earn her keep some way, she's your niece and your responsibility, Bette, and the least you can do is get her off her fat backside and make her do something worthwhile. Why don't you let her help out in the shop? In that way I'll get my chair and my house to myself again and you can take a day off now and then and keep me company.'

None of these suggestions appealed to Bette. 'Oh, no, you don't,' she protested firmly, her double chin merging into her neck as she lowered her head to look at him with a defiance that he knew only too well. 'There's only room for one o' us in the shop, she would just be under my feet all day, asking this, that, and the other. Besides all that, she can't count for toffee. I heard Babs asking her for help with a simple sum and there Maudie sat, adding up with her fingers and still getting it wrong in the end.'

'Well, if she won't go and look for work you'll just have to take her in hand,' Mungo persisted. 'Emily MacPherson might be glad o' some help with all these bairns she has at her skirts. Maudie is supposed to be good with children so now's her chance to prove it.'

'Ach, the laird already has Catrina Blair working for him. She just takes wee Euan along with her and he plays happily with the Crathmor bunch.'

'Cragdu, then,' Mungo went on grimly.' The MacKernon is always looking for help in that castle o' his and if it comes to it. Maudie will just have to wash dishes with the rest o' them.'

But Bette shook her head doubtfully. 'I heard he and his wife are away visiting her family in America and there is only a skeleton staff up there running the place.'

'Bette.' Mungo glared at his other half. 'Do you want to send the girl packing? Straight back to your sister in Partick? Because I'm not having her lazing about here, sitting in my chair, staying up late at night reading and making tea then lying in bed next morning as if she was glued to the mattress. It just won't do, Bette, it won't do at all!'

'Och, don't burst a blood vessel,' Bette replied with more assurance than she was feeling. 'I'll think of something.'

'And of course, there is that other business that has to be sorted out.' Mungo didn't look at his wife as he spoke nor did he enlarge on the subject but Bette knew exactly what he meant and she swallowed hard as she wondered just what she had taken on when Maudie Munro had stormed the portals of No. I of the Row.

For as well as all her other drawbacks there was a disturbing innocence about Maudie that her aunt was at a loss to deal with. Though the girl had the body of a woman she still had the outlook of a child and loved playing games with her three young cousins: hide and seek, hunt the thimble, I spy, being high on the agenda of favourites. The trouble was, she had no sense of propriety when it came to other more personal matters and thought nothing of stripping off naked in front of everybody in order to bathe herself in the zinc tub beside a roaring fire.

The first time it happened only Bette and Babs had been in the kitchen, but last night Joe had been there too and his eyes had gone round with amazement at the sight of his cousin blithely peeling off her clothes and stepping into the tub. For several minutes his mouth had hung open as he gaped in wonder then an event had occurred over which he had no control. When his mother came in and saw the bulge in his trousers she had taken his arm and had propelled him out into the pouring rain to 'cool off' before turning back into the house to seize a bucket of cold water from under the sink and pour it over Maudie's head.

The girl had gasped in shock, her mouth opening and shutting like a fish out of water as she tried to see through spikes of soaking wet hair. 'Why ever did you do that?' she had spluttered indignantly as soon as she could get enough air into her lungs to enable her to speak.

'Don't you know, Maudie?' Bette had said ominously. 'Don't you really know?'

'No, Auntie, I don't, and it wasn't very nice o' you to do such a thing to your very own niece. I could catch my death o' cold just sitting here in the bathtub and how would I explain that to Mammy and Daddy?'

'How would you, indeed? Unless, of course, they do the selfsame thing themselves and wouldny bat an eye at anyone else doing it.'

'But, Auntie.' Maudie's good nature was returning and she sounded placating. 'People do that in families. You did it yourself when you were a girl. Mammy told me how you and she and your other sisters steeped yourselves in the tub and washed each other's hair while you were at it.'

'I *was* only a girl,' Bette had answered faintly. 'A very young girl who hadn't yet developed properly.'

'Och well,' Maudie had rapidly recovered from her experience, unperturbedly swishing soap over one large breast as she went on, 'it isn't easy to be private in a tenement with no facilities. Daddy washes himself in front o' me and my sisters and none o' us mind a bit. It's always been like that, ever since I can remember.'

'Your father bathes naked – in the sight o' his daughters?' Bette was aghast.

'Oh, ay.' Maudie gazed pityingly at her aunt. 'The human body is a very natural thing, Auntie. We all used to walk around naked before Adam and Eve made it all wicked and evil. It's too cold to do that sort o' thing now, of course, and we would need more than a fig leaf to keep us cosy. But it's nice and warm in the tub here by the fire and I won't be minding if you and Uncle Mungo do it too and let me wash your backs while you're about it. Just think o' the hot water you would save and how good you would feel if I told you one o' my stories while you were soaking yourselves.'

Bette had always been a woman who could stand her own ground in any sort of situation. Speaking her mind was as natural to her as breathing and no one was ever left in any doubt as to what she was feeling and thinking. But now she couldn't think of anything appropriate to say that might instill some sense of modesty into her niece. She would never get through to the girl, never, and she was really beginning to feel that it would be better for everyone if Maudie went back to her parents in Partick and let life at No. 1 of the Row return to a semblance of the order that had existed there before she had managed to disrupt it so effectively.

Bette thought about that for a long moment. Oh ay, it had been orderly all right, and when Mungo was at home it had often been positively restricted, especially in the long nights of winter when he'd be away at these kirk meeting of his and she'd be left, the bairns in bed, whittling away at her carvings, sometimes wishing that something would happen to change the dull routine of her life.

Well, something had happened. Maudie had arrived, carefree, lovable, good-natured Maudie, her fund of songs and stories and downright harmless mischief entrancing them all and keeping them amused for hours on end. It hadn't mattered at all when Mungo took himself off to his meetings and committees and anything else that meant so much to him but nothing at all to Bette.

There had always been Maudie, sitting with her at night when the young MacGills had gone to bed, talking in her calm yet enthusiastic manner, commiserating over troubles great and small in that nice sympathetic way of hers.

And later, firmly ensconced in Mungo's chair, legs splayed wide to the heat, she loved making toast on the long fork held close to the fire. When there was a great pile of crispy golden-brown squares she lavishly walloped butter over them and she and her aunt sat back to drink cocoa and eat the piping hot toast, the butter running down their dimpled chins, their grunts and groans of pleasure mingling agreeably because they could be like that with one another, uninhibited, free, easy.

'This is better than a man any day o' the week,' Maudie had said once, scooping melted butter from her chin back up to her mouth. 'You could never do with a man the sort o' things you do with a well-done slice o' toast. Men go all soggy on you after a while but a good slice o' crunchy toast stays firm right to the last mouthful.'

Bette had never thought of it like that and she had stared at her niece in some bemusement as it began to dawn on her that the girl was more a woman of the world than she made out.

'A lass has to learn, Auntie,' Maudie had said in answer to the inevitable questions. 'And it's as well to find these things out sooner rather than later. Oh, I'm no' saying I've been a loose sort o' lassie, no, no, I was never a one to take down my drawers to a lad just because he was anxious to show me what he was made of, if you see what I mean.'

At this point she had grinned and winked at her aunt before going on sagely, 'A wee bit fun is fine in its place but I'll wait till I get a ring on my finger before I go the whole hog. After all, I have Mammy and Daddy to consider and my reputation to think of as the eldest o' the family. If you can't respect yourself how can you set an example to your wee brothers and sisters, and that's what I always tell myself when I'm up a back close after a night at the pictures, my finger on my halfpenny and a prayer on my lips for it isn't always easy to be strong when it seems the very de'il himself is biting your leg off.'

The revelations had stunned Bette and she had remained silent for quite some time before erupting into gales of laughter that had set Maudie off too so that the kitchen had rung with the sounds of their unrestrained merriment.

That same feeling had been with Bette as she gazed at Maudie standing in the tub, humming a little tune as she applied a long-handled loofah to her glistening body. A bubble of mirth had risen in Bette's throat and she had collapsed into Mungo's chair to fall helplessly about, her rolls of fat shaking and quivering while Maudie had looked at her and had said how glad she was to see her aunt in such high spirits as she had been 'a wee bit serious this good whilie back.'

Mungo had come into the room at this juncture, the church committee meeting having finished earlier than usual. To say he was surprised at the sight of Maudie in all her naked glory would have been putting it mildly. He simply gaped at her in astonishment while she merely smiled at him in her winsome way and went on washing herself with gentle energy, soap bubbles flying off her bosoms, everything about her rosy and bright and some bits standing regally to attention, her young muscles able to support those parts of her anatomy that had long ago given up the fight in Bette.

Mungo licked his lips. Unwillingly he tore his eyes away from his niece through marriage. This would never do. He was a kirk elder. A respected member of the community. If anything of this nature leaked out he would be the talk of the place. And Bette didn't seem to be in the least bit put out by any of it but was actually laughing – like a hyena – all moist-eyed and gasping and giving every impression of enjoying these heathen practices going on within the walls of a home that had once been orderly and sane.

'Why is Joe standing outside in the rain?' Mungo's voice seemed to come out of some hollow place in his head . . . Maudie's breasts had given an extra vigorous bounce as he was speaking and quite unable to help himself his eyes were drawn to them like a magnet.

The room was suddenly very warm, all that steam and soap . . . sweat gathered on his brow, he ran a finger inside his starched collar and felt it would do him no harm to join his elder son outside for a few moments.

'Oh!' At his words Bette's hand flew to her mouth. 'I forgot all about him. Get out o' there this minute, Maudie, and wrap yourself in a towel before Joe comes back in.'

Maudie made to step out of the tub and Mungo hastily averted his eyes. Never in all his born days had he experienced anyone like Maudie and as soon as he got Bette alone he would tell her just what he thought of her for allowing such indecent behaviour to go on under her own nose.

Now it was the next day, Mungo had said his piece, and Bette was never so glad to escape to the shop and pour her woes into the willing ears of her cronies who shook their heads in sympathy and uttered ready words of comfort but little in the way of sound advice.

Not that Bette would have listened anyway. In her present state of mind all she wanted was a shoulder to cry on. She knew she shouldn't have given away so many of her family's 'internal affairs' but that was Bette all over, on one hand resentful of 'outside interference', on the other only too ready to unburden herself to those she considered worthy of her trust and who now listened with interest to all the tasty little details of Maudie's trangressions.

'Mungo didn't know where to look.' Bette somehow managed to convince herself of that even while she remembered her husband's face when he had beheld the unclothed form of his niece through marriage. The steam had almost come out of his ears at the sight and his eyes had been bulging out of his head. The dirty bodach! Just wait till she got hold of him to tell him what she thought of a kirk elder who enjoyed gaping at such forbidden fruits . . .

'Are you quite sure o' that, Bette?' Mattie's tones were laden with mischievous sarcasm. 'I was always under the impression that Mungo was never a body to let opportunity slip by. Any man worth his salt would know where to look wi' a lass like Maudie flaunting her naked flesh under their noses.'

'Ay, that's right enough,' nodded Rita Sutherland, who was only too well aware of the truth of Mattie's words. A devoted member of the Free Kirk Ramsay might be, but given half a chance he would have done the selfsame thing as Mungo – and maybe a bit more besides. 'Men are like that, the whole jing bang o' them, never satisfied with what they've got but always hankering after what isn't theirs.'

'Mungo didn't hanker.' Bette was beginning to be sorry she had opened her mouth. 'He was just there and he couldn't help seeing.' She hesitated. 'Mind you, Maudie isn't really a bad lassie, just thoughtless and young and more innocent than most. She has a lot o' good points and she and I have had many's a laugh since she came to live with us . . .'

Bette thought once more of all the things she had come to like in her niece and she determined there and then that she would give the girl a chance. Tomorrow she would leave Mary Law in charge of the shop and personally escort Maudie along to Crathmor to see if there was any work going in that quarter. Mary was in local domestic service but was always eager to make an extra bob or two and Bette knew for a fact that the girl had an afternoon off every Wednesday.

Jessie MacDonald came into the shop and Bette quickly became brisk and businesslike. She had not yet forgiven the little woman for the rumours she had spread concerning the escapade with Granny Margaret, and if Jessie got wind of this latest happening she would undoubtedly tell everyone that the proprietress of the village store not only indulged in drunkenness but encouraged orgies in her home as well!

Chapter Twelve

The following day, Bette bundled her niece into the family trap, despite that young woman's protests that she had promised she would go along to the creche in Calvost to help out with the pre-school tots.

'No excuses, my girl,' Bette said firmly. 'It's a proper job you're needing and I'm going to try and make sure you get one. Up with you this minute and don't wriggle about too much or you'll upset Mrs McGinty. She finds it hard enough going with just me to pull along and won't like the extra weight of you as well.'

'Mrs McGinty.' Maudie sounded a little sulky. 'What a name to give a horse. And I suppose Mr McGinty bolted when he saw that marriage to a carthorse wasn't going to be all wine and roses and walks by the sea in the moonlight.'

Bette looked at Maudie, Maudie looked at her aunt, they both burst out laughing and rumbled along to the laird's house in the best of spirits.

The laird's driveway was long and winding, shaded with rowans and silver birches that opened up halfway along to reveal rolling grasslands and paddocks and a little duck pond where two swans gracefully preened and an assortment of ducks poked and quacked around a tiny island in the middle. In the distance, glimpses of the sea could be seen; the red-tiled roof of the stable block hove into view; men were busy in the gardens, among them Dokie Joe who tilted his hat and scratched his head in some surprise as Mrs McGinty and the two womenfolk went sailing past his vision.

Crathmor was a lovely old house, rustic and rambling with red ivy growing on the walls and tiny little mysterious windows set into an older L-shaped building that enclosed a circular arrangement of flowerbeds that were aglow with huge bronze and yellow chrysanthemums and blue lobelia tumbling over the edges.

Maudie had never seen anything like it and she gazed at the house in wonder, beginning to think to herself that it might not be so bad to work in such a place after all. Bette brought the trap to a halt and after tying a nose bag to Mrs McGinty she took her niece by the arm and led her over to the studded arched door set into an impressive pillared stone portico that jutted out from the main entrance.

'Don't you you think we should make an appointment, Auntie?' Maudie sounded unusually nervous as Bette's hand went up to the bell. 'Captain MacPherson might no' like people calling on him all cheeky and casual like.'

Bette looked surprised. 'The same mannie does the very same thing himself and never stands on ceremony for anyone. Many's the time he's sat in my kitchen drinking tea and eating jammy pancakes and sometimes even supping soup as well when he's been hungry after a walk in the hills. This isn't your west end, Maudie, this is Kinvara. The gentry are different here and the laird o' Crathmor is so different he's unique, as you will see for yourself soon enough.'

The door was opened by a neat little maid called Dora who smiled when she saw Bette whom she knew well and was about to pass the time with when she remembered her manners and gave a cursory bob as she ushered the visitors inside.

'I'll just tell the mistress you're here.' Dora nodded, instructing the women to take a seat in the hall after she had ascertained the nature of their visit.

The hall was oak-panelled and impressively adorned with stags' heads, shields, and fierce-looking swords; wonderful tapestries hung suspended from the ceiling; ancient paintings of MacPherson clansmen gazed proudly down from lofty perches; nooks and crannies held Chinese vases on polished occasional tables.

It was all very grand and traditional and Maudie sat with her aunt on a striped Regency sofa that was full of lumps and thought very seriously about getting up and simply fleeing away. It was all so different from what she was used to, the home she shared with her mammy and daddy and small brothers and sisters in Partick; the tenement close and the plaster walls; the cludgie on the landing and the drab backcourts; the pubs and the clubs and the Saturday night drunks at the street corners eating fish and chips out of last week's newspaper.

She couldn't imagine any of that in these hallowed halls. Here there were flowers and sunshine, lightness and brightness, wealth and prosperity. Sanctity seemed stamped on the pictures hanging on the walls and she gave a little shiver as she felt the eyes watching her, potent images of people that had been grand and powerful and not at all approving of a humble lass from the city . . .

Then her eye was caught by a coat stand in a corner, hung with an assortment of well-worn outerwear, beneath it a pile of wellingtons and a pair of tartan slippers placed strategically to just slip on when their owner felt like it. After that she noticed more homely touches: a little alcove hung with a child's drawings; the laird's bone-handled crook propped against a wall; fishing rods and baskets tucked into a recess together with a large dog basket liberally strewn with hairs and well-gnawed bones.

Maudie began to feel at home. Impressive the paintings might be but the people in them were dead and buried long ago and gaping down from a wall was about all they could do now. And while the furniture was good it had seen better days and was as ancient as the folks in the pictures. Mammy had better stuff in her house in Partick and it was maybe true about toffs being careless and sometimes down on their uppers as well. According to Aunt Bette the laird had fallen on hard times after the war and had been forced to sell off some of his properties to make ends meet. But Aunt Bette had also said he was a fly old rogue who had always watched the pennies and it was more than likely that his money was tied up in stocks and shares and other such investments.

Maudie didn't know anything about stocks and shares and didn't want to know. The most Daddy ever indulged in was a flutter on the horses when he had a copper or two to spare, which wasn't often and could hardly be described as an investment since any winnings he got were promptly spent in the pub on a Saturday night.

Dora was coming back, throwing a curious glance at Maudie as she said the lady of the house would see them now, and leading the way to a door near the stairs. When Dora opened it to announce the visitors the laird's wife came forward to greet them and draw them into the fireside. She sat down rather awkwardly herself since she was into the seventh month of her fourth pregnancy and feeling as if she had been in that state for years as she told the visitors with a rueful smile.

Emily Stables Abercrombie was a young woman of almost thirty with blue eyes and fair hair and a face that was sweet yet full of character. Her husband proudly called her his bonny English rose; on the main she was even-tempered and easygoing and never happier than when she was in the great outdoors with her family, rambling with them through the countryside, teaching them to ride and fish, showing them how to paint and sketch and to appreciate the bounties of nature. She also made them toe the line when the need arose and take their share of domestic chores; these included mucking out the stables, cleaning their father's Lanchester and his AEC lorry, and generally lending a helping hand since the advent of war had seen the need for reduced staff and stricter economy in running the household.

Emily had been a great asset to her husband right from the beginning, helping him to sift and sort through paperwork and answer letters and all the other boring but necessary tasks that made him groan and grumble and take himself off on his wanders with his spaniel dogs and his cat till his head cleared and he could come back refreshed and ready to face the more mundane matters of life.

Everybody agreed that the laird and his lady were a good team, despite the difference in their ages. They enjoyed the same things, the countryside was a delight to them, they rode and rambled, walked and talked, were tolerant of each other's shortcomings and never seemed to tire of one another's company. They adored being parents and doted on their children but agreed that discipline was a necessary part of growing up and wielded their authority accordingly.

The people of Kinvara loved and respected them as they were good mixers and seldom stood on ceremony with anyone. After a few minutes in Emily's company Maudie began to relax and to enjoy her visit and to comment eagerly on everything she had seen on the trip to Crathmor and that 'it was a fair treat to meet the lady of the house and to know she was as human as the next body even though she lived in such a grand place.'

Bette cleared her throat at this and after the first few pleasantries she soon let it be known that she hadn't called with her niece that day for purely social reasons.

'It's about a job, Mistress MacPherson,' she began, deciding that it was better to take the bull by the horns and just come right out with it, 'a job for Maudie. She is a good and willing lass and is a dab hand at keeping bairnies amused and with you having another on the way I was thinking you might be needing some extra help about the place.'

The lady of the house made no comment to this and Bette was about to enlarge on the subject when the door opened to admit Catrina Blair with a laden tea tray which Maudie rushed to take from her, tripping on the edge of the carpet in her hurry to show just what a good and willing lass she was.

The gesture cut no ice with Catrina. Her green eyes flashed as she glowered long and hard at this newcomer with her big flowing breasts and her rosy eager face. Dora's tongue had been busy; Catrina knew all about Maudie's quest for work and Big Bette's last remark had just confirmed her suspicions.

Catrina was the youngest of the Simpson sisters, as they had been and still were known, despite the fact that both Cora and Catrina were now married, leaving their elder sister Connie to carry the flag alone.

All three sisters had harboured ambitions to marry well but young men of any sort had been thin on the ground since the war and Cora had been glad enough to take black-bearded Ryan Du as her husband while Catrina's marriage to Colin Blair had been more out of necessity than love, instigated by the fact that she had been carrying the child of Ramsay Sutherland who had raped her at Vale o' Dreip one stormy night when Rita had been lying ill and helpless upstairs.

Few in Kinvara knew about the part Ramsay had played in Catrina's rush to get Colin's ring on her finger and Catrina had never forgiven the master of Vale o' Dreip for taking away her freedom of choice in the marriage stakes. It was small consolation to Catrina that he paid for little Euan's upkeep. In her opinion he had gotten off lightly while she had been tied down too young and too soon. Colin was a good hardworking man, one who treated her with respect and affection, but still she hankered after what might have been and had started putting away small amounts of her earnings for a rainy day. She was therefore jealous of her job at Crathmor, even though it was just part time, and was not at all pleased to see Maudie whom she regarded as a potential usurper, while Maudie, who took life as it came and didn't have a devious bone in her body, nevertheless interpreted the meaning in the other girl's eyes and retired back to the sofa with a rather crestfallen expression on her countenance.

The laird, his curiosity getting the better of him, came in

at Catrina's back, rubbing his hands at sight of the tea-things and cocking an inquiring eye at Maudie as he came further into the room. Emily dismissed Catrina with a slight nod and that young lady departed the scene with a certain amount of bad grace, desperate as she was to know what the outcome of Maudie's visit would be.

Outside the door she encountered Dora, who gave her a meaningful glance. Catrina smiled, Dora smiled back; as one they bent to the door and took turn about at the keyhole, all the while remaining alert lest anyone should come along and catch them eavesdropping on a private meeting between the master and mistress and the two visitors whose appearance had caused such a stir among the household staff.

Over tea, Bette repeated the conversation she'd had with Emily for the benefit of her husband, ending, 'I just thought you might be interested in Maudie, Captain MacPherson. As I've said before, she's a good lass and by way of commendation I have in my bag the very letter sent to me by my sister before her daughter's arrival in Kinvara.'

The laird *was* interested in Maudie but for all the wrong reasons. His eyes were positively gleaming as he beheld the overflowing figure of the young woman before him, her unfettered bosoms straining against her frock and the bonny sweet face of her all rosy and bright and as fresh as the mountain dew.

By this time, however, Maudie wasn't feeling entirely at her ease. All that talk about letters and commendation and the laird looking at her as if he could eat her in one gulp, his wife looking as if *she* would like to eat *him* and spit him out in little pieces.

Bette was rummaging about in her bag but before she could withdraw the epistle Maudie burst out, 'It isn't a proper reference, Captain MacPherson, sir, it's only from my mammy in Partick to my aunt in Kinvara saying she thought I was needing a wee holiday and it would be that nice if Auntie could put me up till I found my feet again.'

'Partick.' Captain MacPherson's eyes lit up even more while

Bette looked as if she would like to dismember her niece there and then. 'I know the place well,' he went on enthusiastically, 'a chap in my regiment came from there and I went to visit him after the war. Corporal Bobby Beattie, maybe you've heard of him, lass.'

'Mammy and Daddy know the Beattie family well,' cried Maudie eagerly, utterly entranced by the turn of events. 'Bobby was the eldest of six children and he used to come and visit us regularly. Oh, wait till I tell Mammy and Daddy about this! They'll never believe it.'

'Ay, ay, it is indeed a small world.' The master of Crathmor was quite carried away by now and both Emily and Bette could only stare as he continued, 'Bobby and me had a high old time of it in Partick. Went on a pub crawl and ended up eating fish and chips out of newspapers and talking about the army till the cows came home.'

He sighed and shook his head, causing one errant strand of white hair to descend over his brow. 'He died, the effects of mustard gas, but he was a great lad and to this day I think of him and remember my time with him in Partick: the art galleries; the Kelvingrove Park; the cafés serving mushy peas and vinegar and the quaintness of the alleys and the closes.'

Maudie was enthralled. She had never thought of Partick as quaint before but now the laird made her see it in a new light and he and she had a wonderful time, talking, reminiscing, retracing the steps he had taken with Corporal Bobby Beattie through the streets.

When he had talked himself to a halt, the laird was silent for a moment, before peeking at his wife through his bushy eyebrows to say coaxingly, 'Well, what do you think, Emily? Maudie would get on well here, there must be something that she could do, even if it is only part time.'

Emily could have throttled her husband for putting the onus of the decision on to her. As matters stood, there was simply no room for Maudie at Crathmor; the household budget was strained enough as it was and Maudie, for all she was a happy blithe spirit, looked as if she was quite happy just being

Maudie without the added strain of actually working for her keep as well.

Emily's lips twitched. She had never seen anybody who could dispatch food like Maudie. The swiftness with which the sandwiches and cakes had disappeared! Followed by a look that suggested she hadn't eaten a thing and could quite easily have murdered another plateful!

'It's all right.' Maudie's voice gently broke the sudden silence. 'It's kind of you both to try and help but I don't think I'd be much use to anybody wi' my bad ankle. I hurt it as I was getting into Auntie's trap and though I didn't think much about it at the time it's starting to give me gyp and it might be best if I just went home and bathed it.'

'Oh, but my dear child, we wouldn't even consider letting you leave this house in pain and distress.' The laird looked as if he himself would very much like to do something about Maudie's ankle. 'We could bind it for you or get Cook to apply a fomentation to help the swelling. She's very good at first aid and always sees to the little aches and pains of the children.'

'No.' Maudie stood up and hobbled a few steps rather unconvincingly. 'Auntie will see to it, she's a dab hand at that sort o' thing and we've taken up enough o' your time.' She turned to gaze fondly at Bette. 'To tell the truth, Auntie thought I was bored being at home all day with just her and the bairns but I'm not. In fact I love it, and while I might be glad to get a job later I thought it would be nice to have a wee holiday first – isn't that right, Auntie?' she added with gentle reproach.

Auntie's face was like thunder. A tortured grunt issued from her throat. Oh, wait till she got that Maudie home! Turning up her nose at the opportunity to work at Crathmor! Telling lies about her ankle! Making a fool out of her very own aunt after all she had gone through to introduce her to the laird and his lady.

But not by one twitch of a muscle did Bette allow anyone to see how mortified she was feeling. Graciously she extended a hand to Emily and thanked her for the tea. With a regal inclination of her head she did the same to the laird. Beckoning to her niece she puffed out her magnificent chest and sailed majestically across the room to open the door.

Three bodies fell in. Namely Dora, Catrina, and the children's governess, Miss Dorothy Hosie. Miss Hosie was short, plump, and wore a pince-nez, and she was not at all amused at having to explain her inelegant entry into the room. She had only come down to ask Mrs MacPherson for a book and now it looked as if she had been listening at the door alongside those two dreadful girls . . .

Her voice was high as she tried to exonerate herself. Behind her, Dora and Catrina smothered their giggles while Maudie and her aunt made good their escape. But not before Catrina had stuck her tongue out at Maudie and had thrown her a look which conveyed all too plainly how glad she was to see the back of such a cheeky upstart.

'So, you've hurt your ankle,' Bette began grimly as she and her niece drove away from Crathmor House. 'A fine excuse I must say! You made a right fool o' me in front of everybody and I've a good mind to choke you with my own bare hands after all the bother you've caused!'

'Oh, but I did hurt it, Auntie, I gave it a twist on the rug when I helped that Catrina in with the tea and it's throbbing something awful. I saw the way she was glaring at me wi' those green witch's eyes o' hers and I got that flustered I didn't look to see where I was going.'

'Ay, she wasn't very nice to you,' Bette said thoughtfully. 'Catrina's changed a bit since she went and married Colin Blair and had wee Euan. She used to be full o' fun and mischief and I'm thinking it's more than marriage and motherhood that's made her that way.'

Maudie gave vent to a mighty sigh. 'I've been thinking, maybe I'll just go home to Partick to be with Mammy and Daddy. I know Uncle Mungo thinks I'm just a lazy good-for-nothing and I'm beginning to feel I'm just no' wanted in your house any more.'

A great pang of guilt seized Bette. This was what she had wanted, what Mungo dreamed of, the answer to all their problems and prayers. Yet the thought of life without Maudie made her feel suddenly bereft.

'I'll tell you what, you can come and help me in the shop,' she stated rashly. 'At least it would get you out o' the house – and maybe help to lighten my load a bit.'

'Och no, Auntie.' Maudie's voice was filled with the conciliatory tones that Bette was beginning to know well. 'You know that would never work in thon polky wee shop. There wouldn't be room for two of us behind the counter and you would only get under my feet all day. Just leave things be for the moment. I was always a one to look on the bright side and something is bound to turn up. I've a wee hunch you'll be proud o' your niece one o' these days but I just need time to get myself sorted out.'

'You're no' as green as you're cabbage-looking, Maudie Munro,' Bette said wryly.

'No, Auntie,' Maudie agreed placidly. Bette's stomach gave a wobble, so too did Maudie's, and they rumbled their way homewards with the sounds of their merriment drifting agreeably into the mellow air of the October day.

Chapter Thirteen

The Fountainwell Orphanage was not the gloomy forbidding place that Hannah had imagined it would be. Magnificent horse chestnut trees marched along on either side of the driveway, their red and gold leaves littering the ground beneath; through the branches the countryside rolled away to distant hills that seemed to drift and dream against the intense blue of the late October sky.

The serried ranks of trees gave way suddenly and now there was sunshine as well as shadows and rolling lawns bordered by flowerbeds where late roses bloomed in the sheltered hollows and two benign-looking stone lions sat on their haunches and gazed in eternal contemplation of a graceful fountain cascading into a small pool in front of them.

The orphanage itself was no shabby dwelling but a fine old country house with an exterior of weathered grey stone covered in rambling roses and clematis and a turreted tower that rose up into the sky with quite dignified splendour. On the top floor, little casement windows peeped out from banners of red virginia creeper; white wrought-iron railings encircled ivy-draped balconies; the entrance door was of stained glass that caught the light and made it seem as if rubies were trapped in the panes. It was all very different from what Hannah had expected yet for all these good first impressions she was very glad that she and Janet had made up their differences, as that young lady had willingly agreed to accompany her neighbour to the orphanage to get Andy measured for his callipers.

Doctor MacAlistair had kept his promise to come along to No. 6 of the Row to visit Andy and explain just what a set of callipers could do for his walking problems and why he had to see someone who would measure and assess him so that he could be fitted out properly.

The little boy had been delighted by all this. He didn't mind anything that would help him to get around better and in his excitement he had become totally inarticulate and hadn't been able to express any of his feelings to the doctor.

'It's all right, I understand anyway.' Doctor MacAlistair had ruffled the little boy's head affectionately and had turned his attention to Hannah to gaze at her over his specs and ask if there was anything further she would like to ask him about the proposed visit to the orphanage.

'No, nothing, doctor.' She had kept her eyes averted as she spoke and had made a great show of setting cups and saucers on the table and pouring boiling water into the teapot.

'Fine, fine.' The doctor had sipped his tea and looked thoughtful before barking out, 'And you, Hannah, what about you? Anything troubling you? You seem strained somehow, as if you're bottling something up and are loath to get it off that damned stubborn chest o' yours.'

Hannah, caught off guard, had reddened and stared at him. 'There's nothing wrong with me, Doctor, I'm fine and well but just missing Rob about the place.'

'Ay, ay, so you say,' the doctor had muttered and had subsided back into his chair to gaze into the depths of his cup as if he was mesmerised. His next attack took Hannah by as much surprise as the first. 'Not sickening for something, I hope! Cold? Flu? Impetigo? Measles? Pregnant, perhaps?'

'Really, Doctor MacAlistair,' Hannah had stuttered, wondering for one wild moment if she should just unburden herself there and then and be done with it. But to bring it out in the open would make it too real somehow, and it wasn't real to her, not yet anyway. What could Alistair MacAlistair do even if she were to confide in him? That Effie would likely get to hear of it, Jeannie MacAlistair too; before you could blink the whole place would be looking at her and asking her questions and wondering among themselves if her next child would turn out to be like Andy.

'A worry shared is a worry halved,' the doctor said, his voice softer now, more persuasive. 'I am bound by my profession never to divulge a confidence, you do know that, Hannah, don't you?'

'Ay, doctor, I know that.' She looked at him, a real country doctor if ever there was one, reassuringly homely in his tweed cape and deerstalker hat, his pipe sticking out from his whiskers like some extra part of his anatomy because it was nearly always there, lit or otherwise. The people of Kinvara loved and trusted him though often he 'scared the shat' out of them with his forthright manner and blunt way of speaking.

It was hard to imagine anyone more fatherly looking than Alistair MacAlistair. Though he and Jeannie hadn't produced any children of their own they knew how to get the best from them and were generally looked upon with great affection by youngsters of all ages, not least of these being Andy who often called in at Butterbank House on his travels to partake of Jeannie's homemade buttery scones and creamy milk while enjoying the gossip of the many womenfolk who came and went from the house.

Hannah had come to like and respect the doctor also and felt herself to be teetering on the brink of capitulation to his persuasive tongue, especially when he laid a hand on her shoulder and said kindly, 'I'm always here if you ever need me, lass, even if it's just to talk to. You will remember that, won't you?'

'Ay, doctor, I'll remember,' she said huskily and watched at the door as he galloped off on his 'big stallion brute' Dandy, a glossy-black magnificent beast who tossed his head, rolled his eyes, and pawed the ground when he was getting impatient and wanted to be up and running.

'A motor car would be better for someone in Alistair

MacAlistair's position,' Dokie Joe had said but the doctor couldn't afford to keep anything more expensive than a horse whose only requirements were bed and board. He paid for these in sound measure by providing generous dollops of manure for the rose garden that was the pride and joy of both Jeannie and her husband.

After the doctor left, Andy had been so excited about his forthcoming trip to the orphanage he had insisted in getting into his cart and going to tell Johnny Lonely all about it. Hannah had let him go, glad of some time to be alone for a while with her thoughts before writing to Rob to let him know of the latest happenings in the family. She did this fairly regularly. Nothing elaborate or too long, just quick little notes to keep him up to date about everything.

The one thing she should have told him but didn't was her fear of another pregnancy. She knew he would see it as something wonderful, an event to look forward to and be proud of while she had none of these feelings. Also, to put it down in black and white would make it seem like a definite thing when all the time it wasn't. She still couldn't be sure, there had been no more of these dreadful flutters in her belly and she had never had any sensations of sickness.

Not like she'd had with Andy. That was all too real and horrible to think about and at this point she had pushed the whole frightening subject to the back of her mind and had tried to forget it as much as she could.

She had instead turned her thoughts to the row she'd had with Janet, an incident that had caused her a good deal of anxious soul-searching since she had soon come to realise that her angry denials of Janet's comments could easily be taken as an admission of truth.

The girl's words had been a mite too personal for Hannah's liking, but even so, she hadn't deserved to be shouted at so harshly. There and then, before she could change her mind, Hannah had gone cap in hand to make her peace with Janet, who had been only to willing to bury the hatchet and be on friendly terms once more.

And now here they all were, riding along in Janet's trap with Andy and Vaila beside them and complete with Cousin Kathy, who had decided that she wanted to come along 'for the jaunt' much to the dismay of Hannah who always found herself at a disadvantage in Kathy's company. It was hard enough trying to decipher her whimsical mode of speech without the added distraction of hearing her counting stitches under her breath and reading aloud from her knitting pattern.

'It looks no' too bad a place,' Kathy commented as they pulled up at the door, her needles cast aside for once. She had wanted to enjoy the journey to the orphanage which was a mere two miles from Kinvara but seemed longer with all the twists and turns in the road and the steep little hump-backed bridges dotted along the way. 'Mind you,' she craned her neck and looked upwards, 'I see they have bars on some o' the windows so we'd better watch they don't lock us up and throw away the key. That happened to an uncle of mine when he went over to the mainland to visit a sick relative in hospital and never came back to the island. Folks said he went queer in the head with loneliness and ended up hanging himself from the rafters with his very own trouser braces. That was told to me by my own dear father when I was just a girl living in the Hebrides and to this day I will never forget the sadness on his face when he was speaking. He never got over the loss of his elder brother and even now he cries whenever he mentions Uncle Tam's name.'

'Och, come on, Kathy.' Janet laughed as she saw the startled look on Hannah's face. Cousin Kathy loved an audience and enjoyed telling yarns of an unusual nature when she was in the mood to do so. 'We all know fine that Uncle Tam got locked up in jail for being drunk and disorderly and tried to throttle one o' the guards in the process. He never came back to the island because he liked it better on the mainland

and ended up marrying his sick relative who was his second cousin on his mother's side. It's a well-known fact that Morag was as wild and unruly as he was himself and still is from all accounts.'

Kathy laughed. 'Ach well, it was worth a try, and it was always a good story to tell at the ceilidhs. I myself like my version best, and there's no knowing which o' the stories is true since Uncle Tam never came back to tell the tale and for all we know could be dead and buried in some foreign land wi' his very own trouser braces wrapped around his neck. He was never short of a bob or two and Morag herself might have killed him for his money. She liked the men, did Morag, and could have met somebody who just swept the feet from under her. It would be interesting to look them up someday just to find out what really did happen the day Uncle Tam sailed from the island and never returned.'

Hannah had to smile at this for whatever else Kathy did she was certainly adept at lightening the atmosphere. All of them climbed down from their seats in good spirits, Hannah taking Andy's hand, Vaila clinging on to one each of Janet's and Kathy's.

The children gazed in some awe at the house and at the great glass door looming in front, and finally at the bespectacled woman who came to open it and take their names before ushering them inside to a small dingy waiting room with scuffed rugs and a strong smell of aniseed. This issued from the breath of a rustic-looking man who had just topped up a rather smoky fire and was turning to make his way out again.

'You've been smoking that pipe of yours again, Angus,' the woman accused him, looking at him suspiciously and patting her severe bun as she spoke.

'It isny me, Mrs Dunn, it's the fire,' Angus maintained gruffly, adding in aggrieved tones, 'and what makes you think it was me even if it wasny the fire? It could have been anybody creeping in here for a fly puff.'

Mrs Dunn sniffed and patted her bun again. 'The aniseed,

Angus, the aniseed, you always give yourself away with the aniseed.'

With that she took herself off, leaving Angus to pull his lit pipe from his smouldering pocket and gaze at both in some astonishment. 'Och, my,' he tutted, 'just look at that, another pair o' good trousers to be mended. That woman has eyes on her like a hawk and a nose that would sit better on a ferret. We call her The Dragon around here but she isn't as bad as she makes out and they aren't all like her so don't worry.'

The children watched fascinated as he dipped two horny fingers into the depths of a nearby vase and used them to extinguish the charred remains of his pocket.

'Who is she anyway?' Janet asked curiously.

He grinned. 'My good lady wife, of course, as she has been for the last twenty years. She's the housekeeper here and I'm just the odd job man but we make a good team, Amy and me, and later on, when we're sitting by the fire, she'll scold me for smoking but will mend my trousers just the same while we go over the events o' the day together.'

With that he touched his forelock and departed, leaving Hannah and Janet to raise their brows at one another while Kathy said it just went to show that appearances counted for nothing and it was a good thing they hadn't voiced their thoughts on 'the good lady wife' before Angus had made her marital status known to them.

After that a silence fell over the waiting room. Hannah fixed her eyes on a painting of a large cow opposite her chair and wondered why its udder was purple when the rest of it was brown; Kathy rummaged in her lapbag to produce her knitting and soon her needles were clicking away busily, mesmerising Janet who found her eyes growing heavy as she watched her cousin's flying fingers and saw the wool being eaten up as if by some hungry hairy predator.

'Knit one, purl one, knit one, purl one,' Vaila chanted and collapsed in a heap beside Andy to giggle into his hair while he rolled his eyes and snorted and then fell silent as the minutes ticked away and the cow on the wall became the focus for every pair of eyes except Kathy's.

'Hallo. My name is Bonny.'

Everyone jumped. The cow on the wall was forgotten. The child who was Bonny came further into the room to fold her hands behind her back and stare at them out of eyes that were big and bright and darkly beautiful.

'My name is Bonny,' the little girl repeated. 'I'm four years old and I would like to come home with you.'

She put her thumb in her mouth; her steady gaze roved over the row of surprised faces in front of her before it finally came to rest on Janet. Janet said nothing. There was nothing she could say that would make any sense during that first encounter with Bonny, a tiny fragile child with fair ringlets tumbling about her face and little legs that were so twisted and deformed with rickets it was a wonder to anybody that they held her up at all.

An instant pang of love and compassion shot through Janet's heart. She was captivated by the child's fair little rosebud of a face: her melting blue eyes; the small mouth that looked to be trembling on the verge of tears yet might just as easily break into smiles. Over and above all, there was an aura of strength about Bonny, a toughness and determination that could only have developed in a child who had endured hardship and difficulties in her life.

Four years old. Only four years old . . .

'This is where you are!' A plump. good-natured looking nurse came into the room and went straight to Bonny to lift her up and give her a little shake. 'I've been looking all over for you but might have known you'd be in here giving everyone your blethers.'

'Ach, well, bairns will be bairns, knit two purl two together.' Cousin Kathy did not look up as she spoke but kept her eyes fixed on her flying needles which had come only to a brief halt at Bonny's intrusion into the scene. 'But, of course, you will be knowing that already with yourself looking after them every day. Och! Dammit! Now I've lost the place. I've done hundreds of them in my time but it's never easy turning a heel when folks keep popping up from nowhere.'

She began rummaging in her lapbag while the expression on the nurse's face suggested that she had lost the place also and wasn't quite sure how to deal with such an unusual personage as Kathy.

Janet came to the rescue. Standing up she touched Bonny's cheek and said softly, 'Can you tell us about her? Where she comes from. Who she is.'

The nurse nodded. 'I suppose you could say she is an indirect casualty of war. Her father died two years ago from wounds he received and after that her mother couldn't cope and went to pieces. Deprivation, squalor, poverty, they all took their toll. The Barrs are a big family. Bonny came to us in a dreadful state and we've been trying to build up her strength ever since . . .'

She glanced at the little girl's legs and shook her head. 'A bit late in the day but her general health is better than it was and she's certainly active enough. One day her mother will come back for her. She'll go home to Glasgow where she belongs and though it isn't much it's what she knows best and chatters about all the time.'

'Mamma.' Bonny clasped her hands together in a quaintly old-fashioned gesture. 'Home to Mamma.'

Janet bit her lip and looked appealingly at the nurse. 'Please, could I take her for a walk in the garden? Just for a little while? I promise she won't come to any harm and I'll bring her back safe and sound.'

The nurse looked doubtful. 'She's got an appointment to see the doctor but I suppose . . .' She glanced at Andy waiting patiently beside Vaila. 'Oh, all right, the little boy can go first. I'll just let Matron know and then I'll get Bonny into her coat. If she wants to go with you that is.'

Janet held out her hand. The child took it, her tiny fingers holding on as if they would never let go. Janet held her breath. It was as if she had waited for this day all of her life and she knew she would never forget those strangely poignant moments of meeting little Bonny Barr for the first time.

'She's perfect,' she said to the others as Bonny was led away to get dressed in outdoor clothes.

'But – she's dreadfully handicapped,' Hannah couldn't help saying.

'That's right.' Janet's face was glowing. 'A perfect handicapped little girl. I love her already, and I'm hoping I'll maybe get to take her to Keeper's Row for a holiday one o' these fine days.'

Hannah sat back in her seat while Kathy nodded her agreement with Janet's words. After a while she produced a large bag of sweets from her lapbag and gave one each to Vaila and Andy before popping one into her own mouth.

'Cousin Kathy.' Janet's lips twitched. 'I saw a jar of these in Wee Fay's shop only the other day. Surely you didn't actually go in and buy them after telling everyone about the dangers of too much sugar.'

'That's right.' Kathy, cheeks bulging, was bending her head once more to her knitting. 'Only I didn't buy them, Wee Fay gave them to me in return for a scarf I made for Little John, and you of all people, Janet, should know it is only manners to accept payment of any sort – even those that are bad for you.'

Janet looked at Hannah. Hannah's eyes sparkled; without further ado they both helped themselves from Kathy's bag of sweets and sat sucking contentedly till the nurse came back with Bonny and it was Andy's turn to go in and see the doctor.

KINVARA

Winter 1926

Chapter Fourteen

Big Bette took two pairs of her husband's long johns from a drawer in the dresser and examined them for wear and tear. With the progression of autumn into winter the air had sharpened considerably and last night Mungo had decided that the time had come for him to wrap himself in his warmer underwear.

'New elastic,' Bette decided as she gazed at the stretched waistbands. If she could get Kangaroo Kathy to sew it in it would save her a job she hated and delay the purchase of new garments into the bargain.

Bette went downstairs. Maudie was sitting by a roaring fire, eyes closed as she kneaded the ruff of Toby, a big ginger tom who had recently walked into the house and had so persistently refused to leave that not even Mungo's drastic attempts to discourage it had been successful.

He had poured a bucket of cold water over it; he had laced a saucer of milk with vinegar and when that had failed he had spread zinc ointment on its paws and had watched in despair when it licked it off with relish and in a state of high contentment settled down to preen its fur as if it had just partaken of some wonderful treat.

As a last desperate resort he had tied a tin can to its tail and had sent it packing with a none-too-gentle nudge from his boot, much to the surprise of his neighbours in Keeper's Row whose heads had popped from their windows to watch as the startled cat had rattled and clanked his way along the road. Eventually he had sought refuge in a woodshed at the back of Purlieburn Cottage where he had remained for two days, resisting all of Effie's well meaning attempts to coax him out with saucers of milk and tasty titbits. In fact he had made it plain to everyone who dared come near him that he had taken a thorough dislike to anything that moved on two legs, proving his point by spitting and hissing and ferociously displaying his gleaming fangs whenever anybody approached.

The good folk of Kinvara muttered darkly about Mungo's heartlessness towards a dumb animal and 'him a kirk elder too'; while his very own offspring cold-shouldered him for days and took every opportunity to show him that he was not a very popular member of the MacGill household and never would be until Toby was returned to the fold and made to feel welcome in it.

Maudie soon joined forces with the young MacGills. Behind Mungo's back the cat was persuaded to return to Keeper's Row to take up temporary residence in the hayshed behind the house where Mungo kept winter feed for his horse and his three breeding cows. In this abode, Toby was made as comfortable as possible with blankets and hot water bottles and choice portions of food sneaked to him from the kitchen table.

For a while he was as contented as any stray feline could be until a curious Breck discovered his presence in the shed and began giving him a hard time of it by poking and sniffing around all the nooks and crannies and jumping up at the window to peer in through the cobwebs in the hope of catching a glimpse of the unhappy creature inside.

It soon occurred to Toby that this way of life was definitely not for him. On a morning of heavy hoar frost and bitter draughts sneaking under the door, not to mention Breck's whimpers and whines filtering through every crack, Toby decided he'd had enough of the shed. He went stalking boldly back to the house to present himself in the kitchen, tail waving high in the air, all purrs and bristling whiskers and rubbing himself against Mungo's legs as if in greeting of a much-missed and valued friend.

Bette, Maudie, and the children had stared defiantly at the head of the household, daring him to make one threatening move in Toby's direction while that same animal had fawned and fussed over the head keeper of the light in a most shameless fashion and had employed every one of his tomcat charms to get himself accepted into the bosom of the family.

'Oh, all right,' Mungo had eventually decided after a bit of blustering and blowing, 'Let it stay, waifs and strays seem to be a feature o' this house just now so what difference does one more make. Not in my chair, though,' he added as a last stand. 'If I catch it there with its hairs and its fleas it will be out that door with the toe of my boot up its arse and that will be the end o' the matter for once and for all.'

With memories of being decanted from that same chair in a somewhat painful manner Toby had no intention of incurring further humiliating experiences. He was soon wise enough to wait till Mungo himself was in occupation of the chair and was in a good enough mood to allow a furry bundle on to his knee, 'fleas and all'.

So it was that Toby stayed and grew big and sleek and spoiled, not least by Mungo himself, who soon came to realise the cat's worth as a mouser and a catcher of rats or any other sort of vermin that dared to twitch one enquiring whisker in the vicinity of the house.

In his turn, Toby came to love all the MacGills that ever were born; but more than anyone he loved Maudie with her cosy available lap and the knack she had of making him feel special and wanted and very much a pampered cat with all the immediate world at his feet.

The almost perpetual sight of Maudie at the fire with the cat on her knee, very often in 'the chair', had done nothing to improve Mungo's opinion of the girl as 'a lazy good-for-nothing'. Now Bette looked at her niece and felt some of her husband's frustrations rubbing off on her. Feeling in need of a rest, she had put young Daisy MacNulty of

Quarrymen's Cottages in charge of the shop for a day or two and she was determined that she was not going to jeopardise her precious free time for anybody.

'Maudie,' she said sharply. 'Put that cat off your knee and open your eyes.'

'Ay, Auntie?' Dutifully Maudie did as she was bid and looked at Bette sleepily.

'Mungo needs new elastic for his winter drawers and I want you to go along to the draper's shop in Balivoe and get some.'

Maudie glanced at the window. 'But it's raining, Auntie, and I'll get wet.'

'And about time too, you sit around far too much for a young girl and will take root in that chair if you don't start moving your backside a bit more.'

'All right, Auntie.' Maudie heaved herself out of her chair and gazed at Bette rather reproachfully. 'But you do know, don't you, that I have a tendency to be chesty, and dampness of any sort always brings on my cough.'

'Ay, chesty in more ways than one,' Bette returned grimly. 'If you covered yourself a bit more it might be better for everybody. Wrap yourself up and get along out. And while you're in the village you can get me a few supplies for the larder. I've never known it to be so bare though I keep topping it up till it's about bursting,' she finished meaningfully.

Maudie didn't notice. She had dispatched herself to the lobby to don her outdoor garments and was soon back for Bette's inspection.

'Just look at you,' Bette tutted her disapproval of Maudie's rumpled appearance. If there was one thing that Bette could not abide it was sloppiness. Her own children had known her none-too-tender administrations from an early age and Maudie's slovenly attitude was truly beginning to get on her nerves. 'Collars and buttons undone, no gloves, no scarf. Didn't your mother teach you anything? A big girl like you should know better and will have to learn a few things before you're very much older.'

Like an obedient child, Maudie stayed still while her aunt set about tidying her up, finally shoving a shopping bag into one hand, a purse into the other, and the instructions ringing in her ears not to be late back as there was nothing in the larder for tea that night.

The Knicker Elastic Dears had never met Maudie before and watched in fascination as she roved round the shop, fingering the goods on the sales rack, gazing with lanquid interest at some ribbons and bows displayed at one end of the counter.

'Could we get you something else, dear?' Tillie asked as she wrapped up the elastic for Mungo's long johns. 'We have some very nice corsets in stock, flesh-coloured of course and just the thing to keep the contours firmly under control.'

'Corsets?' Maudie tore her attention away from the ribbons to focus it on Tillie.

'Yes, indeed.' Tottie joined forces with her elder sibling. 'A very popular line with our more discerning customers, a wee bit expensive perhaps but they do their job very thoroughly, very thoroughly indeed.'

Maudie looked blank. 'It isn't something I'm familiar with – maybe if you showed me . . .'

'Certainly, certainly.' Tottie beamed and rushed to bring several boxes to the counter. Carefully she removed the garments from their tissue wrappings and laid them out lovingly. 'Wonderful quality.' Her fingers glided over the material. 'Like silk against the skin, allows it to breathe you know and – er . . .' She gave a discreet little cough. 'Perspiration is kept to a minimum so that the wearer is made cool and comfortable. We have these facts on good authority, recommendation, word of mouth, that sort of thing. When something pleases our ladies they generously allow others into their little secrets.'

Maudie nodded pleasantly. 'My Aunt Mary from Belshill wears them and she kept nothing secret when she came to stay with us in Partick. Full of ridges she used to say, the worst torture any woman could endure. She couldn't wait to get them off at night in order to breathe properly and give herself a good scratch.'

'Oh these aren't ridges.' Tillie was offended. 'They're bones, sewn into the material in order to control the waistline.'

'I know all about bones.' Maudie looked as if she was really enjoying herself. 'I broke one when I was five years old jumping down from a wall and to this day I still have a wee twinge in my arm to prove it.'

'Quite.' The sisters were non-plussed. They had never met anyone like Maudie before and they raised their brows to one another in a gesture that said she wasn't really 'all there' and 'allowances must be made'.

Maudie grinned at them engagingly. 'The colour *is* nice,' she said placatingly. 'And Aunt Mary did look neater when she had hers on.' Her eyes travelled slowly to the buxom but well-restrained figures of the two sisters and she nodded her head in full approval. 'Yes. I see what you mean, very elegant ladies, both, and a great advertisement for your own corsets. But I was never a lass who could make up her own mind easily and it would really help if I could have a wee quick peep under your frocks to see for myself what's holding you up. We could go into the back shop if you're feeling shy about it. No one would ever know except me and I was aye a body who could be trusted to keep my mouth shut – as my Aunt Bette herself would surely tell you.'

The sisters were utterly aghast at this suggestion and glared tight-lipped at Maudie as she went on to say flippantly, 'Och well, it was only an idea, no need to get your knickers in a twist over nothing. If it helps at all I'll go home and tell Auntie about your corsets . . .' She grinned again. 'Though mind, she's a bit like me in that respect, and as far as I know only ever wears her stays if the minister is coming to tea or the laird popping in for a cuppy. Weddings too, of course, and the Sabbath, oh, ay, always on the Sabbath. Otherwise she just lets gravity have its way and Uncle Mungo doesn't seem to mind – but och, that's men for you,' she added indulgently. 'They enjoy the wobbly bits and never like anything that restricts freedom – as I myself have found out from experience. The minister too must like them, for I've noticed how his wife just lets hers fly in the wind when she's out riding that bicycle o' hers, skirts up and bosoms unanchored – just the way nature intended.'

Hardly daring to look at the two stunned faces in front of her Maudie opened her purse and counted out the coins, placing each one on the counter with a businesslike snap before gathering up her little package of elastic and departing the premises with a pleasant 'Good day' and a vigorous jangling of the doorbells.

The sisters winced and glanced at one another. 'From the town, of course,' Tottie said decidedly.

'Oh, definitely from the town,' Tillie agreed as she scooped the corsets from the counter to tuck them back into their respective boxes before placing them once more into a drawer discreetly marked 'Cor. Skin Tone. Size 16 upwards.'

Chapter Fifteen

Bubbling with laughter, Maudie made her way along the street, going over in her mind her little interlude in the draper's, the things she had said to the Murchison sisters, the expressions on their faces and their reactions to her revelations concerning her aunt and uncle.

'Oh.' Clapping a hand to her mouth she leaned against a wall and gave vent to her mirth. Perhaps she had said too much but she simply hadn't been able to help herself – that bit about them giving her a private strip show; Aunt Bette's personal habits; Uncle Mungo's preferences regarding the female form. Actually she didn't really know when her aunt wore her stays and had only guessed at her uncle's views on the matter but it had been so good to tease the two and watch their faces as she did so.

Then there were the wobbly bits – and the minister's wife – and the horror on the sisters' faces – and them such devout Sunday School teachers too! 'Oh, dear God! Dear God!' Maudie clutched her stomach and screeched and couldn't have cared less if the minister himself had come walking along the street, so helpless was she with agonised laughter.

A rumble of wheels on the pavement vaguely penetrated her senses and only when a voice said at her elbow, 'Can we share in the joke or is it a private matter?' did she recover sufficiently to see Janet's face smiling at her and Hannah hovering in the background with Andy who, with the aid of his new callipers, could get along fairly well now. That day he had generously given up his cart to little Bonny Barr who sat in it quite happily, her small delicate face whipped to roses in the wind blowing up from the sea, her halo of golden curls brisking out from a woolly red bonnet knitted for her by Cousin Kathy.

Some weeks had passed since Janet's first meeting with the little girl and in that time, with her mother's written permission, Bonny had been a regular visitor to No.5 of the Row. Janet had never been happier or more fulfilled. Brimming over with enthusiasm she had prepared a room for Bonny in readiness for her first overnight stay, Cousin Kathy willingly running up curtains and bedspreads and anything else to delight a child who had spent so much of her short life away from her own home.

'I hope you don't get hurt by all this,' Hannah had warned. 'You'll have to remember that Bonny has a family of her own and a mother who could come back for her whenever she feels like it.'

But Janet hadn't listened. 'Her own mother isn't well enough or capable enough to look after the family she's already got, never mind a special child like Bonny. It could be years yet before she goes home – if she ever does – and meanwhile I'll be here for her as long as she needs me. If all goes well, Jock and me could become her foster parents, or even adopt her if we possibly can. She would have everything she ever needs or wants and most of all she would have love. I adore her already, it's as if she's my own bairn and our paths were meant to cross.'

At that point, and much to Hannah's surprise, she had thrown her arms around her neighbour and had said softly, 'And it's you I have to thank for everything, Hannah Sutherland. If we hadn't made up, if I hadn't gone with you to the orphanage, I would never have met Bonny and I wouldn't be as happy as I am now. I feel as if I've been given the little daughter I've always wanted and nothing anyone can say or do will ever take that away from me.'

A small fear had touched Hannah then, a sense of unease that wouldn't be stilled no matter how hard she tried to push it away. She saw very clearly that Janet had shut her mind off to reality and wasn't prepared to listen to the hard facts concerning the uncertain future of little Bonny Barr. In Janet's view, the child was already hers, and nothing anyone could say was going to rob her of that illusion.

The thought of this made Hannah feel strange and breathless because at that point she remembered her own unwillingness to acknowledge matters concerning her own life and that of the child growing within her. She could no longer ignore it. Every day it was getting stronger and stronger, moving about in her belly, kicking her, never letting her forget its presence for a minute.

She was about four and a half months 'gone' as Dolly Law would have said, and never a moment of sickness to show for it, never a pain nor an ache nor any of the other discomforts normally associated with pregnancy. She wasn't even very big yet and had only started to feel a tightness in her clothing that was easily solved by moving a button or two and wearing baggy cardigans that disguised anything that bulged.

She hadn't said a word to anybody about her 'condition', though at times she had longed to unburden herself to somebody. The idea of writing to her mother had briefly entered her head but she had quickly decided against it, as news like that might easily bring Harriet rushing to Kinvara and what earthly good would that do anybody? She would just upset the entire household with her interference and probably voice the fears and doubts that were uppermost in Hannah's own mind.

No, no, Harriet was the last person she could confide in. She wasn't going to tell Rob just yet either as she felt it was far better to wait till he was home rather than put it down on paper. It didn't do to put news like that in black and white, it was too awkward, too impersonal, and anyway she wouldn't know how to word it.

Christmas wasn't all that far away; in just a few weeks she

would see him, talk to him, let him discover the truth for himself. Meanwhile it was her secret, tightly locked within her, giving her some strange sense of satisfaction to think about it as such. No one had guessed that she was pregnant, no one suspected, with the exception perhaps of Janet who had never mentioned it again after the row they'd had.

But she hadn't reckoned with the twinges of conscience she felt every time she saw Janet with Bonny and realised how unfair the twists of fate could be. Still, that was life, as Donald of Balivoe said often enough, and she had ample problems of her own without having to concern herself with those of other people.

Yet still she felt guilty about matters as they stood and in an effort to compensate she began going out of her way to please Janet. They became friends as well as neighbours and were often to be seen together, walking, talking, getting each other along the road to the village.

Today they had gone out with the intention of meeting the children from school but first they met Maudie and were soon laughing along with her as she regaled them with a humorous account of her visit to the Knicker Elastic Dears.

Babs and Tom, Vaila and Joss, came running up and there was a clamour of voices when they saw Maudie and tried to gain her attention, Babs in particular being very clingy and demanding and hanging on to her cousin's hand in a most possessive manner. But Maudie was too taken up with Bonny at that point to be bothered with much else and plucking the child from the cart she swung her up high and began to sing to her in an unexpectedly melodious voice.

'Oh little Bonny Barr went flying far.
Yes, little Bonny Barr went flying far.
Well she landed on a star
Because she had travelled far.
Yes, Bonny Barr had landed on a star.

'Now little Bonny Barr began to sing.

Yes, little Bonny Barr began to sing.
The stars went ting-a-ling
And did a Highland fling,
Because little Bonny Barr began to sing.

'Well the sun up in the sky winked his eye,
And the fairies of the moon went flitting by.
The birds and bees were there,
With flowers in their hair.
And the cat he sat in Uncle Mungo's chair.'

The little song came to an end. Bonny chuckled and asked for more. Andy was enthralled by Maudie's clever use of words, while everyone else showed their appreciation of the impromptu entertainment. Only Babs remained unimpressed as she said in a melancholy voice, 'How can the sun and stars be out at the same time? And birds and bees don't have hair, they only have wings and stings.'

'That rhymes too,' Maudie laughed and promptly wove the words into another verse. 'The birds were on the wing and the bee had lost his sting because little Bonny Barr began to sing.'

'Why can't I be a fairy in one of your songs?' Babs' lower lip jutted as she spoke.

'Because you're too big to be a fairy.'

'If you had any imagination at all you would know you'd never get two inches off the ground even if you had ropes holding you up,' Tom told his sister heavily. 'You're more like an elephant than a fairy.'

'No, I'm not!' Babs cried passionately. 'And anyway,' she added scornfully. 'How can *she* be a fairy? She's got broken legs.'

'She doesn't need legs when she's got wings.' Vaila was determined not to let Babs have the last say.

'No, she doesn't. She's just Bonny Barr from the orphanage and she'll never fly in a million years.'

'Oh, yes she will.' Joss, always quick to defend Bonny,

glowered at Babs. 'She's got wings in her mind and she can go anywhere she wants in the whole wide world.'

The hot tears of anger and humiliation sprang to Babs' eyes and she showed every sign of throwing a tantrum. It was all Maudie's fault. Making such a fuss of that Bonny Barr who was just a newcomer to the place and not a very attractive one at that. Those legs of hers, for instance, all twisted and bent and weak so that she had to ride in Andy Sutherland's cart because she couldn't walk very far. They were both alike, him and her, she with her funny legs and he with his slavers and grunts and his big head lolling about on his bony shoulders.

Yet for all their ugliness they got all the attention and just because she was a little bit fat she got none and would never ever be a fairy in one of Cousin Maudie's stories. Her lip trembled, she wanted to strike out at someone, and lifting her hand she made to cuff Tom on the ear. But he ducked and ran a safe distance before turning to make faces and rude signs at her. She felt her heart near to bursting with frustration and downright temper because she knew she would never catch up with him to pay him back. He was the agile one of the family, Joe was the strong one – while she – she was just plain old Babs who was too big and too heavy for her age and who had hair that was lank and mousy brown and teeth that protruded slightly.

'Come on, Babsy,' yelled Tom. 'Race you to Wee Fay's! I've got tuppence in my pocket and I'll buy you a sugar-olly twist if you can run all the way to The Dunny without tripping over your own big feet.'

Oh! Brothers were horrible! Horrible! Babs bit her lip. Joe was superior just because he was working and Tom was cruel with his taunts and his jibes. She hesitated. The thought of what a penny could buy *was* alluring. Tom *was* wicked but he could also be kind and he had always been good at sharing what he had with her. Pride and temptation fought a short bitter battle within her but in the end she succumbed to the latter and went running to join the others who were peering at the mouth-watering array of sweets displayed in the window of The Dunny.

Bonny pointed to a large dish of marshmallows. 'Like Maudie,' she decided mischievously.

'A pink one,' Vaila added because she knew she could say such things to Babs' cousin and get away with it. 'All squishy and squashy.'

Janet smiled. 'You are a bit like a marshmallow, Maudie, soft and sweet and fluffy.'

Maudie was not offended. 'I couldn't think of anything nicer to be, and I vote we should go in and get some before the bairns from school snap them all up.'

Babs looked immensely cheered by this and temporarily casting aside her sulks she went inside with everyone else and even quite pleasantly allowed Andy to go before her as they stood at the counter waiting to be served.

Once home, however, and most of her sweets eaten, Babs' grievances against her cousin returned anew and she went stomping away upstairs in the highest of dudgeon, hoping Maudie might follow her and coax her into a better frame of mind.

But Maudie was having none of that. She had discovered that the best way to deal with Babs was to leave her to smoulder and fester and snap out of her moods in her own good time and with this in mind she left her young cousin to her own devices and took herself into the kitchen where she threw her hat and scarf on to a chair and flopped down beside them.

'Oh, I've had a lovely day, Auntie,' she enthused as she grabbed hold of Toby and cuddled him to her bosom. She had brought the tang of salt fresh air into the room, her face was dewy and glowing; she looked altogether the picture of youthful health and vigour as she sat there with the purring cat on her lap.

'Your outing has done you good, Maudie,' Bette said

approvingly. 'Wasn't I right when I said you should get out and about more?'

'Of course you were right, Auntie, you're never far wrong – as Uncle Mungo has a habit o' saying. I met Janet and Hannah and the bairns and we had a rare old chin wag on the way to the shops. But first I went into the draper's as you asked and you'll never guess what I said to the Knicker Elastic Dears.'

She proceeded to give her aunt a word-for-word account of her little interlude with the Murchison sisters. Though Bette thought it was hilarious she also looked worried at the mention of the minister's name and those of herself and her husband.

'Kerry O'Shaughnessy might no' like it if word o' this gets around. That two have never approved o' her as a minister's wife and would be only too glad of the chance to bring her down a peg or two.'

'Och, Auntie, it was only a joke, I never said anything bad about her at all and I'm sure she would only see the funny side if it *did* get to her ears.'

'Kerry might, but the minister would surely have something to say if he thought folks were talking about his wife behind her back. Your tongue has indeed been busy, my girl, and while it was all right to make a passing remark about my stays I hope you didn't go blabbing your mouth off too much. What I do behind closed doors is my business and I don't want the likes o' that Jessie MacDonald finding out anything she shouldn't. It's enough that she's already branded me a drunken Jezebel without adding a shameless hussy to her list as well.'

'Och, no, Auntie.' Maudie turned an innocent face. 'The Knicker Elastics would never say anything like that about you for I told them you always respectfully wore your stays to weddings and on the Sabbath.'

'Funerals too,' Bette said faintly.

Maudie looked shocked. 'Och, Auntie! That goes without saying! I myself borrowed some from a friend when Uncle Dick went and died on us. I felt so stiff I might as well have been in the box beside him and couldn't wait to get the damt things off.' Scooping Toby from her lap she stood up. 'I must go and see how Babs is doing. She was mad at me earlier for making too much o' Bonny and not enough of her and went marching away upstairs in the huff.'

Bette clicked her tongue. 'I don't know what's gotten into Babs these days. She used to be a nice-natured wee lass but now all she ever does is sulk and moan and find fault with everything.'

'She's just getting to be that age, Auntie,' Maudie said knowingly. 'She wants to be everything she isn't and will have to learn to accept herself as she is before she's very much older.'

It had never entered Bette's head that her daughter's surliness might owe itself to the not-so-simple matter of growing up and she eyed her niece thoughtfully as she said, 'You're wise in the ways o' the world, Maudie Munro. To me Babs is just a wee lass yet but now that I come to think of it, she *is* getting to be that age now.'

'Oh, ay, and taking everything to heart in the process, especially the teasing and tormenting she gets from her brothers. It isn't easy for her being the only girl among boys. Brothers can be buggers at times and I should know, mine made my life a hell at Babs' age. It was only when we got up a bit that we began to really like one another. I was always on the plump side, and didn't think much o' myself till I realised I was born to be big and people loved me as I was. Now I couldn't be happier or more contented and I hope Babs will grow up to feel like that too.'

She smiled her dimpled smile and hoisted up one large breast with the back of her hand. Laughter spurted from Bette's lips. 'No, Maudie,' she agreed, 'no one could be more contented than you but you're young yet and shouldn't allow yourself to get too settled. There will be time and enough for that when you're old and grey and have nothing else to do but sit at the fire gazing up the lum. You must get out more, go to the dances and the ceilidhs and meet all the young men who are just waiting their chance for a nice lass like you to come along.'

Maudie made a face. 'There aren't so many o' these in Kinvara. The war took the best and those that were left are bound to have been snapped up long ago.'

The wisdom of her words gave Bette food for though as she went to put the kettle on. Maudie was right, there were very few eligible young men left in Kinvara, but surely, oh, surely there must be one lurking out there who would fall head over heels for a winsome wench like Maudie, a girl who was so good with children and who would never stray very far from her own fireside.

Mungo came in looking for his tea, his eyes going at once to the vacant chair by the fire and his brows lifting in surprise at the sight. 'I don't believe it,' he said sarcastically. 'I've become so used to seeing your niece pinned to that seat with the cat on her knee it's as if something's amiss when she isn't there.'

'Oh, she's been out and about,' Bette said airily as she nudged him aside to reach for the teapot. 'And I wouldn't worry your head about her if I were you. Maudie's a good strong healthy lass and already quite a few o' the lads have their eye on her. She's been keeping her head down since she came here but all that's sure to change given time. She's young and she's ready and the wedding bells will be ringing before any o' us have a chance to realise what is happening.'

'Really?' Mungo looked unconvinced as he sat down and accepted a mug of steaming hot tea. 'I've never seen any sign o' that for myself but then I'm not so much at home these days and you know better than anybody the kind o' things your niece gets up to in her spare time. One thing's for sure, she's got plenty o' that, and since it looks as if she's got no intention o' getting a job she'd do well to find herself a man who can afford to keep her in the manner she's come to expect, and the sooner the better as far as I'm concerned.'

Bette stirred her tea and wished she'd kept her mouth shut. Her double chins sank to her bosoms as she mulled the matter over. She had put her foot well and truly in it this time and had no earthly idea how she was going to wriggle herself out of it. She glanced at her husband. He was looking thoughtful

– no, smug was the word. Already he was visualising having his home to himself again. Bette sighed and began going over in her mind the names of all the available youths in Kinvara. She could think of none. She would start with the first letter of the alphabet. That often helped when she couldn't sleep and lay on her back going through the lists of flowers, animals, etc.

'A,' Unconsciously she spoke the letter aloud.

'Eh?' Mungo blinked.

'Oh, nothing – I mean not that kind of eh, the other sort, only it doesn't matter now because it has all gone out o' my head anyway.'

Heavy feet sounded on the stairs and Maudie came into the room. 'Uncle Mungo,' she acknowledged cheerfully as she sat herself on a stool beside him and bit into a jammy scone with relish. 'I thought I heard you coming in. I think you must smell it when Auntie's making the tea because you always seem to arrive just as she's filling the pot.'

'Snap,' Bette muttered dourly.

'What was that?' Maudie asked.

'Back to normal,' Mungo grunted and grabbed at a scone before his niece through marriage could finish them all.

The door opened and Babs came in, looking much happier as she hummed a catchy tune under her breath and perched herself on her father's knee.

'That's what I like to hear,' Mungo told her heartily. 'My little girl singing. Do it aloud and we'll all join in.'

Babs, looking ready to burst with pride, plunged straight into the song.

'Babs MacGill's a very pretty girl.
When she goes out the boys are in a
whirl.
But she pushes them aside
And takes it in her stride,
'Cos Babs MacGill's a very pretty girl.'

'Oh, very good, ay, very good indeed,' Mungo said warily,

as if he knew what was coming. 'Where did you learn it?'

'It's a Maudie song!' Babs blurted out. 'Written specially for me. There are lots and lots of verses. Would you like me to sing them to you, Father?'

Mungo knew when he was beaten. Babs' voice droned on, praising herself to the nines, faithfully chanting every word her cousin had written. A resigned expression crept over Mungo's face. Bette winked at Maudie and handed her the plate bearing the last scone but one. That was reserved for Babs when she came back to reality and was able to enjoy the more earthly pleasures of life once more.

Chapter Sixteen

Connie was listening at the door of the minister's study into which room he had disappeared barely five minutes ago with Big Bette MacGill of Keeper's Row.

Up until that time Connie had been anxious to finish her duties at the Manse, since she had promised to meet her young man at the foot of the drive in a matter of fifteen minutes. But when she saw Bette, the alarm bells had sounded and now she hung back, placing herself strategically at a small occasional table conveniently situated just outside the minister's room.

In one hand she held a vase, in the other a duster, both items suspended in mid-air as she cocked her ear to the door and concentrated all her attention on the buzz of voices on the other side.

The Manse however was a sturdily built house with walls and doors of sufficient thickness to ensure a great degree of privacy for its occupants and for anybody else who came within its impressive portals. The only things that ever got in and out of a closed Manse door with any measure of success were the draughts that sneaked all round the house in great abundance on a windy day.

Connie was only too well aware of these drawbacks and always came prepared with an extra cardigan when the sea was riding high and every breeze that sprung up from the waves seemed to find its way to the house atop the hillock.

This had been just such a day and Connie had been kept

busy lighting fires and tending them till several of the chimneys were puffing busily away and the smoke blowing hither and thither according to the wiles of the wind. But while the rooms were cosy and warm it was a different story out here in the hall and Connie was sorry now that she had been in such a hurry to remove her cardigan along with her apron as she felt the chilly air creeping up her ankles and seeping through her clothing. Uncomfortably she moved her cold feet and was about to give up her vigil when Bette's laugh boomed out and a name filtered through the door, muffled but reasonably distinct for all that.

Connie held her breath. So she had been right after all! She knew all about Bette MacGill and her quest to find a job of work for that stout and slothful niece of hers, Maudie Munro. Word had spread about the trip the pair had made to Crathmor to see the laird and his lady and Catrina had been only too ready to fill her sister in with the details, adding a warning to be on her guard should Bette appear in the vicinity of the Manse.

'Seemingly Maudie's a wizard with children,' Catrina had gone on to say. 'Kerry just lets these bairns o' hers run wild and the minister might easily take to the idea o' having a nursery maid and a housekeeper combined. None of the nannies he's had so far have stuck it out for long but nothing ruffles Maudie's feathers and she and Kerry would get on a treat. Money's always tight in the Manse and having someone do two jobs for the price o' one would just suit the MacIntoshes down to the ground.'

After that, Connie had been on her guard where the MacGills were concerned. She had come across Maudie in her travels and had taken to her at once but had no intention of letting sentiment get in the way of practicalities. Now here was Bette, laughing with the minister in his study, discussing Maudie, having a rare old blether to themselves.

Connie's green eyes glittered and she edged closer to the door, all pretence of work forgotten as she endeavoured to catch any snippets of conversation that might filter out from the study and provide her with a clue as to the reasons for Bette's visit.

* * *

In actual fact, Bette had only made the trip to the Manse to give the Reverend Thomas MacIntosh a message from Mungo, to the effect that he was suffering from a bad head cold and would be unable to come out that night to the meeting of kirk elders of which body he was the Session Clerk.

'He will no doubt attend to the paperwork he took home with him last time,' Bette went on to say, adding rather sarcastically. 'Even suppose he was dying he would still see to that.'

'Quite, yes, he is a very thorough man in that respect but must learn to take things easier when he isn't feeling well.' The minister, while attempting to appear sorry at Bette's news, could not, however, suppress a feeling of relief since Mungo was apt to take his duties very seriously indeed and often annoyed everyone, not least the minister himself, with his ponderous manner and his insistence on adhering to every rule in the book when it came to matters of the church.

'Tunnel vision,' Donald of Balivoe was wont to say and secretly the minister could not agree with him more. The idea of a cosy session meeting in the Manse sitting room without Mungo's presence cheered the minister immensely since it meant that everyone else could enjoy a glass of sherry without his disapproving eye upon them.

The Reverend MacIntosh was also not enamoured with the way in which Mungo tried to boss him about and interfere with his arrangements of kirk affairs. This often resulted in a clash of personalities as the minister was an extremely self-willed man in his own right and did not take kindly to this sort of meddling.

He was therefore quietly pleased to see Bette and offered her a sherry which she readily accepted, a twinkle in her eye as she noted the relief in his even while he strove to look suitably sympathetic about her husband's malady.

'Och well.' Bette sat back comfortably in her seat and sipped her drink. 'It is the way o' things, none o' us are immune to a wee head cold now and then, no' even Mungo for all he's got the kirk in his blood and thinks it will fall down altogether if he isn't here to hold it up.'

The minister looked at her, she looked at him; in a moment of complete understanding they both burst out laughing after which enjoyable interlude he went on to ask her how the rest of the family were faring.

'Oh, they're grand, just grand, growing bigger every day and eating me out o' house and home.' She hesitated for a moment before plunging on, 'Then of course, there's Maudie, my niece who's come to stay with us from Partick. I like fine having her about the place but Mungo thinks she – hmm – isn't as active as she should be for a lass o' her age and I'm that torn between the two I don't know whether I'm coming or going sometimes.'

'Mungo, yes.' The minister's shrewd brown eyes were thoughtful. 'And Maudie. She hasn't been to church yet, as far as I know, but I've spoken to her once or twice in the village and thought how cheerful and likeable she was.'

'Oh, she's that all right.' Bette gave vent to a mighty sigh. 'That really is part o' the trouble. She's got the sunniest nature of anyone I've ever known and it's very hard to be angry with her even when I feel she deserves it. She's very easygoing is our Maudie and hardly does a hand's turn in the house. It really annoys me sometimes and I often feel like braining her, but just when I've worked myself up to giving her a right good scolding she turns around and smiles at me and I find myself melting like a big soft piece o' butter.'

Bette sighed again. 'The bairns adore her, they gather round her like bees to honey. She would make a wonderful mother and an excellent wife for someone but though she's started to get out and about a bit more she's still very contented just being at home and hasn't shown any inclination to socialise properly or get a job as yet. Mungo thinks she's got a few admirers lined up and seems only too eager to get her married off. It's his chair, you see, Mr MacIntosh. Maudie spends a lot o' her time in it with the cat and it's aye been regarded as Mungo's, even when he's away on light duty and not here to keep an eye on the things he considers to be rightly his as head o' the household.'

The minister disregarded that last part of the conversation as being too trivial for his attention but for the rest he was able to pat Bette's hand and say reassuringly, 'I'm sure Maudie will have no bother finding the right man when he comes along. Meanwhile you ought to enjoy her while you've got her. I've heard how entertaining she is and she must be good company for you when your husband is engaged in his various interests.'

'To be honest, Mr MacIntosh, other than her laziness I love having Maudie in the house,' Bette said warmly, quite relieved to be able to talk to someone about matters that were troubling her. 'She does get on my nerves occasionally, the way she just laughs at life, but somehow I can't imagine what it would be like without her now.'

The minister hooked his thumb in his lapel and regarded Bette thoughtfully. 'Perhaps I shouldn't say this but Maudie reminds me of my wife, bubbling over with the joy of living, daft and young and lighting up everything in her path.'

Pride and love shone out of his face as he spoke and Bette saw another side to the sober Sunday man that everyone knew. 'Kerry changed my life when she did me the honour of marrying me, and I can honestly say that these past years have been the happiest I've ever known. You see, she's natural, like Maudie, and doesn't put on airs and graces for anyone.' He shook his head. 'In the beginning I found this rather daunting as I had been brought up always to put on a face and never to let my real feelings show. Now I see it as refreshing and unique and while I myself will never be able to change my ways completely I'm learning not to take myself as seriously as I once did.'

He smiled a smile that transformed his thin face completely. 'The Kerrys and the Maudies of the world teach us all a lesson. I treasure my wife and you should do the same with Maudie. She's young and she's bound to spread her wings and won't always be there at your fireside in Mungo's chair, telling you stories and making you laugh. One day you'll look back and remember all the good things about Maudie and you'll perhaps think how comforting it was when she was living with you and keeping you cheerful.'

Bette was greatly uplifted by his words and also felt extremely honoured to have shared his confidences about his wife. Not only that, he had compared her to Maudie, and if Maudie did as well in the marriage stakes as had Kerry O'Shaughnessy then that would indeed be a feather in the girl's cap and something for any aunt to be proud of!

Quite carried away by her imaginative thoughts, Bette stood up and puffed out her impressive bosom. 'Mr MacIntosh, I can't tell you how much I've enjoyed talking to you, it's been a pleasure, a real pleasure.' Her plump face with its dimpled cheeks and double chins beamed gratitude all over the minister. 'May the good Lord forgive me, but I have to be honest and say how glad I am about Mungo's cold. If it hadn't been for that I wouldn't have had the chance to enjoy such a rare old blether with my very own minister and we might never have gotten to know one another as well as we have done today.'

Taking his hand she pumped it so hard he winced. 'Thank you, thank you for everything,' she bellowed in her fat meaty voice. 'I'm so pleased for my Maudie I could kiss you, that I could, and if it wasn't for the fact that we are both respectable married people I would have no second thoughts about it, of that you can be assured.'

The minister repossessed his hand and hastily moved back a step or two. 'Yes, well, very good, I may say I too have enjoyed our little tête à tête.' He fingered some notes on his desk. 'Dear me, I never realised I had so much work to catch up on . . .'

He allowed the remainder of his sentence to hang meaningfully in mid-air but Bette was in too much of a rosy haze to notice. The sherry had mellowed her mood, the minister's kindly words about her niece had done the rest – and if she could just take one more minute of his time to tell him about Babs and how cleverly Maudie was managing to restore the child's self-esteem . . .

Outside the door, Connie's mouth fell open. The minister and Bette, kissing! Or at least, discussing the act. She hadn't been able to help herself hearing. That Bette had a voice like a foghorn, so loud it had penetrated right through the thickness of the door and out into the hall. And she had said something about being pleased for Maudie's sake. Did that mean the minister had said he would give the girl a job? Perhaps – Connie shivered – *her* job?

'Oh, you're still here, Connie. I thought you must have gone when you didn't answer the door just now.'

At the sound of Kerry O'Shaughnessy's voice right at her elbow, Connie jumped and spun round. In her panic the vase she had been holding slipped from her grasp and before she knew what was happening it had smashed itself to smithereens all over the polished linoleum at her feet.

A little squeaky shriek escaped her as she stared down aghast. 'Oh, no! Oh, God! I'm so sorry, Mrs MacIntosh, I'll pay for it – unless, of course, it's a priceless antique and can never be replaced. I didn't mean it, I've never done anything like this before, I'm always so careful but I got such a fright . . .'

The deep blue eyes of the minister's wife twinkled. Laying a hand on Connie's arm she said through a bubble of glee, 'It's myself who should be paying you for getting rid of it. It was a present from my husband's mother on our wedding and I've hated it every waking day of my life. I hoped when the children were very small they might knock it over and break it but no such luck – until now – and . . .' She glanced down at the broken pieces. 'You've made a very thorough job of it and for that I can never thank you enough.'

'Really?' Connie, who had been on the verge of tears, brightened up considerably. Taking her hanky from her sleeve she applied it to her nose to give it a very loud and satisfying blow, after which she threw Kerry a watery smile and said again, 'Do you really and truly mean that, Mrs MacIntosh?'

'Of course I mean it, and call me Kerry. Surely to goodness you know me well enough by now to drop the formalities.' She paused and inclined her head towards the study door. 'No sign of my husband coming out just yet, go and fetch a dustpan and brush and we'll get this mess cleared up before he sees it. Fingers crossed he'll never even notice the vase is gone, especially if I put something else in its place and keep the rest of the ornaments exactly where they always are on the table.'

'Och, you're a sport, Kerry O'Shaughnessy, indeed you are,' Connie said a few minutes later, blowing back an errant lock of red hair and puffing a bit in her excitement.

'Think nothing of it.' Kerry's ready smile flashed out. 'We must help one another in this world as Thomas himself would surely agree, and now I must go and see to tea before the hungry horde descends. They're like a pack of ravening wolves – the minister included.'

She giggled infectiously and was halfway up the hall when she came to an abrupt halt and turned back to hand Connie a note. 'I almost forgot about this. One of the village lads called with it a few minutes ago and I gathered it was from your young man.'

She went off once more, leaving Connie to unfold the piece of paper and read its contents. It was indeed from John, telling her that he was suffering from a sore throat and wouldn't manage to meet her that night as arranged but would be in touch with her as soon as he was feeling better.

> *I have something rather important to say to you, Connie,* he had gone on, *but best to wait till we are face to face as it's not the sort of thing I would want to commit to paper.*

Connie snorted as she stuffed the note into her pocket. Something important to tell her indeed! Perhaps he was planning to give her the brush-off and if that was the case then it really might be for the best all round. She was growing tired of John and his ailments. The least sign of a sniffle and he was in bed feeling sorry for himself. A mammy's boy if ever there was one. An only son who was mollycoddled and pampered and who often compared her cooking to that of his mother.

That last time, for instance, he had said she put too much salt in the soup and should have left the sugar out of the apple pie. 'I like mine tartish,' he had intoned seriously. 'Mother always leaves flavouring to personal taste and I've become used to eating my food with only very small amounts of additives.'

These rather prim attitudes of his might have had something to do with the fact that he and his mother lived in a large Victorian dwelling on the fringes of Balivoe and considered themselves to be a better class of people than most. In days gone by, a household staff had existed at Bougan Villa with maids to do all the menial tasks about the house and a nanny and a governess to look after John when his parents were off on their frequent travels around the world.

All that ended, however, when his father had lost out on various business ventures and had died a premature death through worry and drink, leaving behind a widow who was poorly equipped to handle the domestic affairs of a house without staff and a son whose privileged and sheltered background had made it difficult for him to adjust to a rather more ordinary way of life.

In his late teens he had joined the army and had somehow made it safely through the war. Now twenty-nine, possessed of brains but too lacking in ambition to use them, he muddled along as a clerk in the office of the Balivoe Fishery, earning very little and certainly not enough to keep himself and his mother in the style to which they had once been accustomed.

The roof of Bougan Villa was leaking; unused rooms lay cold and empty; the gardens which had long ago bloomed with colour and life were now choked and overgrown; spiders and beetles thrived in the outhouses; mice scampered in the cellar; stray cats had taken up residence in the abandoned staff kitchen and altogether it was 'no fit place for man nor beast' according to Dokie Joe MacPhee who didn't know about the cats and the mice since the 'lady of the manor', as she was known, had never encouraged anyone near Bougan Villa for years.

The local children called it 'The Ghostie House' because of the shadows and the thin lights flickering in the windows and loved to dare one another to set foot inside the tangled garden but seldom got as far as the gate since John had a knack of appearing out of nowhere and soon sent them packing with a few choice words he had learned in the army.

'Down on their uppers,' Granny Margaret was fond of telling her eldest granddaughter. 'The house is falling into ruin about their lugs but that doesn't stop them from being uppity. Oh, no, she's a snob is Prudence Taylor-Young with a hyphen and it's more than likely she can't cook for nuts. No wonder John doesn't like salt or sugar, they probably can't afford to buy any and might be suffering from malnutrition for all we know. Whichever way, he's only after you for a decent roof and a place to lay down his head when his mother is no longer alive to look after him.'

'But, Granny, this isn't our house,' Connie would protest. 'We only rent it from The MacKernon and who knows what will happen in the future? Besides all that, ours isn't a decent roof, it's leaking like a sieve with buckets in the bedrooms and great holes in the gutters under the eaves.'

'That's only because Harry Hutchinson didn't fix it properly that last time he was here, and to think he has the cheek to call himself a skilled tradesman. He charges The MacKernon good money for nothing and I could have done the job better myself with a ladder and some nails. Even so, it's a better roof than the one at Bougan Villa and John knew which side his bread was buttered when he cast his beady eye at you, Connie, my lass.'

Connie could have told her granny that John wasn't keen on butter either because his mother had said it was bad for his arteries but she had long ago learned it was no use arguing with Granny Margaret when she had made her mind up about something or someone.

Perhaps she was right at that. John was too settled in his ways to make a good husband for anybody and Connie was beginning to feel that she might be better off staying single after all. In fact, she was starting to go off men altogether, if the ones her sisters had married were anything to go by. Cora was happy enough with Ryan Du but always had to keep her eye on him when there were other women around and what kind of life was that for any self-respecting woman?

As for Catrina, she had never been the same since she'd wed herself to Colin Blair. Not that Connie believed for one minute that it was all Colin's fault. He was a good hardworking man, rather dull and unexciting, but at least he was faithful. Strange how a vibrant girl like Catrina had allowed herself to get mixed up with Colin to the point of having to marry him to give her child a name.

Connie thought about little Euan. He reminded her of someone – only at the moment she couldn't think who. He certainly didn't resemble Colin in the least, and Connie wrinkled her brow as she tried to think just who it was that her nephew looked like . . .

Chapter Seventeen

Connie's musings were rudely interrupted by the arrival of nine-year-old Bram MacIntosh on to the scene. Along with him he brought a large hairy hound called Busker, named so because he always sang for his supper in a most unnerving fashion at precisely six every evening, never stopping till his doggie bowl was set before him in exactly the same spot under the kitchen table where he could keep a watchful eye open for the two thieving cats and the other large hairy hungry dog.

The boisterous activities of the Manse animals were the bane of Connie's life. Wherever they went they left trails of wet pawprints and reams of discarded hairs all over her clean floors and it was even worse when a very large angora rabbit, which went by the name of Humphrey, was smuggled in from his hutch on cold winter nights to sleep in Bram's bed and leave little round black calling cards under the furniture.

But at least Bram had the sense to confine the rabbit to his bedroom when he brought it indoors. If seven-year-old Shaun or eight-year-old Maureen performed the same deed it often led to disaster, as on the night Humphrey got into the minister's study and ate his Sunday sermon before anyone had a chance to save even the smallest portion.

On another occasion Humphrey had made merry with the contents of Kerry's underwear drawer and had dragged a pair of pink silk bloomers into the kitchen for all to see and snigger at.

Worst of all was when he raided the personal and private belongings of nanny number three and had devoured one cherished family photograph, two love letters, and a half of one she hadn't even read yet. Everyone had been in tears that day, most of all Nanny herself who had resisted all attempts of consolation, including a small rise in pay, and had promptly given in her notice.

There had been no more nannies since then and Humphrey had been conspicuous by his absence, but still there were the dogs and the cats to contend with and Connie, smarting over the contents of John's note, was not at all pleased to see Busker coming into the hall with Bram, especially when his paws went in all directions on the polished lino and left a series of dirty skidmarks everywhere. However she had no chance to voice any sort of protest as Bram, gazing at her out of large expressive dark eyes, asked her if she was meeting John that night.

'No, Bram, I'm not. He sent me a note to say he isn't feeling very well so I'll just have to spend the evening alone with Granny Margaret.'

The eldest son of the Manse had been saying outrageous things from the day he could talk and doing outrageous things since the day he could walk. No one knew what he was going to get up to next and Connie, wondering what was on his mind, looked at him askance.

Bram considered her words for a few silent moments before taking her hand in his rather grubby one and saying with the utmost sincerity, 'If you aren't married by the time I'm grown up I'm going to marry you myself and kiss you all night when we're in bed together. I do it with the girls at school. They love it and always want more but I don't like them the way I like you, Connie. They haven't grown bosoms yet and aren't nearly as cuddly as you are and even though you'll be quite old when I'm about twenty I know you'll still be soft and warm to touch.'

Connie stared at him, then quite suddenly she began to laugh, so merrily that Bram laughed too and Busker let out a few little whines and whimpers as if to show that he knew exactly what was going on.

'Oh, Bram.' Connie wiped her eyes with the hem of her skirt and placed her hand on the boy's curly head. 'You're a little devil, that you are, but I haven't felt so good in ages and I'm fair honoured by your bid for my affections. If I'm still single when you're twenty and you still want me to be your wife I'd be only too glad to accept, though, I warn you, I might be needing a couple o' sticks by then to hold me up.'

Bram nodded solemnly and was about to depart when he thought of something else. 'Say you won't tell Father I said all that. He doesn't know about the girls at school and with him being the minister of the parish he maybe wouldn't understand if he heard I had proposed to you.'

'Cross my heart, I won't tell, it's our secret and will never go any further than you and me and I'm sure Busker won't say anything either.'

The boy and the dog scampered off just as the study door opened and Bette came out with the minister. Connie couldn't help noticing how lingeringly Bette held on to his hand and the way in which she tried to make her voice sound husky and low as she said her goodbyes to him.

Not that the Reverend Thomas MacIntosh was taking her on in the slightest. He was looking positively anxious to retreat back into his den and this he did a few moments later when he at last managed to free himself successfully from his visitor and was master of himself once more.

'Ach, but is he no' a fine man, just?' Bette gazed fondly at the closed door. 'When I awoke this morning I was feeling strained and worried and unsure about everything. Now I feel as if a great weight has been lifted from my shoulders and I have my minister to thank for that.'

Connie took a deep breath. 'I know how concerned you've been about Maudie's future ever since she came to bide with you at Keeper's Row – and it just struck me that you might have come here today to ask the minister if he could give her a job.'

'A job?' Bette looked puzzled. 'Oh, ay, there's that as well, but it isn't so important now and will keep for a whilie. She's a good kind lass is our Maudie and for the moment I'm pleased to have her at home wi' me. She wasn't cut out to hurry or worry herself and will no doubt get a job when she's ready – and Mungo will just have to put that in his pipe and smoke it!' she ended on a note of defiance.

Connie released her breath in a whoosh. 'I always thought you were a wise woman, Bette MacGill, and now I know I was right. Maudie is very lucky to have such an understanding aunt and I'm sure she won't let you down in the long run.'

She was wriggling herself into her coat as she was speaking and when she had fixed her buttons she linked her arm companionably into Bette's. 'I must get home before Granny puts tea on for three. If not she'll chop my head off. John sent a note to say he can't manage tonight so to save time I'm taking the short cut through Sweetheart Lane. I'll get you down as far as the Inn and we can keep one another company on the way.'

Privately Bette thought it was John who deserved to get his head chopped off and she was about to convey this to Connie when Kerry reappeared to say laughingly to Connie, 'I heard you being waylaid by Bram coming in from school just now. I hope the young rascal wasn't saying anything he shouldn't. He's getting more precocious by the minute and takes a positive delight in shocking people. The Murchison sisters have never approved of me but seem to be glowering at me more than ever of late and I wondered if it had anything to do with Bram. I know they don't like having him in their Sunday School class because he knows more about the Bible than they do and often puts them in their place when they get it wrong.'

She seemed to look pointedly at Bette as she spoke and that lady squirmed as she remembered Maudie's remarks to the Knicker Elastic Dears about Kerry's carefree bicycle rides. But Connie jumped into the breach, speakingly glowingly about Bram, telling Kerry that she had nothing to worry her on that score as he 'couldn't help being clever and would no doubt put his mind to better uses as he grew older.'

'Surely to goodness, you might be right at that, Connie.'

Kerry spoke absently, her lively eyes still on Bette who, muttering something about getting Mungo's tea, wrenched open the door and made good her escape, Connie following on her heels a few moments later.

Sweetheart Lane, was, as its name implied, a popular rendezvous for lovers, situated as it was behind Balivoe's main street, well away from curious eyes. It was a quiet spot, dark too in the nights of winter, rather eerie when the shadows of night fell over it and distorted everyday objects into ghostly shapes.

So it looked to Connie as she stood at the entrance with Bette, hesitating a little as she peered into the gathering darkness. 'I don't know if I should now,' she said rather fearfully. 'It gets blacker the further in it goes – like a cave – and I can't help thinking about the ghost that's said to walk there, the young lad who hung himself from a tree because his sweetheart never came to him after he had waited nights on end. Donald of Balivoe tells the story at the ceilidhs and it's so sad I just howl my eyes out every time I hear it.'

'Hmph,' snorted the unromantic Bette. 'A likely tale if ever I heard one. Every lover's lane has a lad or a lass who ended up killing themselves for a lost love. Hanging yourself from a tree is as good a way as any if you want to do yourself in, but I have gone down that lane countless times and have never yet seen a ghost swinging from a tree.'

'That's only because you don't have the power or the sensitivity to draw the spirits,' Connie said nervously. 'I have had both from an early age. I've heard things, I've seen things; Cora and Catrina were scared of the stories I told them when we were all girls growing up together.'

Bette shifted her feet impatiently. 'Oh, all right, I'll see you halfway along, though I promised Maudie I would meet her outside the inn round about four thirty. She was picking up some stuff for Janet at Kathy MacColl's house and won't want to come all the way back by herself in the dark.'

Connie breathed a sigh of relief and was very glad of Bette's comforting bulk beside her as they plunged into the depths of Sweetheart Lane where menace seemed to lurk in every corner and the river could be heard swishing and gurgling its way along the boulder-strewn banks below.

'It was near the river,' Connie suddenly hissed in a stage whisper.

'What was near the river?' Bette enquired in a matter-of-fact voice.

'The tree, where the lad was found, strung up like a Christmas turkey.'

'Christmas turkeys hang by their feet, at least the ones in Jake Ferguson's windows do. The Henderson Hens must make a lot of money round about this time o' year,' she went on thoughtfully, 'selling turkeys and ducks and chickens. Effie Maxwell too, and she has the bonus of suckling pigs. I have often thought of starting up pigs and turkeys myself but Mungo won't hear o' it because he says they cause too much work and smell terrible – at least the pigs do. I myself like pigs, there's something very self-contained in the way they conduct themselves and don't worry their heads about anybody. The only way Mungo likes them is fried on his plate at breakfast or as trotters for his dinner. Other than that he has no interest in keeping them which is a pity because to me they are a lot less trouble than cows . . .'

'Shh! Shh!' Connie whispered urgently, clutching frantically at Bette's arm. 'Up ahead, people – at least, I think they're people.'

Bette peered into the gloaming. Sure enough, two shadowy figures were flitting along in front, some distance away, but Bette's eyes had grown accustomed to the dimmess and she was soon able to distinguish the shapes of Ryan Du and Mollie Gillespie, walking very close together, heads touching, hand in hand, lost in one another, never a glance behind to see if anyone was coming.

Bette conveyed all of these impressions to Connie who shook her head and almost failed to keep her voice down as she returned hoarsely, 'I knew it! I just knew they were up to their old tricks. Mollie looked very strange thon time she came to the doctor's surgery and Effie mentioned something about young mothers and their pregnancies. I thought the besom was getting fatter this whilie back and now I know why. I don't believe for one minute it's Donnie Hic's bairn either. Oh, it's sinful! Sinful! Oh, Cora. My poor sister . . .'

'Keep your voice down.' It was Bette's turn to be cautious. 'We're going to follow that two and see what they get up to. Don't talk, just walk – and do it quietly.'

Mollie and Ryan Du were going a little faster now, gradually melting into the night, and masterfully Bette seized hold of Connie's arm and began hurrying her along.

'They're going into Granny's hayshed,' Connie said after a while, her voice hushed in disbelief. 'Of all the cheek, right there in front o' her nose. I know she doesn't use it anymore but Donald of Balivoe does and I don't think he would like the idea o' that two cavorting in his hayloft.' She stopped dead in her tracks, her hand going to her mouth as a thought struck her. 'Ramsay Sutherland. That's who it is! All along I knew it but couldn't see for looking. Poor Catrina, poor Cora, I don't think I'll look at any man again after this . . .'

'Have you taken leave o' your senses?' Bette's voice was heavy with sarcasm. 'It's Ryan Du we're dealing with here, not Ramsay Sutherland – though I wouldn't put anything past him the way he ogles every skirt that passes him by.' She became brisk. 'I want you to stay here, Connie, while I go and get Maudie. That pair in there are about to get the fright o' their lives so just you keep guard and I'll be back in two shakes o' a lamb's tail.'

She went off before Connie had a chance to voice any objection and very soon her sturdy figure was swallowed up in the shadows.

Connie gulped, her mouth went dry. An owl hooted from a nearby branch and her heart galloped into her throat. The only comfort in those fraught moments was the faint light coming from a back window of Struan Cottage, and Connie spent the next few minutes wondering just how long it would take her to cover the distance that separated her from the haven of home – should the need arise.

Chapter Eighteen

Maudie was ensconced on a bench outside the Balivoe Village Inn, humming a catchy little tune as she swung her legs and waited for her aunt. Although she had managed to hitch a lift to Vaul it had been a fair walk back but it had been worth it. As well as all her other attributes Kangaroo Kathy was an excellent cook and those fluffy hot crumpets of hers had been scrumptious – a mite on the sweet side perhaps, especially for someone who was supposed to dislike sugar, but nobody was perfect and they had soon disappeared anyway.

Maudie shivered a little. A cold breeze was skittering up from Camus nan Rua and she pulled her scarf closer round her neck as she gazed at the dusky horizon and thought how different it all was from her home in Partick where the noise and bustle could go on well into the night.

Here there was silence and peace and time to think about the wonders of the universe and Maudie was growing to like that more and more as time went by. She had come across Johnny Lonely once or twice in her travels and he had spoken to her about such matters in a very knowledgeable way. Now she was able to look at the stars in a new light, as it were, and think what the world must have been like in the making.

Maudie drew in her breath. The upheaval must have been terrible, worse than anything she could imagine. Johnny had told her about the earth moving and shifting and how Cragdu had once been an active volcano spewing out fire and ash and lava.

Then had come the ice ages, and the great glaciers carving out valleys and rivers and leaving strange boulders in places where they didn't belong . . .

At that point in her very enjoyable musings her aunt arrived, puffing a bit from her exertions as she grasped the girl's arm and yanked her to her feet.

'Quick, Maudie,' she imparted urgently. 'I want you to come wi' me at once. I need you to sit on someone.'

'Sit on someone!'

'Ay, that's what I said, you're just the lass for the job. Do exactly as I say and don't ask questions. It's for a good cause and you'll find out soon enough what it's all about.'

'But, Auntie,' Maudie objected. 'I've just come all the way from Vaul, I'm tired and I'm hungry, and I'm having a wee rest before the walk home.'

'Rest nothing,' Bette returned hard-heartedly. 'What you are about to do is a stand for womankind everywhere. You'll know what I mean when you have had a chance to work it out for yourself.'

Wasting no more breath on talk she urged Maudie along at a pace which did not suit that young lady in the least. But she sensed the urgency of their mission and held her tongue as her aunt propelled her along Sweetheart Lane where the owls were out in full force and a ghostly moon was casting phantoms into the deep dank recesses of the woods. To Maudie they seemed to be moving, gliding out from secret hiding places, reaching out to grab at her and carry her off in their evil clutches to some dread dark den over yonder in the night-black hills . . .

She gave a little shriek as a twig pulled at her hair and the next minute the wood witches were on her, plucking at her clothing, dragging her down . . .

But it was only Connie, sobbing in relief at seeing them, seizing hold of them and saying how glad she was that they had come at last.

'They're still in there.' She nodded towards the hayshed. 'But maybe you'd better not go in,' she added rather fearfully. 'Just in case . . .'

Bette wasn't listening. She was explaining hastily to Maudie the role she had to play in the affair, ending with,' Right, now, my girl, just remember you're of MacGill stock and don't let the side down.'

'No, Auntie.' Maudie tried to sound brave and strong but couldn't keep a tremor out of her voice as she stood by her aunt's side and waited for her orders.

Ryan Du never knew what hit him. One minute he was murmuring sweet nothings into Mollie's ear, the next he was face down in the hay, a terrific weight on his back, the breath squeezing from his lungs, his hands going up to his head in an attempt to ward off the blows raining down on him.

Ryan Du was a man of great height and tremendous physique, one who had always been able to defend himself. His fists were like iron, his strength legendary; no one took him on unless they were stupid or drunk or both. Big Bette was none of these but she had her own methods for dealing with troublemakers and one of these was the element of surprise.

Ryan Du wasn't the first man she had flattened nor would he be the last. Quite a few Kinvara stalwarts retained painful memories of Bette felling them outside the inn when they'd had one over the top and were making nuisances of themselves. Stottin' Geordie, the village policeman, just a little bit scared of Bette himself, nevertheless maintained that she was the best advocate for law and order this side of Scotland and deserved a pat on the back for every one of her heroic interventions.

'She's only a woman,' the men would scoff behind her back.

'Ay, and a dirty fighter at that. She never goes by the rules and would stab you in the back as soon as look at you and expect a medal for doing it.'

'But she doesn't fight, that's the point, she just squashes people with yon great arse o' hers and expects them to live afterwards. No wonder Mungo's the grumpy bugger he is, she probably sits on him every night and makes him do things he doesn't want to do just by sheer force.'

'Ay, that's likely the reason they go through beds like syrup-o'-figs through a constipated bowel. The springs can't stand the stress and strain o' Bette bouncing about on them like a rubber ball.'

But despite their grumbles, and with only a few exceptions, the menfolk of Kinvara had a healthy respect for Bette and always tried to keep on her right side if they possibly could.

Ryan Du, however, was one of the exceptions. No one could take advantage of him and get away with it, at least that was what he had thought, until Bette had caught him well and truly with his trousers down. God Almighty! There must be twenty tons on top of his shoulders, pinning him to the floor, making it impossible for him to move. But no, there was more to come, another twenty tons on his spine, forcing him to yell out in pain.

Maudie, having mastered her initial shock on seeing Ryan Du's well-rounded bottom staring at her in the darkness, had joined forces with Bette, and was trying not to think of Ryan Du's state of nakedness as she straddled him and prayed that Auntie knew what she was doing when she had tackled a man of such considerable size.

And all the while Mollie wept in anguish and Connie said silent prayers to the Almighty and asked Him to forgive all of them for the mortal sins of the flesh.

'Say you'll never see Mollie again.' Bette stopped pummelling long enough to grind out the words.

'None o' your bloody business,' Ryan Du gasped in a desperate attempt to show that he was still master of himself.

Bette shook him. 'Say it, or I'll get Connie to sit on you too. Don't forget whose sister she is and who would have every right to expose you for what you are – and by that I don't just mean the cheeks o' your bum. There could be trouble ahead for you, my lad, if you don't start to behave yourself. Just think, Donnie Hic wi' his shotgun, Cora with her two vengeful sisters, Granny Margaret on the warpath, quite a formidable quintet if you stop to think about it.'

'All right, I give in, just get your fat arses off me and let me go in peace.'

'Politely, my lad, politely.' Bette sounded dangerously calm.

'What do you want me to do? Eat dung and say I like it?'

'If need be.'

'Please then. Please let me go. I won't see Mollie again, that's why we came here tonight – to say goodbye.'

'Ay, wi' your breeks at your ankles and your hands inside her frock. All very romantic and sad and if you say any more you'll have me crying in a minute.'

'You're a hard woman, Bette MacGill.' Ryan Du was on his feet, dusting himself down, laying his hand briefly on Mollie's shoulder before he was off into the night, cursing as he went, muttering under his breath, stripped of his dignity and only too glad to shake the dust of the hayshed off his heels.

Mollie, her tears now turned to anger, swung round on the womenfolk and said fiercely, 'You didn't have to treat him like that. We were seeing one another for the last time and you had no right to interfere.'

'Oh, ay, we did,' Connie returned with equal asperity. 'You and he needed to be taught a lesson, both for Cora's sake and for my own satisfaction – and if I see you near Ryan Du again you might just get a dose of what he got – so you'd better be careful.'

Bette nodded her agreement and rubbed her hands together. 'A good job well done and no one else need be any the wiser about it. Come on now, Maudie, you and me will get along before Mungo sends the police out looking for us – and I for one could be doing with a cuppy.'

The women dispersed. Only Mollie remained where she was, her heart full to bursting, eyes big and dry as she gazed unseeingly ahead. For a very long time she remained motionless, her cold fingers pressed against her lips, lonely, sad, afraid, as she wondered what the future held for her. Then she put her face in her hands and wept for the loss of the romantic love she had known with Ryan Du, a love she had hungered for and which would be hers no more . . .

Something outside of her own grief and misery recalled her to reality. She couldn't see anyone but she could sense a presence, could feel the stealth and watchfulness in the living darkness around her. Her eyes raked the shadows, she knew that some other creature was creeping about close by, but she could see nothing.

Her scalp prickled suddenly. A dark shape had detached itself from the other dark shapes around her and she knew that Johnny Lonely had been waiting and watching and that he had seen everything that had taken place that night.

'Justice had to be done, Maudie,' Bette told her niece as thankfully they made their way out of the lane and on to the road. 'Ryan Du and Mollie have aye been soft on one another but they're each wed to other people and have to learn to behave themselves.'

'Yes, Auntie, I understand about that. I myself wouldn't like it if I was married to a man who did the same as Ryan Du even though it happens all the time with royalty and the gentry.'

'Ay, Maudie, I know about that, but different rules apply to different people and that two come into neither category.'

Her hand tightened on the girl's arm and she went on urgently, 'Forget the gentry and forget royalty, it's village folks we're concerned with here and I don't want you to breathe a word about this night to anyone. Be like the three wise monkeys and I'll buy you something nice for Christmas.'

'But, Auntie, I was just wondering how Ryan Du is going to explain to Cora about his ripped shirt and his scratches and all these other marks he has on him.'

'Knowing him he'll think o' something. He's always scrapping with the lads and though he's got more balls than brains he was aye quick-witted when it came to telling lies.'

'But, Auntie . . .'

'No more buts.' Bette was growing exasperated. 'Just do as I say and let's get home for our tea.'

'Yes, Auntie, but I was just thinking about Donnie Hic and

wondering how Mollie is going to explain to *him* how her frock got torn and . . .'

'Maudie,' Bette growled ominously. 'How would you like me to brain you and send you to bed without any food and *your* clothes in tatters.'

In the darkness Maudie gave an appreciative grin and linking her arm into Bette's she said not another word for the rest of the way home.

'You're late, lassie?' was Granny Margaret's greeting to her granddaughter the minute she stepped through the door. 'The tea's been ready for ages and you know how much I hate food that is overdone.'

'Oh, Granny, I'm sorry, but I couldn't help it.' Connie, pale and nervous after her experiences of the evening, was in no mood to deal with a crotchety grandmother as well and she sounded edgy as she spoke. 'I got kept late at the Manse and took a short cut through the lane and was kept back by Bette and her niece who were taking a short cut as well.'

'Ach, you're a poor liar, Connie.' The old lady sounded smug. 'What would Bette and her niece be doing in the lane when they live in Keeper's Row, I'd like to know.'

'They must have been visiting at one o' the farms and came in through the lane at the field entrance.'

'Connie, you should realise by now that you canny teach your own granny to suck eggs. I know fine where you've been and why you've been kept so long. It was that hussy, Mollie Gillespie, and that womanising cheat, Ryan Du, up to their old tricks, wasn't it? I saw them for myself the other night when I was out at the bunker getting coal. There they were, sneaking about in the lane near the hayshed, and I've been racking my brains ever since wondering what I should do about it.'

'You *saw* them?' Connie stared. 'But you never said anything, not a word to me or Catrina when she was in seeing us the other day.'

'Well, I thought it wouldn't do to spread a thing like that

about, and Catrina was aye a lassie to say more than she should about family affairs. Before you could blink she would have spread the word to Cora and that would have been a pity as what she doesn't know can't harm her.' Granny Margaret shook her head sadly. 'Ay, me, the lassie would go mad altogether if she found out what that man o' hers has been up to. She thinks the sun shines out his backside and shuts her eyes to his philandering ways, but this would be the last straw. That last time Mollie and Ryan Du were carrying on he nearly lost his job at Vale o' Dreip and he was lucky he didn't lose his head as well when Donnie Hic when storming down to the Balivoe Inn and threatened to blow it off with his shotgun.' She looked at her granddaughter. 'Well, tell me what happened, I've been on tenterhooks ever since I took a wee walk down the garden earlier and saw you going into the shed with Maudie and Bette.'

Connie plunged into an account of the night's happenings and Granny Margaret's eyes began to sparkle halfway through the telling of the tale. Describing herself as 'seventy and a bit' she was a person of small stature with shrewd eyes and genteel appearance; those who took her at face value saw just another elderly lady with nothing more important in her head than the day-to-day challenges of keeping body and soul together.

But there was more to Granny than met the eye. She was in fact as tough as leather and could smoke, drink, and gamble with the best of them. When her grandchildren were occupied elsewhere she liked nothing better than to nip next door to Jake Ferguson's cottage to play cards and partake of a dram or two while enjoying a cigar or perhaps a puff or two of Jake's pipe.

Widowed early, with a young and wilful daughter to raise, she had soon learned to fend for herself and had become even tougher when that same daughter had gone off to Glasgow to meet and marry a man as selfish and as pleasure-seeking as herself. The pair had gone from bad to worse, eventually 'dying drunk under the wheels of a coal cart', leaving behind three infant daughters to be cared for.

Granny Margaret had risen nobly to the occasion and had provided the girls with a home and even her own good name, never giving them any inkling about their parents' sordid manner of living or the nature of their demise, preferring instead to weave a more refined tale around them for the sake of the children and embroidering it just a little bit as they became older and began asking more questions.

The Simpson sisters had grown up to love and respect the woman who had reared them and they had never stopped showing it. They had filled her life with their youth and high spirits but now only Connie remained in the nest, torn between her allegiance to her granny and her natural instincts to make her own way in the world.

Tonight, however, all that was far from Connie's mind and she was only too glad to get home and offload some of her anxieties on to Granny Margaret, whose approval of the punishment meted out to Ryan Du and Mollie was unashamedly enthusiastic.

'Ay, she's a good soul is Bette.' Granny's voice was warm with approval. 'She has aye been a body to stand up for those who canny do it for themselves and next time I see her I'll tell her so to her face.'

'As long as you don't drink one another under the table in the process,' Connie laughed, lighthearted with relief now that the night and all its strangeness was behind her. 'Bette hasn't lived down that last little episode you and she shared. I always knew you were fond o' a droppy but not until that day did I realise what a rogue you really were – and Bette got the blame for it.'

'Ay, well, you'd better get your coat off and get your tea.' Hastily the old lady changed the subject. 'The John lad will be wondering what's keeping you.'

'John?' Connie's brow furrowed in puzzlement.

'Ay, who else? You said he was coming for his tea and he's here in the parlour waiting.'

'Waiting? For me?'

'No, for his salvation,' Granny Margaret said drily, but she was smiling a little as she put her hand on Connie's shoulder and pushed her out of the kitchen.

Chapter Nineteen

Connie took a deep breath; her heart was beating faster as she crossed the lobby to 'Granny's best room' where an overstuffed sofa and matching chairs reposed in all their plump splendour and glass-fronted cabinets held leather-bound books and good china and numerous knick-knacks that had been collected over the years.

In pride of place stood an ancient piano, damp-smelling and fusty but treasured by Granny who retained happy memories of the stirring melodies her husband's agile fingers had extracted from it as he sat before it on the tapestry-covered stool, his hair gleaming in the lamplight, smiling at her as she darned and sewed and listened.

When the girls were little they had found the piano to be a fascinating and challenging pastime but nowadays nobody played it; the only attention it ever received being an occasional tuning, a weekly polishing, and a fond pat from Granny's hand as she paused beside it for a while and thought about the old days when her husband had been alive.

Normally the parlour was the coldest room in the house but tonight a cheery fire leapt in the grate and Connie quickly realised that her Granny Margaret, for some unknown reason, had made a special effort to ensure that the place was warm and welcoming.

'Connie.' John came forward to take her hands as soon as she appeared. 'I know I sent the note but I had to come. Mother wanted me to stay in bed but in the end she gave in and I came straight here as I knew you would already have left the Manse.'

At his words a glow warmed Connie's heart. She gazed at him. He was pale and drawn and his nose was red but for her he had risen out of his sickbed to keep their date after all.

'Connie, listen,' he said eagerly. 'I've got a much better job now with good wages. Before The MacKernon left for America I went to see him about a job that was in the offing and he promised he would give me first refusal when he came back. Well, he's home now, and he's taken me on as his private secretary with a bit of accountancy included in the deal.'

'Oh, John, that's wonderful,' Connie cried. 'I'm so pleased for you.'

'For us, Connie, I'm asking you to marry me now that I have some future prospects to offer you.'

'Where would we live?' Connie came back to earth with a bang as she voiced the question.

'The MacKernon also offered me a house to go with the job but it's quite small and I really don't see . . .'

'You'll bide here with me of course.' Granny Margaret entered the room at that crucial moment and glared defiantly at John.

'Oh, but I couldn't leave Mother all on her own.' Connie noticed the determined lift of John's chin as he went on, 'I've got a much better idea, why don't you come and live with us at Bougan Villa? I've talked it over with Mother and she thinks it's a great idea as she gets lonely there all day on her own.'

'In that bug-ridden hole?' Granny Margaret hooted rudely. 'With your mother? I'd rather live in a cave in the hills with the wildcats for company.'

'Mother isn't so bad when you get to know her. She's always spoken well of you and told me how splendidly your husband looked after the gardens at Bougan Villa when he was alive. She also told me how you used to bake cakes and scones for my father who swore there was no finer cook in all the land than Mrs Margaret Simpson of Struan Cottage.'

'Ay, ay, that's as may be but that was a long while ago,' Granny Margaret had noticeably pulled in her horns at John's conciliatory words. 'Bougan Villa was a fine big place in those days but it's nothing but a ruin now and I'm damned at my age if I'm going to change one leaky roof for another – even if it is a posh one with fancy wood round the eaves.'

A look of triumph flitted over John's handsome face. 'It won't be a ruin for much longer. Father didn't leave much in the way of hard cash but he collected antiques on his travels round the world and I've just had one or two pieces valued to my great satisfaction. Mother hung on to them, you see, sentimental and all that, but she's a sensible woman and wants nothing more than to see Bougan Villa restored to its former glory. When everything is settled we should be able to afford a housekeeper and a maid too so you'll be well looked after, Granny, and can have all the privacy you'll need in rooms of your own.'

'I'm not your granny.'

'You will be when Connie and I are married – that's if she'll have me, she hasn't said "yes" yet.'

Connie's green eyes were sparkling, her cheeks were pink as she murmured, 'Ay, John, I will that, now that everything's been agreed about Granny and your mother I'd very much like to be your wife.'

'Wait a minute!' Granny Margaret broke in. 'I haven't said yes, yet!'

'Oh, Granny, please don't be awkward,' Connie said pleadingly. 'You know you want this as much as I do – for both our sakes.'

'Can I take my piano?'

'Of course you can,' John said with a laugh. 'I'd be annoyed if you didn't – I've been admiring it ever since I came in. It's a fine instrument but it lacks usage and Mother and I between us will see it gets plenty of that. We used to enjoy playing ours till it got ruined by rainwater and Mother is always saying how she misses it.'

On impulse he sat down on the tapestry stool and flexed

his fingers before placing his feet on the pedals of the piano. It wheezed and grunted in an elderly fashion but John was an excellent musician and under his expert touch it soon sprang into exuberant life.

Granny Margaret's eyes grew misty. He was playing a tune that she knew well, one that her husband had played in long-ago days when they had both been young together with all the world at their feet. The music sheet had been propped on the stand for years and was now yellow and brittle with age, but John was still able to read it, and it seemed to her that it was her Alec who was sitting there, playing, playing, filling her heart and the house with his melodies . . .

'This calls for a celebration dram.' Granny Margaret's voice was shaky as she spoke. 'We'll have it in the kitchen, it's cosier in there.' Abruptly she went out of the room and fumbled for her hanky in the lobby.

Connie went over to John and bending down she kissed him full on the lips.

'You'll get my germs,' he told her softly.

'I don't care, I love you, Granny loves you, I've never seen her looking so happy in a long time.'

'Even though she was grumbling.'

'Because she was grumbling. She only does that with people she feels at ease with and your playing did the rest.'

'Come on.' He stood up and held out his hand. 'Let's go and get our tea before it gets cold and Granny changes her mind about me. Tonight has been quite an ordeal in one way or another and I don't feel able to face any more upsets.'

Later that night, after John had gone home and it was just Granny Margaret and Connie by the fire, the latter said tentatively, 'Granny, I can't get over this strange feeling that you knew John was going to propose to me tonight. Why else would you have lit the fire in the parlour and made your special steak and kidney pie?'

The old lady's face took on a look of studied innocence. 'Put it down to experience, lassie, I saw how fidgety he was getting this whilie back and knew he was working himself up to popping the question so I decided I'd better prepare myself for it. That's all.'

'Granny, that is *not* all. I know fine you've been up to something. I've lived with you all my life and know you better than you know yourself. You knew John had been to see The MacKernon, didn't you? And you also knew that he got the job he was after.'

'You could say a little bird told me.'

'You mean that nosy old cronie o' yours who works in the castle kitchens? Her with the shifty eyes and the sharp nose and the way she has o' poking it into other folk's business.'

'Now, now, Connie, there's no call to speak ill o' your elders. Polly and me have aye been good pals and when she comes here to visit it's only natural she should give me little snippets o' information concerning Cragdu. She would be a strange body indeed if she went about with her eyes closed and it wasn't her fault if she happened to be passing when The MacKernon was shaking John by the hand and congratulating him on getting the job he was after.'

'Are you really glad for John and me, Granny? I know you didn't want me to get married for fear you would be left on your own.'

'I aye wanted you to be happy, Connie, just as I did all my lassies, but I have to admit I was feart of an old age alone. I don't have to worry about that now however and Prudence isn't really snobbish, just lonely since her man died on her and I know only too well how that feels.'

'But you said . . .'

'I know what I said but I didn't mean it, I just had to make it seem that way. I've got my pride, lassie, just like anybody else, but now that the ice is broken I'm looking forward to living at Bougan Villa and getting to know Prudence again – and her roof is better than mine – even though I say it myself.'

She sighed and looked around the homely kitchen. 'It will be strange leaving Struan Cottage and all the memories o' Alec but he would be the last one to keep me back and a body is never too old to make a new life for themselves.' Getting to her feet she cocked a beady eye at her granddaughter. 'There's plenty o' whisky left in the bottle. How about a wee nightcap before bed? It's been a long day for an auld wifie like me and I could be doing with something to pep me up.'

'Oh, all right.' Connie let out a giggle. 'What better way to end what has been a perfect evening – except for the first part of course,' she hastily added.

'Ay, well, that too turned out for the best and was in its way just as successful as the rest. We'll drink to that too – but I'll keep a wee drop for Polly when she visits me tomorrow. She'll be that pleased to hear about you and John she'll be longing to tell everybody – but not until you've spread the word yourself, my lassie, oh, no, not until then.'

With alacrity she sprachled away to fetch the whisky bottle and Connie smiled as she lay back in her chair and thought about John. She felt so good and happy about him now and tried to visualise how she would feel living with him at Bougan Villa.

Not that it would be all plain sailing. Three women in a kitchen didn't bear thinking about but perhaps by the time she and John were married there would be someone in to do the cooking. That wouldn't be a problem for his mother; she had been used to that sort of thing for most of her existence. Granny Margaret, on the other hand, liked her independence and had always been fond of cooking . . .

Still, it would all sort itself out in the end, the main thing was that she and John were soon to be man and wife. And to think she had imagined he didn't love her when he had sent that note to the Manse! It just went to show that life was full of surprises and that all things were possible if you waited long enough for them to happen.

A thought struck her and she laughed to herself with glee. John's proposal of marriage hadn't been her only one that day. Bram MacIntosh might only be nine years old but already he was a charmer where women were concerned and knew exactly what to say to damsels in distress. Tomorrow she would take Bram to Wee Fay's and let him have the pick of the sweets in the shop. Tonight she was perfectly content to just sit by the fire and do nothing – except think of all the pleasant things the future held for her as the wife of John Taylor-Young with a hyphen.

That wasn't the end of the surprises. Not long afterwards Hannah too got one, though in her case it was more of a shock than anything else. With only three weeks to go before Christmas the children were preparing for the event and had learned to make paper chains at school. Piles of them lay on the table at No. 6 of the Row, fascinating little Bonny Barr whom Joss had brought along to share in the fun and to whom he was now demonstrating the art.

Vaila had abandoned the decorations in favour of writing a letter to her father and she was bent over the table, her tongue sticking from the corner of her mouth in concentration, Andy beside her, reminding her of the little happenings that had taken place since Rob's departure for lighthouse duty.

It was very peaceful in the room. Hannah was seated comfortably at a glowing fire, reading a book, the feel of Breck's head on her feet giving her a sense of wellbeing. It wasn't often she felt as relaxed as this but there was a feeling in the air, of Christmas, of Rob coming home. Thoughts of him had been very vivid in her mind lately and already she could feel his strong arms around her, holding her close, relieving her of some of the burdens that had weighed her down so heavily . . .

'Cooee! Anybody in?'

Everybody jumped at the intrusion, especially Breck who woke abruptly from his dreamings to sit erect on the rug, ears unfurled as he cocked them towards the door, the feathery white tip of his tail beginning to twitch in anticipation.

'Don't worry, it's only me, not disturbing anyone, I hope.'

'Mother! You never said you were coming!' Hannah's mind went into a spin as she gaped at the dark-haired, striking-looking woman who was her mother. She thought of the unaired guest bedroom, the contents of the larder, wondering if there would be enough in it to feed an extra mouth for dinner and if not would she be able to get to the shops before they shut.

Her throat went tight with panic. 'Mother,' she managed to get out again. 'You should have told me, you should have written . . .'

She got no chance to say another word. The room erupted into noise, movement, confusion, the opposite to what it had been only moments before. Breck simply hurled himself at Harriet Houston from Ayr and she laughed in delight because with his spotty nose and paws he reminded her of dear old Ben Pepper, the cross-collie that had been hers as a girl growing up at Dunruddy Farm in Ayrshire.

'Don't eat me!' she laughed as she tried to extricate herself from the dog's loving embraces. Glancing up she saw her grandson coming towards her, almost tripping himself up in his hurry to get to her. 'Andy!' she cried. 'Just look at you! Walking like a wee soldier! And Vaila! How you've both grown. I feel as if it's years since I last saw you.'

The children surrounded her, giving Hannah a chance to pull herself together. How could her mother do this to her? Just arrive. Without a word. Not as much as a by-your-leave.

'Fear not!' Harriet boomed, as if reading her daughter's mind. 'I'm not going to land myself on you . . .' She broke off to eye her daughter approvingly. 'Hannah, you've filled out, I've never seen you looking so well. Kinvara is certainly agreeing with you.'

Caught off her guard, Hannah reddened and began talking too fast. 'Ay, but half the time I'm not agreeing with it, there's always someone not talking to someone else and privacy is a word they've never heard of here.' She paused, a softness flitted over her features. 'You're right, Mother, it is agreeing with me. I'm getting on better with everyone and have made quite a few friends, especially Janet next door.'

'Ay, Janet, a bonny kind lass.' Harriet looked at Joss and then enquiringly at Bonny.

'She's my new wee sister,' he said proudly.

'Your sister?'

'Janet is fostering her till her own mother can look after her again,' Hannah explained. 'Bonny loves it here and has settled in well.'

'I wish you had told me all this in a letter,' Harriet reproached her daughter. 'I've been waiting to hear from you but never the scrape of a pen.'

'I could say the same about you, Mother.' Hannah was on the defensive at once. 'You should have written to say you were coming. How am I going to feed you? Where am I going to put you? The blankets on your bed will be damp and fusty, the . . .'

'She can have my bed,' Andy offered eagerly.

'And mine,' Vaila added quickly.

Harriet ruffled the two little heads affectionately. 'I wouldn't dream of putting anyone out of their beds. No, no, I have other arrangements. I've decided to make Kinvara my home, Hannah, and just stopped by to say hallo to you and the bairns before heading for Butterburn Croft.'

'Butterburn Croft?' Hannah braced herself. Her mother's unpredictable habits had once been a sharp thorn in Hannah's side. With the passing of time she seemed to have quietened down on that score but now Hannah wondered – was she up to her old tricks again?

Harriet's next words confirmed her daughter's worst fears. 'Ay, Hannah, Butterburn Croft. It wasn't a spur o' the moment decision as you might be thinking. When your father died I had a lot o' business to tie up – as you yourself very well know. It took some time to sort everything out but at last all was settled and I had time on my hands to think about my future. There was nothing much left for me in Ayr after the hotel was sold and that was when I decided to come and live here in Kinvara, to be beside my daughter and my grandchildren but most of all to make a new niche for myself.'

'A new niche?' Hannah repeated the words slowly and carefully.

'Ay, you heard.' Harriet picked one of Breck's hairs from her mouth and looked at it thoughtfully. 'The hotel life was never really for me. I was brought up with animals and that is what I am going back to – at Butterburn Croft with Charlie Campbell – far enough away from you not to be a nuisance but near enough if you ever need me to hand.'

Harriet really quite enjoyed dropping that bombshell. For days she had wondered how she was going to deliver it to the best effect and now she knew she had done it very well indeed because her daughter's face was a picture as she digested her mother's news in fraught and utter silence.

Chapter Twenty

'But, Mother,' Hannah said at last, staring at the older woman as if she had taken leave of her senses. 'Charlie Campbell himself bides there – you can't stay under the same roof as a bachelor man like him.'

Harriet remained entirely unruffled. 'I can and I will. We have made an arrangement. Charlie is away a lot at the fishing and finds it difficult to look after his croft as well, so I will see to that side of it and also do a bit of housekeeping. In return I am to have rent-free accommodation with my own rooms and as much freedom as I want. It's much better than buying a place o' my own though I might think o' that later when I've had a chance to adjust to living here.'

'But, Mother! The whole place will talk about you behind your back. You'll be known as a fallen woman in no time at all.'

'Now, Hannah, there is no need to jump the gun. Of course there will be talk, there is always talk in a rural community like Kinvara. I'll be an incomer; whatever I do, whatever I say, will have the tongues wagging, so . . .' She shrugged and made a face. 'I might as well give them something to get their teeth into and will just have to grin and bear it till the dust settles.'

'That's hardly fair on me, Mother. It took me ages to get myself accepted and now it will start all over again, the pointing fingers, the nudges and the tight lips, the silences whenever I appear.'

'Och, don't fret, Hannah, you always did take yourself far too seriously. In a way I'll be doing you a favour. Their sympathies will be with you and all you had to suffer having me for a mother.'

Janet came in just then, putting an end to further argument between Harriet and her daughter. Bonny immediately toddled over to the newcomer and held up her arms to be lifted.

'You have a big heart, Janet,' Harriet observed as the young woman cuddled the child to her bosom and planted a kiss on one soft cheek.

'Ay, and it's bigger still since Bonny came into it. She's special and dear to us already and I can hardly wait for Jock to come home so that he can see her and hold her for himself.'

'A pity,' Harriet said with a shake of her head as soon as the trio had departed. 'That young woman is a natural born mother; she looks at Bonny but doesn't see her faults, only the beauty that shines out of her face and the little arms reaching out for comfort and love.'

Harriet looked at Andy. After a shaky start she had come to accept and feel a strong affection for her small grandson. He was different, there was no doubt about that; it was easy to be impatient with him and to want to shake the words out of him instead of waiting for that slow, tortuous speech to make some sort of sense.

Yet, how much more frustrating it must be for him, to know what he wanted to say but unable to do so because of an accident of birth. Those big bright eyes of his burned with the need to be understood and listened to. 'Andy.' On impulse she picked him up and tucked his dark head under her chin. He chuckled and cooried into her and she knew that the affection she held for him had somewhere along the way turned to love; she was more glad than ever that she had decided to make the move to Kinvara to be beside her family.

Word about Harriet's intentions to move in with Charlie Campbell spread round Kinvara like wildfire. The tongues didn't just wag, they positively sizzled with speculation and gossip and right in the forefront was Jessie MacDonald, consumed with indignation at the very idea of any woman other than herself making merry with a duster in this particular bachelor abode.

'Mind you,' she snorted self-righteously, 'I'm no' surprised at anything that goes on in that house. Charlie Campbell's aye been worth the watching. Oh, he's been careful all right, and there's no way o' telling who goes sneaking in and out o' his bed at night. Just because he's single he thinks he can do anything he wants with anybody and hell mend him if this latest venture turns sour on him. Harriet Houston from Ayr is a bossy domineering woman and 'tis small wonder her own daughter is the queer cratur' she is.'

'Och, Harriet's a decent enough body,' protested Effie, her long nose twitching with delight as she liked nothing better than a good going argument and would have said black was white just to stir up proceedings. 'She is a bittie overpowering, I have to agree, but she's learned no' to throw her weight around too much and is a lot quieter than she used to be. As for Hannah, she has improved since she's been here and it isn't fair to judge her on her mother's wee indiscretions. Charlie's a good sort too and I'm surprised to hear you talking about him in such a manner, Jessie.'

'He's a Campbell and he's tarred wi' a black brush.' Jessie's retaliation was immediate. 'And he has been ever since his murdering gang slaughtered me and my kinfolk while we slept innocently in our very own beds in yon dour dark glen miles from anywhere. We will never forgive him for that! Never!'

'Ach, Jessie!' Maisie Whiskers was moved to exclaim. 'You canny personally blame Charlie for things that happened long ago! He might have some peculiar wee ways about him but he's no' a bad man for all that.'

'He's a Campbell!' Jessie's claws were really starting to show. 'Once a Campbell always a Campbell and I wouldny trust him as far as I could throw him.'

'Oh, is that a fact?' Mattie snorted. 'Well, if you don't

mind me saying so, I aye had this funny wee notion that you were sweet on Charlie yourself. Could it be that you're a mite jealous o' Harriet from Ayr, getting what you yourself have been hankering for all these years o' knowing him?'

Jessie's nostrils flared. 'Jealous! Of a Campbell! Never, never, never! I wouldn't give tuppence supposing I wasn't to see him again! Fancy him wanting a housekeeper – the – the philanderer that he is. As if it was too much trouble for him to flick a duster over the house himself. Oh, I admit, I have myself, on the odd occasion, swallowed my pride and taken pity on him as a bachelor man but it was a waste o' energy. As soon as my back was turned the place was a boorach again. Harriet Houston will have her hands full wi' him – and serves her right too – the harlot that she is!' She sniffed, folded her hands across her stomach, lifted her chin and looked down her nose as if preparing herself for a confrontation with the said harlot.

Tottie Murchison tightened her lips and nodded her approval of all this. 'I agree with Jessie, the disgrace o' such a thing happening in Kinvara! What will the minister have to say about it, I'd like to know? Surely he will see that it isn't right and proper for a man and woman to be living under the same roof and her without a wedding ring on her finger.'

'Oh, but Harriet Houston has still got her old one.' Tillie lowered her brows and glanced round meaningfully at all the interested faces. 'Don't forget, she's been wed before, and maybe she's got it into her head that one ring gives her a lifelong passport to any man she fancies.' She cast her eyes heavenwards. 'As for the minister, you won't get any support from him, Tottie, that Irish-born wife o' his has changed him beyond all recognition. Whenever I try to speak to him about my bothers all he ever says is, "We have to move with the times, Miss Murchison, and keep open minds and hearts."'

'In my opinion,' said Cousin Kathy, 'if everyone took up knitting there would be none o' this talk now. The devil makes work for idle hands and tempts those who are easily tempted – even men.'

'Rubbish!' snorted Jessie. 'While I might be mad at Charlie I can't imagine him sitting knitting by the fire at night. He's a man when all is said and done and it isn't at all decent for men to do women's work.'

Mattie gave a wicked snigger. 'Maybe you prefer the idea o' the idle hands, Jessie, just as long as they're up your skirts and doing all the things you yearned for in your younger days.'

'Really! You get worse with each passing day, Mattie MacPhee!' exploded Jessie and walked stiffly away to her cottage, there to make herself a good strong cuppy laced with a drop whisky while she thought of all the opportunities she had missed when she had been young and willing and only too ready for adventures of an intimate nature.

That Mattie! That Harriet! That Charlie! Oh, she should have been bolder when she'd gone to see him bearing offerings of soup and home baking and all the other little treats she had dreamed up to try and win him round. Now it was too late. A stranger had stolen an eligible bachelor right from under her nose – as if one man hadn't been enough for her! And it had to be Charlie of all people. The one Campbell that Jessie had doted on all these years of waiting and hoping. And her an incomer too! Entirely lacking in the graces that Jessie associated with her own fair sex!

Jessie drank her tea and closed her eyes. It wouldn't last, of course. He would soon see the error of his ways with a woman like Harriet Houston from Ayr bossing him about at every turn.

The thought made Jessie feel better. She took out her hanky and blew her nose and smiled a little to herself. She would be here waiting when Charlie finally saw the light and this time she would not hesitate to let him know how she felt about him – by God and she wouldn't!

Harriet merely shook her head when the gossip reached her ears. The van bringing some of her more personal possessions had been and gone from Butterburn Croft and she was far too busy to bother herself about much else.

'It was inevitable, Charlie,' she told him when the removal van had rattled away down the road and she and Charlie sat drinking a well-earned cup of tea. 'You and I know it's just a business arrangement but people will talk and I just hope you won't let it worry you too much. Given time, it will die down. Meanwhile I know we'll be happy with matters as they stand and I for one will be far too occupied to let the likes of Jessie MacDonald get me down.'

Charlie, a strong, ruggedly handsome man of fifty, couldn't have agreed more. He had spent a good part of his life avoiding possessive women, including his mother and his elder sisters whom he had left behind in Argyllshire as soon as he was old enough to do so. His mother had been widowed young, none of his four sisters had married; he had been the only man in a household filled with 'chattering skirts', all trying to make him bend to their will and do what he was told to do.

Not that he didn't have a healthy liking for the fair sex. As a very young man in the Merchant Navy he'd had the proverbial girl in every port and had been only too keen to love them just as long as he could leave them behind when he went on his way.

When he had settled in Kinvara he had been careful not to get too involved with any one woman but had been hard put trying to fend off those who couldn't resist the lure of his 'seaman's eyes' and the promise of romance in the husky overtones of his voice. These physical qualities of his, while giving him the ability to win over most females who took his fancy, were nevertheless often a drawback when it came to breaking away from those with matrimony on their minds.

Because Charlie had no intention of becoming ensnared in the ties that bound. Beddings without weddings was his own personal motto and he was perfectly happy with that. He was more than able to take care of himself and could cook and clean, darn his own socks, even knit his own pullovers when he had to.

If Jessie had found out about this last attribute she would surely have gone up in smoke and would have told him yet again that he needed a woman about the place. But Charlie had learned some handy lessons of survival in the Merchant Navy and had no intention of letting Jessie take over the running of his home.

She had been a thorn in his side for a long time now and had done everything in her power to try and win him over, but the more she persisted the more determined he had become not to allow himself to be monopolised.

All he wanted was to be left in peace to do as he wanted and Harriet Houston had been the answer to his prayers. He had come to know her very well indeed on her visits to Kinvara and after her husband's death she had corresponded with him, telling him of her desire to break away from her old way of life and start afresh in Kinvara.

The idea of inviting her to be his housekeeper had taken root only slowly and had at first been utterly ridiculous to him. But the more he thought about it the more reasonable it became. Harriet was a woman of great strength and resilience. She would be a buffer for him, someone whose very presence would repel the Jessies of the world and allow him to go on his way unhindered.

I need a woman. He had penned the words before his courage could desert him, being very blunt and almost rude in his efforts to ensure that she understood exactly what was required of her. He had gone on, outlining his plans, telling her that everything would be on a strictly business level and that each of them would lead entirely separate lives.

He had posted the epistle as soon as it was written for fear he might change his mind and when she had written back saying yes he had spent a whole week quaking in his shoes and wondering if he had done the right thing.

But Harriet herself had had enough of marital commitments and wanted only a quiet harbour in which to take stock for a while. Hers had been a no-nonsense letter, brisk and to the point and letting him see very plainly indeed that she had only agreed to the arrangement because it suited her own ends; if it didn't work out she wouldn't hesitate to pack her bags and go.

Now, here they were, companionably drinking tea and eating the little seed cakes that Harriet had made that morning. 'I hope you won't regret inviting me to share your home, Charlie,' Harriet said as she topped up his cup from the pot. 'It won't be easy at first, the whole place will talk about us for a while, but I think, like me, you're an individual who has been used to some controversy in your life and will manage to hold your head up despite it.'

Charlie swallowed a mouthful of seed cake. It was as light as air and glided agreeably over his tonsils. It was better than anything he had ever tasted before. She was a damned good cook. He had to give her that. Baking was something he had never had patience or time for and and it had always been quicker just to buy anything of that sort from the village store.

He looked at her. She was an attractive woman, well built, smooth-skinned, a good generous mouth on her, a copper glint in her hair where it caught the light.

His heart skipped a beat. Damn this attraction he felt for any good-looking woman who chanced his way. It was a compulsion that had always been there, right from the time he'd been in short trousers chasing the girls after school.

Gently he moved away from Harriet and went to the window to focus his deep blue gaze on the heave and toss of the waves in Niven's Bay. He would be all right once everything calmed down and he could get back to his routine again. The sea was the element he knew best. Right from the start it had given him a sense of freedom, separating him from dull domesticity, taking him away from everything that oppressed him and tied him down . . .

'No regrets, Harriet,' he said evenly. 'I'm very glad you came and I'm sure our arrangement will be a satisfactory one for us both, you in your small corner and I in mine. What could be better for two people who want only breathing space in their lives to fill it how they will.'

'Ay, what could be better?' Harriet agreed as she collected the dishes and took them to the sink to be washed, humming a little tune under her breath as she did so. It was good to be here in Kinvara in this house with its stunning views of the bay and the sea and the small isles of the Hebrides visible on the horizon. She knew she had made a right move coming here to Butterburn Croft and she felt so uplifted it was as if she was a girl again, young and fancy-free with all the world at her feet.

KINVARA

Christmas 1926

Chapter Twenty-One

Big Bette was wallowing in bed with the flu, snorting, sneezing and snuffling, feeling very sorry for herself indeed and blaming Mungo for giving her his cold germs. 'You never used your hanky enough,' she accused him baldly. 'Just blasted us all wi' your snotters and sniffles and nary a thought for all the suffering you might cause to others.'

'Och, poor Auntie,' Maudie said with some concern as she beheld the sight of Bette's red nose and swollen eyes. 'You're in a terrible state, that you are, but don't worry about a thing, I'll see to the bairns and the meals and anything else that needs doing, so just you lie there and I'll get Babs to bring you up a nice hot cuppy in two shakes o' a lamb's tail.'

Bette subsided into her pillows, groaning and moaning at the thought of her niece making merry in the kitchen, producing weird and terrible concoctions that would no doubt be unpalatable to say the least and would probably end up in the bin. And all those dirty dishes piling up! The kitchen like a midden! Everyone taking advantage of her illness and turning their backs on the chores . . .

She released a mighty sneeze. Her head felt like bursting, her nose like a piece of raw meat. Oh, to hell with it! Why should she care if the place ended up looking like a pigsty? She was far too ill to be bothered about anything any more. When Toby jumped up on the bed to miaow into her face she was too weak to chase him away but cooried him into her massive bosom instead and gave herself up to misery.

But while Bette was lying ill in the upper regions of the house a miracle was taking place downstairs – the breakthrough with Maudie that Bette had always longed for and which in the end she missed through no fault of her own. She had always maintained that her niece would one day prove herself and now she did so in a way that nobody was prepared for, far less Mungo whose faith in Maudie's capabilities had never been strong and whose opinion of her as 'a lazy good-for-nothing' was one that he felt she would carry with her throughout her life.

When she enveloped herself in one of Bette's voluminous aprons and tucked her hair into a mutch cap not one member of the MacGill household took the least bit notice but went on with their everyday pursuits: Mungo in his chair, his lips moving as he devoured yesterday's newspaper; Joe, Tom, and Babs, sprawled round the scrubbed kitchen table in a variety of slovenly poses as they perused the contents of comic papers and occasionally raised a languid arm to add a piece to a jigsaw puzzle that had seen better days.

'Right!' Maudie's voice sliced through the silence. 'I want this table cleared – now – and I want you, Babs, to make your mother a cup of tea and take it up to her without spilling a single drop in the saucer. When that's done you can come down here to fetch and carry for me while Tom goes to the shops and Joe stokes up the stove. Oh, and Uncle Mungo, you could maybe move your chair a bit to let me get more room round the table, and if you don't mind, I think you should fill a bottle for Aunt Bette's feet and have a wee look in the medicine chest for the cough mixture. She is in a bad way and could be doing wi' some tender loving care from her very own husband – as I'm sure the minister would very well tell you if he could see her for himself.'

A bomb might as well have been dropped in the room, so great were the shockwaves caused by her words. Babs was frozen in the act of stuffing a toffee into her mouth; Joe and Tom simply gaped; Mungo's eyes appeared over the top of his paper to stare in some awe at the sight of his niece through marriage standing with hefty arms akimbo as she waited with some impatience for her orders to be obeyed.

'But, Maudie.' Babs shook her head in bewilderment, 'You never tell us what to do, it's only Ma who does that and she's ill in bed so we don't have to do anything we don't want.'

'Oh, is that so?' Maudie reached for her cousin and plucked her to her feet as if she was a feather. 'Tea, this minute, and if you say you won't do it I'll put *you* to bed for the rest o' the day and see how you like that.'

Crimson-faced, astonished beyond belief, Babs went to put on the kettle while her brothers uncurled themselves from their seats and went meekly to carry out their allotted tasks, though Joe couldn't resist muttering a bit under his breath as he disappeared out to the coal bunker.

That left Mungo, with his paper at half-mast, definitely amazed and decidedly worried by this latest turn of events. To rise to the bidding of Mighty Miss Maudie, as he immediately christened her, would be to undermine the authority he was only just beginning to regain after the rocky start to his leave. That wouldn't do. It wouldn't do at all. He was the master of the household. It would look very bad indeed if he allowed himself to be intimidated by a mere relative who had insinuated herself into his home without as much as a by-your-leave or any of the other niceties normally associated with good manners.

Not only that, she was still just a slip of a girl, even if she was huge, and he was buggered if he was going to be bossed about by her or by anybody else for that matter. His brow furrowed. Maudie had implied that he was a neglectful husband, that the minister would surely think so too if he didn't get a good report when he came to visit Bette in her sickbed.

Oh, she was a cute one, was Maudie! She had him by the crutch of his underpants and he could tell by the glint in her eyes that she meant every word she had said regarding his duties towards an ailing wife . . .

Mungo got to his feet. He went to the medicine chest and found the cough mixture, he filled a bottle with hot water, he seized the cup of tea from Babs, found a tray and personally bore the whole lot upstairs to his wife. She eyed him with some suspicion when he tucked the bottle in under the blankets, fed her cough mixture from a spoon and kissed her on one hot cheek before leaving her to enjoy her tea in peace.

'I'll be back in a wee while to make sure you're all right,' had been his parting shot and Bette lay on her back, feeling very uneasy indeed as she wondered what had happened to make her husband behave in such an untypically caring manner.

If she could have glimpsed the scene below stairs she wouldn't have believed the evidence of her own eyes. Maudie was at the table, sleeves rolled to her dimpled elbows, surrounded by baking ingredients, wielding a rolling pin with energy while Babs ran backwards and forwards on chubby legs, fetching and carrying, lifting and laying, not daring to voice one single protest, so alarmed was she by this new and completely unexpected side to her cousin.

Maudie Munro had come into her own at last. A complete metamorphosis seemed to have gripped her in the last half-hour and as the pastries and pies took shape under her expert touch a stunned Mungo was moved to say rather too heartily, 'Well, well, is this no' a turn up for the books? Our Maudie cooking and baking as if she's been doing it all her life. You certainly are a lass of surprises, if you don't mind me saying so.'

'Of course I can cook,' Maudie told her uncle with raised brows. 'I thought you would have known that. Mammy herself showed me how to do it from the minute I could hold a mixing bowl and my Aunt Lottie on my father's side let me in on a few more tricks. She was head o' the kitchen in a big house in the west end and it was all the fancy wee touches that I seemed to take in the most. She had a very deep manly sort o' voice, and I always remember her saying to me how glamour was all very well in its place but the best way to get to a man's heart was through his stomach and girls had to know how to do that if they wanted a wedding ring on their finger.' She sighed. 'It was a terrible pity that she had to go and die before she could get herself a man of her own. Her trouble was food, piles of it on her plate, all the stodge o' the day and too much sugar in everything. Maybe it was just as well she never lived long enough to be married because she might have killed her man through kindness.'

Mungo looked worried by these revelations. His eyes roved to Maudie's well-rounded bosoms peeping over the rim of her frock and catching his glance she laughed. 'Ach, don't worry yourself, Uncle, I know what you're thinking but I'm not about to kill you through kindness. I got a fright when Aunt Lottie died and after that I was always careful wi' the sugar and always cut the fat off the meat. And while I love eating just as much as Aunt Lottie I go on a wee starvation diet now and again just to get myself back in trim . . .'

She giggled at the expression of guilt on his countenance. 'My, my, just look at you, Uncle, all red in the face because you know you've been talking about me behind my back. It's all right, I won't hold it against you. I was just so relaxed in this house I let myself go and ate everything Aunt Bette gave me – even the fat and the sugar. Of course . . .' She slid him a sidelong laughing glance 'I'm also stout because it's natural for me to be that way, just as it is for Aunt Bette and Mammy too. You are built a bittie on the large side yourself, Uncle, but it doesn't matter since you're a man and have to keep your strength up – so don't fret your head any more about anything and go back to your chair and enjoy your paper.'

Meek as a lamb, Mungo did as he was bid but he was unable to concentrate on the words in front of him; the aromatic smells in the kitchen were tempting him beyond all bearing and he could hardly wait for teatime to come so that he could sample some of the goodies for himself.

At last the clock struck the hour. Maudie's skills were about to be put to the test. The family sat round the table, knives and forks at the ready, mouths watering as Maudie set down the dishes and the bowls, the gravies and the sauces.

As head of the house Mungo was given the honour of

serving the first dish, an enormous savoury mince pie, crisp and piping hot from the oven, the rich reek of onions filtering out through the little hole on top. The plates were lined up in front of Mungo; he raised his hand, the knife flashed, rich juices burst out of the crusty steaming depths. Mungo's hand shook slightly as he dished out the portions, feeling it his right as man of the house to serve himself a larger wedge than anybody else.

Everybody dug in, silence pervaded; Maudie waited. The plaudits rained on her from all sides. There was no doubt about it, she was a cook *par excellence*, the cleared plates bore testimony to that, but then the comparisons began.

'Ma always just makes the mince in a pan,' Joe said between mouthfuls.

'Ay, and her tatties are nearly always soggy.' Babs didn't look up from her plate as she spoke.

Tom added his piece. 'Her doughballs are sometimes so heavy they're only fit for banking up the fire at night.'

'Now, now, that's enough o' that.' Mungo rose to the defence of his absent wife in a half-hearted fashion. 'Your mother is out at the shop all day and hasn't the time to make fancy meals. She is a good plain cook and none of us have suffered because o' it – except for the occasional bout o' indigestion that I myself get when I dare to eat one o' her doughballs.'

The last remark was a very ungallant one and Maudie glowered at her uncle as she arranged a tempting repast for her invalid aunt, thoughtfully adding a hyacinth spear in a bud vase as a last touch.

'I'll take it up.' Mungo, anxious to make amends for his unthinking words, grabbed the tray and bore it away upstairs, composing his features into an affable smile as he pushed open the bedroom door with his foot and went inside. Bette, however, was not in the least bit hungry and showed no enthusiasm for the dainty array set before her.

'You have to eat something,' Mungo told his wife in his best bedside manner. 'Maudie has spent all afternoon preparing food with you in mind. She's a grand lass, is our niece, you should see the way she handled Babs and made the boys run to her bidding.'

He went on to give a glowing account of Maudie's activities of the day and only stopped talking when he had run out of adjectives to describe her culinary talents.

'You've changed your tune,' Bette croaked sarcastically. 'She used to be my niece, now she's yours as well, and all of a sudden you're crowing her good points to all and sundry.'

'You're hardly all and sundry, Bette.' He sounded maddeningly placating. 'And I thought you'd be pleased to know that your faith in her has been justified. I wish you could have seen for yourself the way she works and how easy she makes it look.'

He paused for a moment and gazed thoughtfully into space, 'I never knew you could do so many different things with tatties. It just goes to show that we are all learning something every day.'

'I know what I'd like to do with a potato!' Bette yelled hoarsely, gazing at the ones on the edge of her plate in a demented fashion. 'That hyacinth bud too! Maudie had no right to break it off before it had a chance to flower and if you say another word about her cooking I'll – I'll take the pair o' you and knock both your silly heads together!'

Her anger had made her forget her flu miseries. She looked perfectly capable of carrying out her threats, and Mungo beat a hasty retreat when she grabbed the baked potato from her plate and began waving it in the air in a most threatening manner.

Chapter Twenty-Two

'Yoohoo! It's only us, dear!'

Mungo had only been gone a short time when the rallying cry reached Bette's eardrums. The next minute the Henderson Hens burst jovially into the sickroom, all striped butcher's aprons, clumpy feet, wide toothy grins, and bearing gifts of a sensible nature.

Wilma deposited a bag of rosy apples on the bedspread with a flourish, Rona did likewise with a box of mixed poultry eggs, including some large pale green ones of the duck variety.

'Freshly laid this morning,' Rona beamed, fingering the eggshells with pride and affection. 'Just the thing to get you back on your feet.'

When she was 'at herself' Bette liked nothing better than an egg of any sort but now she felt insulted at the very idea of anyone thinking she was fit enough actually to eat one and not a word of thanks did she utter as the sisters made themselves comfortable – not too near the bed; goodwill visits were all very well and one had to be neighbourly but it would never do to catch someone else's germs since 'there was no knowing where they'd been and might be foreign for all one knew.'

Bette's lack of appreciation was not lost on the sisters, but determined to be cheerful at all costs they plunged into vivid accounts of village affairs, being very vocal and witty, each echoing the other, a little peculiarity of theirs that often annoyed Bette and never more than now when she was feeling too ill to concentrate.

Reclusive the two might be but their knowledge of what went on around them was amazingly up to date. They spoke at length about Jessie MacDonald's continuing disapproval of Charlie Campbell's so-called sinful liaison with Harriet Houston from Ayr; how good Johnny Lonely was with young Andy Sutherland and how the hermit had occasionally been spotted visiting No. 6 Keeper's Row and Hannah all alone there without her husband; about Janet Morgan's fostering of little Bonny Barr and their hopes that 'all would end well there as it seemed such a happy agreement for the parties concerned.'

After that, little snippets of more general gossip filled the gap till they remembered something much more eventful and went on to recount the latest talk concerning Carrots Law who had allegedly stolen a sheep from Donald of Balivoe in order to provide a slap-up Christmas dinner for his family.

'No one can prove it, of course,' Wilma stated emphatically. 'Far less the village policeman who ought to be wise to the Laws after all this time.'

She guffawed at her own joke while Rona went on to surmise that the animal would be well and truly slain by now, cooked, carved, jointed, and hidden away from prying eyes.

'One has to make allowances of course.' Wilma pursed her lips and looked as if she wouldn't have made any if one of her turkeys had been stolen. 'Dolly and Shug have always been devious and the elder Law lad is only doing what he was taught to do since he was a babe in arms.'

'People got hanged for sheep stealing in the old days.' Rona's eyes gleamed at the thought. 'I'm sure we could be doing with some of these good old-fashioned methods of punishment nowadays – though nothing as drastic as hanging of course,' she hastily amended.

Bette groaned and moved restlessly. Wait till she got that Mungo! How could he have done this to her? Allowed those two upstairs. All she wanted was to be left alone to nurse her miseries in peace . . .

'We miss you so much in the shop, dear,' Rona said regretfully.

'Yes, we miss you, dear,' Wilma repeated. 'Young Daisy MacNulty is all very well but she does seem to have a perpetually runny nose and her fingernails aren't exactly clean. Rona and me were just saying how unhygienic a person she is and not really the sort we would have chosen to put behind the counter of a food store . . .'

'I couldn't care less if she painted the whole damt shop with her snotters and her dirt!' Bette had had enough, and she didn't mince words as she went on, 'If I was in there I'd be doing the same but I'm not, I'm here in my bed with the flu, too ill to be bothered with anybody and spreading my germs into every corner o' the house! They never confine themselves to any one place and one sneeze goes a long way, a very long way indeed, as I thought the pair of you might like to know.'

The sisters blinked behind their glasses like a couple of surprised owls.

'Yes, well, oh dear me, you have got it bad, haven't you?' Wilma hazarded warily.

'And here we were, only trying to be neighbourly,' Rona put in huffily. She stood up and carefully straightened her apron. 'However, we won't stay where we're not wanted. Come along, Wilma dear, we've done our good deed for the day and can go home with a clear conscience.'

'I'm sure Bette didn't mean it.' Wilma hastened to pour oil on troubled waters. 'When people are ill they say things they wouldn't normally dream of saying.'

Bette opened her mouth to retaliate then shut it again. She was thinking of all the lovely fruit and vegetables the sisters provided for her shop. If she was to get on their wrong side they might take their business elsewhere and she could lose a lot of custom because of it.

'Oh, sit down.' She tried to sound apologetic without actually having to say she was sorry. 'You're right, Wilma, I don't know what I'm saying, make yourselves at home and have an egg – I mean a grape – oh, I'm even worse than

I thought I was but you both know what I mean so help yourselves.'

The sisters sat, they had three grapes each, they gazed fondly at the invalid and harmony was restored between them.

Two days later Bette was sitting in the warmth of the kitchen, Toby decorating her knee, a brightly coloured woollen shawl wrapped around her shoulders, her feet encased in a pair of Mungo's fleecy-lined check bootees because her own slippers had a hole in them. Still weak and shaky, she had no inclination to move from the spot but was glad to remain where she was while Mungo and the children made a gratifying fuss of her and Maudie hummed a catchy tune as she stirred a big pan of soup on the stove.

Since her aunt's illness she had organised the household like a sergeant-major, assigning suitable chores to the younger members of the family as soon as they came home from school or work, doing the same with Mungo but in a less obvious way, making him feel that he was the boss and she was only there to make sure that his orders were carried out.

None of them minded, not even Mungo. They adored Maudie, they adored her cooking, they wanted her to look after them forever and wouldn't have cared less if she had donned a uniform and made them salute her just as long as she went on telling them her stories, kept on making her flans and her tarts, found time to laugh and joke with them as they sat round the fire at night toasting muffins and marshmallows and anything else that tasted good when held on a fork next to the flames.

Bette watched as her niece ladled soup into plates. She saw how Babs, Tom and Joe reacted to every word Maudie said, she noticed how Mungo had stopped glowering at her and was smiling at her appreciatively instead. Bette felt shut out of the happy family scene as she sat in her chair by the fire and accepted the steaming bowl that Maudie brought to her before rejoining the others at the table.

Bette frowned; she told herself how good it was to have someone else take over the running of the house for a change, but somehow she couldn't convince herself of this and she went into a muse as she ate her soup and kept one eye on all the contented faces rowed round the kitchen table.

The next day Bette was able to don her clothes and get up for breakfast. It being Saturday there was no school and as soon as the meal was over Maudie set herself up at the table, Babs running hither and thither as usual and taking quite an interest when her cousin showed her how to make a cake mixture, even allowing her to turn it out into a tin and put it in the oven.

Bette sat at the fire, carving a wooden horse for little Bonny Barr's Christmas stocking, all the while keeping a covert watch on her niece as she stirred and rolled and patted. She began paring down Maudie's capabilities. The girl wasn't exactly working her fingers to the bone, Bette decided, she had a willing slave in Babs and all Maudie did was stand at the table and 'flash her flour' as Bette put it to herself.

And her singing was beginning to get on Bette's nerves. Nothing ever seemed to bother that girl! She had taken to looking after the family like a duck to water, she was kind, caring, and considerate to everyone, especially her aunt whom she tried to please more than anyone, forever asking if she was all right and could she get her anything.

A pang of guilt went through Bette as she thought these things. Even so, she couldn't help feeling just a tiny bit resentful of her niece. She was taking over, there was no doubt about that; she probably didn't mean to make it look that way but it was happening and Bette was beginning to feel more and more like an outsider in her own home.

With all this in mind Bette began to question some of Maudie's cooking methods and was greatly put about when Maudie turned to her and said apologetically, 'If you don't mind me saying so, Auntie, I always thought you put too much baking soda in your pancakes and no' enough yeast in your bread. I never liked to say anything but now that you've brought the subject up I feel it's the right time to mention it.'

Bette did mind. For two whole days she hardly spoke to Maudie; on the third she decided she was being childish and had a long talk with the girl when the rest of the family were occupied elsewhere, coming straight to the point as was her habit when she had something important to say.

'Sit down, Maudie,' she invited. 'I haven't said anything yet about the surprise I felt when it became clear that you had more to your make-up than just sitting by the fire reading a book. You are certainly a dark horse and no mistake. Why didn't you tell anyone you had such a flair wi' the flour? With your skills you could get a job anywhere, The MacKernon is always looking for a good cook, the laird would give his good ear for you, half the gentry houses in the district would kill one another to get you. You could ask what you liked in the way of wages and maybe a bit more besides.'

'Och, you are kind, Auntie,' Maudie said with a coy little flick of her lashes. 'But I'm no' wanting to do work o' that sort for anybody, even if they are gentry wi' plenty money. I just like doing what I do when I feel like it and wouldn't enjoy sweating away in a hot kitchen all day and me wi' my chest to consider.'

'You're quite a girl, Maudie Munro.' Bette eyed her niece in some puzzlement. 'You have achieved things that nobody would have given you credit for. Somehow you have become a culinary genius, somehow you came into this home and made it your own, somehow you made Mungo love you and that in itself is about the biggest achievement anyone could wish for supposing they lived to be a hundred.'

'Yes, Auntie,' Maudie agreed as she got up to don a pair of oven mitts in order to examine the progress of a chicken casserole bubbling away merrily in the depths of the stove. 'I'm that pleased Uncle Mungo likes me at last and wants me to stay on here. I love living wi' you and him and the bairns. I know how worried you were about me and my laziness but now that I've proved myself I'll never go back to that again and I hope you'll go on wanting me and won't ever feel that you have to send me back home to Partick.'

Maudie was singing again as she went to prepare the pudding for lunch. Bette sighed and felt sad. She knew that the time for Maudie to make her own way in the world was fast approaching, but for the life of her she had no idea how she was going to handle such a delicate situation when the day finally dawned for her to have her say.

Chapter Twenty-Three

Bette wasn't the only person in the Row facing impertive decisions for the future. Hannah too was fast approaching a crisis in her own life as she walked along the shoreline of Mary's Bay, deep in thought, worrying and wondering about many things but most of all about her failure to tell anyone of her pregnancy. She couldn't hide it for much longer, she was growing bigger by the day, and she knew now how foolish she'd been to try and keep such a momentous happening to herself.

Rob would be home soon. He would be angry at her for not including him in something so personal to them both, while her mother's reactions didn't bear contemplation; she wouldn't understand the reasons behind her daughter's thinking; her fears about having another child like Andy; her refusal to believe that she was expecting again after trying so hard never to go through that experience again.

She sat down on a rock and gazed out to sea. It was a beautiful day, crisp and so clear she could see for miles. The seals were lying on the reefs, looking for all the world like miniature boats with their flippers in the air and their heads held up as they called to one another.

Her eyes travelled to the Kinvara Light, a lone pinnacle on the blue horizon, surrounded by all that sea and space and endless solitude. She thought of Rob, so tall and dark, so handsome a man, virile, strong, loving. Her heart quickened.

Soon she would see him again, soon they would hold one another, soon . . .

Her breath caught on a sob. It wouldn't be like that. He would be angry at her for shutting him out, he would look at her in hurt and bewilderment and all the old tensions would spring up between them again.

The roof of Oir na Cuan was shining in the sun. No one lived there now but Hannah remembered how smoke had once poured from the chimneys, how lights had shone from the windows. A vision of Morna came to her suddenly. So filled with the joys of living, so vibrant and carefree despite all her tribulations. No wonder Rob had loved her as he had. He would go on missing her for the rest of his life, his memories of her would remain with him throughout his days . . .

Hannah got up. A mist of tears blurred her vision, she stumbled against a hidden spur of rock and went down heavily, twisting her ankle as she did so. Her mouth twisted in agony. She tried to hobble on but couldn't. Needle-like shafts of pain were shooting up her leg, making it impossible to move one foot in front of the other.

A tall dark figure appeared beside her and Johnny Lonely was suddenly there, grabbing on to her, propping her up with his hard shoulders, saying in an oddly comforting voice, 'Just you hold on to me, missus, no need to hurry or worry, just take one step at a time.'

'Johnny!' she gasped gladly. 'Where did you spring from? I didn't see you.'

'No, but I saw you, that's all you need to know.'

A wry smile touched her lips. 'Ay, you're always there, Johnny, watching and listening, but for once I don't care. If you hadn't come along I don't know what I would have done.'

'Ay, well, you shouldn't be out here alone in your condition. You'll have to tell someone about it sometime, Hannah Sutherland, and the sooner the better for your own sake.'

He was speaking in the cryptic tone that Hannah was coming to know well and she stared at him as she cried, 'What do you know of that, Johnny Lonely? Has someone been talking? Janet

Morgan, for instance? She thinks she knows everything about everybody but she knows nothing about me, nothing!'

'Not Janet.' He lowered his shaggy brows and looked at her. 'She's a good friend to you and knows how to hold her tongue.'

'Who, then?' she demanded.

'You did, just now, as soon as I mentioned it. A pregnant woman canny keep forever and I've seen enough o' them in my day to know what I'm talking about. At least you know who the father o' you bairn is. There are some hereabouts who don't.'

Hannah knew what he meant. Mollie Gillespie had been keeping her head down of late, getting 'more and more pregnant' as Dolly Law said and Donnie Hic blissfully believing that he was the proud father-to-be.

'Though mind, he isn't daft, is Donnie Hic, despite being pickled in drink half the time,' Mattie had said with a knowing nod. 'If that bairn comes out looking like Ryan Du there will be hell to pay and Ryan Du might just end up like a castrated bull if that last time in the Balivoe Inn is anything to go by.'

Johnny Lonely had said enough and they set off, Hannah's arms around him as he half-carried her over the sand and the shingle and hardly paused to catch his breath as he soldiered on towards the road.

It was a long way up the beach and by the time they reached the road they were both panting and sweating and Johnny Lonely was forced to stop for a rest while Hannah sank on to the grass verge, too exhausted to remain on her feet for another second longer.

The laird drew up in his Lanchester at that opportune moment. Poking an inquiring face through the window he sized up the situation rapidly and got out of his car to help Johnny get Hannah into it. 'Just you sit back and relax, dear lady,' he directed her kindly as she lay sprawled in the roomy rear seat. 'You must have that ankle bathed and bound immediately . . .' He broke off as Johnny made to disappear in his usual silent fashion. 'Come back here, man!' Captain Rory called. 'I need you to assist me at the other end. No use doing someone a good deed if you can't see it all the way through.'

Johnny hesitated but came back without a word, looking awkward and uncomfortable as he settled himself gingerly in the front beside the laird and scowled at the dashboard.

'It won't bite,' Captain Rory MacPherson said drily. 'Neither will I for that matter so just you sit back, enjoy the ride, and think yourself lucky I came along or you might have had to carry Hannah all the way home.'

Johnny made no utterance to this but sat perfectly still, trying to fathom out the laird's unusual philosophies, trying also not to look too hard at the road ahead as the Lanchester bowled along at a frisky pace, narrowly missing sheep, geese, and other such impediments to the driver's progress. Captain Rory was in a jubilant mood that day. His 'good wife Emily' had just given birth to a 'bonny wee boy' and he was in a hurry to get back to both her and the new arrival.

They were at Hannah's front door in minutes and Harriet, who had been minding the children, looked up in some surprise as her daughter was led into the kitchen supported on either side by Johnny and the laird. Carefully they lowered her on to a chair and the laird was about to depart when Toby, taking advantage of the open door, came in, tail waving high in the air in a confident manner.

Breck's nose twitched but he was growing more tolerant nowadays and had made a pact with the local cat population, allowing them into his house on the condition that they didn't eat his food or sit on his rug. In return he expected the right to chase them on his outside wanders except when he was pulling Andy in his cart and had to exercise a great deal of control over his more basic instincts.

Memories of Breck's former bullying had not entirely faded from Toby's mind but he was more at ease now in the dog's company and was bold enough to march straight up to the laird to rub himself against that gentleman's hairy legs and look appealingly up into his face.

'Hmm.' The laird cocked his head and looked down at the

cat. 'Emily isn't the only one in our house to have given birth. Sheba's just had kittens of uncertain origin – orange some of them – and I was just wondering . . .'

'Half the cats in Kinvara have been having orange kittens,' Harriet told him. 'But the MacGills swear that Toby is hardly ever out of doors and couldn't possibly be the father.'

He gave a rueful grin. 'And here was me thinking that my Sheba never went anywhere without me. Emily was right when she said that cats have lives of their own however much you think you own them.'

He doffed his hat and went off and Harriet went to seek out bandages, leaving Johnny Lonely and Hannah alone in the kitchen. 'Johnny.' Hannah seized hold of his arm and continued urgently, 'I want you to come here to this house for Christmas dinner – oh, please say yes – I don't know what I would have done without you today. You are a very kind and caring man in spite of all your gruff ways and I won't feel right until I've done something to repay you, not just for me, but for all the love and attention you give to Andy.'

Johnny reddened, he shuffled his feet, he rubbed his chin with a calloused thumb and hummed and hawed for quite a few moments before muttering, 'Ay, I'd like that, Morna used to do it, since she died I've had nobody . . .' His Adam's apple worked, he swallowed hard and looked down at his feet and then he was off, without a backward glance, too overcome even to remember to shut the door behind him in his hurry to get away.

Harriet came back, bringing the children who had been playing in their room and who were now anxious to do everything they could to assist her as she attended to their mother. It was while Harriet was bandaging up the injured ankle that Hannah said abruptly, 'I'm expecting a baby, Mother, in March, and I didn't tell you because I thought you would make a fuss.'

'Hannah, Hannah,' Harriet chided with a click of her tongue, 'from the moment I clapped eyes on you I knew you were pregnant again. I'm a woman, lassie, I'm your mother, and I have more in my head than you give me credit for.'

'It seems everyone knows about this bairn except me!' Hannah wailed indignantly.

At this, Andy released one of his explosive snorts, Vaila giggled and clapped her hands. 'Can I have a girl?' she cried.

'No, a boy.' Andy's gruff voice was filled with excitement.

Harriet gathered both children to her bosom and smiled at them. 'You'll take what you get and be thankful for it – whatever it is.'

'A girl,' Vaila repeated.

'A boy,' Andy reiterated with a touch of aggression.

Hannah took her son and her stepdaughter on to her lap and said softly, 'Listen to your Granma Harriet, she's older and wiser than any o' us and knows what she's talking about.'

Harriet grinned. 'So, you've forgiven me for coming to live at Butterburn Croft with Charlie Campbell. Is that what you're saying, Hannah?'

'Maybe. Time will tell all. Meanwhile, could we have a nice cup o' tea together and just sit quiet for a while? It's been quite a day one way or another and I for one am exhausted.'

That night, when everyone was in bed, Hannah sat herself down at the table and picked up her pen. For several moments it remained poised above the paper before she began to write:

Dearest Rob,

I have something very important that I want to tell you . . .

Chapter Twenty-Four

When Bette looked from her window one morning and saw Rita Sutherland coming up the path to her door she had no idea that her problems concerning Maudie were about to be solved. Rita had been in visiting her daughter-in-law Hannah and had been thrilled to learn that she was to be a grandmother again.

Now she regaled Bette with the news as she sat drinking a strong brew of tea and bit into one of Maudie's fluffy jam doughnuts while Bette listened and nodded but couldn't muster up any of her usual enthusiasm for a fireside chat.

Rita paused in her monologue and looked at Bette's face, commenting on how pale she was and asking if anything else was worrying her other than the after-effects of flu.

Bette poured it all out then, finding a willing listener in Rita who stayed silent throughout except for the odd understanding comment. 'I'm finding myself more and more redundant,' Bette ended mournfully. 'Maudie's a good lass and she was undoubtedly a grand help when I was ill but now that I'm ready to take over again she won't let me near my own stove even to stir the porridge in the morning. I'm beginning to feel like an intruder in my own home and I just don't know what I'm going to do about it, short of blowing my top and telling her to go!'

'Send her to me,' Rita said promptly, her kindly face glowing with resolution. 'With Christmas coming on I could be doing with some help and Maudie could be earning herself some money instead o' frittering her talents away for nothing. Since Catrina left I've often thought how nice it would be to have an extra pair o' hands in the kitchen and if Maudie came she would be made most welcome and would have a nice room all to herself and all the animals she wants to keep her happy.'

'Are you sure?' Bette asked a trifle breathlessly. 'I must say it would solve everything – and Maudie would like it at Vale o' Dreip once she gets used to it.'

'Of course I'm sure.' Rita finished the last of her doughnut. 'If this is an example of her baking I should think anybody would want to take Maudie on. I've met her in the village once or twice and thought to myself what a nice lass she is. I'm looking forward to having her at the farm, she'll be company for me and I know Aidan will enjoy hearing some o' these famous stories she tells about her life in Partick.'

Bette shook her head. 'That's all and well. Rita, but I feel it's only right to warn you that life wi' Maudie isn't all a bed o' roses. A good cook she is, a housewife she is not. She never makes her bed, she never clears up after herself, she still sits in Mungo's chair whenever she gets the chance and she is also something of a prima donna when it comes down to the basics of cookery. I have always prided myself on my bread and pancakes but she had the cheek to tell me just recently that my ingredients weren't of the correct quantities and if that isn't an insult I ask you what is!'

Rita merely smiled at this. 'What Maudie does in her own room is her business. No doubt you tidied up after her and spoiled her a bit but she won't get any o' that in my house. When she realises no one is going to make her bed or clear up her clothes she will soon come to her senses. As for the rest, we will cross that bridge when we come to it so don't you worry yourself any more on that score.'

She went off, leaving Bette with much food for thought as she gazed into the fire and awaited Maudie's return from the village, deciding it was better to take the bull by the horns while the going was good rather than let the passing of time weaken her purpose.

Maudie came in, rosy-cheeked and sparkly-eyed, bringing with her the fresh tang of the sea and an eagerness to rhyme off the names of the people she'd met and the things they had said. While she was speaking she was peeling off her outdoor garments, throwing them over the nearest chair, retrieving a tray of large potatoes from the pantry in order to prick them before putting them in the oven to bake for lunch.

It was while she was thus occupied that Bette began to speak, telling her niece about Rita's visit, outlining the proposals that Rita had made, going on to say that it would be for the best all round and that everyone had to make a break sometime in their lives.

Maudie stopped pricking and stared at her aunt in dismay. 'But, Auntie, I don't want to go to live at Vale o' Dreip! I love it here with you and Uncle Mungo and my cousins. I wrote to Mammy and Daddy to tell them so and that I would be staying on here for an indefinite period!'

'Maudie, you can't stay here forever, you must move on and find a new niche for yourself. You and I have been great friends but if we remain in this house together we will only end up shouting at one another and saying things we don't mean.'

'But, Auntie.' Maudie's face crumpled. 'I don't want a new life and I would never shout at you even supposing you were to beat me to death! I've tried my best to be a good help ever since you took ill. I know I've been a disappointment to you in the past but all that's changed and I promise I'll never ever do anything to make you think bad of me again – and – and I'll even stop using Uncle Mungo's chair if it makes you feel any better.'

'Maudie, Maudie, I never thought of you as a bad lassie, in fact you are the nicest niece any aunt could wish to have and I'm going to miss you sorely about the place. But you'll like it at Vale o' Dreip with the cats and the dogs and a nice big cosy kitchen for you to work in. Rita's a fine wee woman, you'll get on well with her, everybody does and nobody has a bad word to say against her.'

Maudie ignored the last part of that statement and picked instead on the first. 'If you'll miss me so much then don't send me away! I'll be an even better niece to you if you let me stay, helping you and keeping Uncle Mungo and the bairns happy. You wanted me to get a job and now I've got one and I don't know what it is that I've done wrong!'

'Not my job, Maudie, as wife, and mother looking after my husband and my children. Oh, what can I say to make you understand? There just isn't enough room for two o' us in this kitchen. I've loved having you here, we've been great pals, but it's over now and I hope in time you will realise it's for your own good and won't think too badly of me.'

Getting up she put her arms round her niece and hugged her close while Maudie sobbed in a heartrending fashion and held on to her aunt as if she would never let her go.

Bette wrenched herself away and went quickly upstairs to have a good weep to herself in the privacy of her bedroom. Down below Maudie had abandoned all attempts to prepare lunch and was sitting in Mungo's chair, staring bleakly into space, for once ignoring Toby when he jumped up on to her knee to rub his face against hers and purr loudly into her ear.

Several times in the course of that day Bette found herself weakening whenever she looked at Maudie's woebegone face and saw the reproach in the big puppy-dog eyes. Matters were made worse when Mungo and the children came home and the inevitable questions began, Babs in particular being very upset and demanding to know what Maudie had done to cause her 'to be banished from the house so suddenly'.

'It isn't as if she's having a baby,' Joe muttered darkly.

'She tells great stories,' Tom growled, glaring at his mother as if she was the big bad ogre personified. '*And* she makes the best doughballs of anyone I know.'

His mourning siblings agreed. Mungo did too though not in so many words; everyone went to bed in the dampest of spirits, hungry, puzzled, and upset, making Bette feel so unpopular she hardly slept a wink that night and thought seriously about going to Maudie's room to beg her forgiveness and to ask for the continuing pleasure of her company.

But no! She had to make a stand sometime! If she wavered now, Maudie would never make a move to support herself, and there really wasn't enough room for two large women in a rather small kitchen no matter how much they loved and cared for one another.

Bette lay wide-eyed, listening to Mungo's snores, thinking about many things, but most of all about how strange life would be at No. 1 of the Row without Maudie's cheerful presence.

When morning came, Maudie packed her bags miserably and slowly, silently watched by Babs, Joe and Tom, who could find nothing to say after all this time of delighting in, and loving, their cousin.

She cleared her photos from the dresser; her collection of furry animals was removed from the bed; her reams of writings she stuffed without ceremony into her case. At the last minute she thoughtfully replaced two of the furry toys on the pillow 'to keep Babs company when she had no one to talk to and laugh with any more.'

Babs could take no more. She broke down and simply howled, rushing out of the room and into the little cubby hole in the stairs where she cried and sobbed and called her mother everything beneath the sun – under her breath of course since the might of Bette's hand was a force not to be reckoned with.

Maudie came downstairs with her cases, feet trailing, shoulders slumped, the sight of her making Bette feel like a traitor sending an innocent person to their execution. Maudie said not a word but went straight outside to climb into Mungo's trap for the short journey up to the farm.

Her cousins came out to stand in a solemn row as they watched proceedings. Bette too came out to say her farewells but Maudie was having none of that.

'I did it for you, Auntie,' was her parting shot as Mungo took up the reins and the trap began to move away.

Joe bit his lip. Tom screwed up his face. It would never do for a boy of his age to be seen shedding tears. Babs rushed back to her cupboard once more to wail and weep and vow that she would never again speak to her mother as long as she lived.

Bette had been too upset earlier to eat any breakfast. Going back into the house she poured herself a large mug of tea and put two slices of toast on a plate. Carefully she laid everything on the table. She looked at it but not a drop did she drink nor a bite did she eat. Guilt tearing her in two she threw her apron over her face and 'bawled like a bairn' as Mungo said later when he was recounting that morning's experiences to some of his cronies.

When Ramsay beheld Maudie for the first time he broke out in a sweat and his blood pressure soared. Her breasts were swelling over the top of her jacket, her hips were swaying seductively as she got down from the trap and came walking over the yard to the door. She was rosy and fresh and very young and Ramsay moistened his lips because his mouth had suddenly gone dry.

Rita watched him and smiled to herself. She enjoyed seeing him squirm like this. She knew his strengths and his weaknesses. She knew how much he liked young women and how successfully he hid this fact from the world. As a key member of the Free Church he had to do what was expected of him and behave in the dignified manner that befitted someone in his position.

But none of that had helped him some years ago, when,

on a night of storm and tempest, with Rita lying ill and helpless upstairs, he had lost his head over Catrina Blair and had ravished her against her will, little Euan Blair being the result of that ungodly union.

Oh, ay, Rita knew her husband all right and now he reddened and turned away as Maudie came inside, Mungo at her back with her cases.

Three-year-old Aidan, Finlay's son from his brief marriage to Morna, was at the table when Maudie appeared, an auburn-haired, highly strung little boy who had suffered asthma attacks since his mother's death despite the fact that he seemed to have settled in well to his new life at Vale o' Dreip.

The arrival of Maudie Munro was like a breath of fresh air for everyone that day, for despite her own personal troubles she came into the house smiling, and Aidan felt the sunshine of that smile as he sat and watched and took in every aspect of the scene before him.

There followed a short pause and everyone started slightly when Ramsay's voice cut roughly through the silence. 'Where did that cat come from?' he demanded as an enquiring whiskery face came round the door followed by a lithe ginger body that proceeded to wind itself round Ramsay's legs in a most winning fashion.

'Toby!' Maudie made a dive for the cat and picked him up.

'He must have come with us in the trap,' Mungo said in some bemusement.

'We don't want any more cats here,' Ramsay stated firmly. 'We're overrun with them as it is and they are *never* allowed into the house.'

'Better take him back, Uncle,' Maudie said regretfully. 'Babs will miss him like anything and she'll be feeling bad enough without losing Toby as well.'

But Toby refused to be parted from Maudie and cooried into her neck, his claws flashing out threateningly when Mungo made a move to pluck him away.

'It is not staying here,' Ramsay repeated flatly while Aidan held his breath and decided that life at the farm with Maudie Munro was never going to be dull.

'Cats will go where they want to go and bide where they want to bide,' Rita said calmly. 'If you take him away he will just come back and we'll all have a high old time of it running backwards and forwards.'

'He will help you to feel at home, lass.' Mungo patted Maudie's shoulder by way of comfort and stared boldly at Ramsay. The two factions did not share the same religious beliefs and seldom crossed paths but when they did Mungo liked to feel that he had the upper hand and he went on in even more defiant tones, 'I'll get Babs another cat, there are plenty o' kittens in Kinvara since Toby made it his home and nearly all of them look like him.'

It was a magnanimous statement coming from a man who had done everything in his power to keep his house cat free and Maudie felt such a great rush of affection for him she stood on her toes and kissed him on one ruddy red cheek.

He blushed and moved towards the door. 'Ay, well, I'll be going now, you take care and come to visit us as often as you can.' Awkwardly he patted her on the shoulder once more and went out just as Finlay was coming in. Rita introduced Maudie to her son but they didn't hear a word. For them it was love at first sight. They just stared and stared at one another and would have kept on doing so had not Rita put her hand on Maudie's arm to lead her upstairs to her room.

Maudie ran to the window; she put her hands to her mouth with delight as she gazed at the view of russet-green fields rolling away to the moors and the hills.

'Oh, Mrs Sutherland, I love it, I just love it!'

'Call me Rita, everyone does.'

A little shyly, Maudie nodded and said softly, 'Ay, I'll do that – it suits this place somehow – friendly and nice.'

Rita went out and Maudie fell on the big feather bed to

bounce on it and laugh before getting up to gaze once more at the vista that was going to be hers and which she hoped she didn't have to leave 'for a long long time'.

Chapter Twenty-Five

Life was never the same at Vale o' Dreip after that. Maudie and Finlay flirted and giggled together, they ran and played like children, they were besotted with one another and it was all they could do to keep their feelings to themselves. The farmhands ogled Maudie and whistled appreciatively whenever her bountiful curves sailed past their vision but they never got anywhere with her; she had eyes only for Finlay and he for her and they met wherever and whenever they could and tried very hard to appear normal if they thought anyone was watching.

Rita and Maudie got on famously from the start and worked together harmoniously, the older woman leaving the younger to produce glorious meals in the kitchen while she went about the more mundane household tasks, occasionally going back on her own word as she tidied Maudie's room and excused her actions by telling herself it was only till the girl found her feet and that 'such a lass had better things to do with her time anyway.'

It didn't take Aidan long to fall under Maudie's spell. He could never get enough of her stories, she played with him and talked to him and made him laugh with her nonsense and mischief and he loved it when she gave him 'wee tastes' from pots and pans and trays while she was in the midst of her culinary preparations.

Because Maudie always seemed to make time for these things when everyone else was too busy to be bothered. Her joy in her new surroundings was fresh and infectious so that those around her began to see everyday objects in a new and revealing light as she pointed out various aspects that they had never noticed before.

As for Ramsay, Maudie's sunny nature and buoyant personality soon softened any objections he might have had regarding her presence in his home. She lightened and brightened mealtimes; her cheerful observations about life in general and her hunger for knowledge always invited lively discussion and Ramsay found himself warming more and more to her as the days went by.

He became mellower, he told Rita she had done the right thing bringing the girl to Vale o' Dreip, he watched Maudie and his son going off with Aidan to feed the chickens or the ducks, the cows and the pigs, and he thought it was really quite pleasant to see all the young people getting on so well together.

He changed his tune when he found Maudie and his son romping in the barn one night, locked half-naked in each other's arms 'like a pair o' heathens without heed to the laws o' decency'. After that he went daft altogether and began ranting and raving about 'strangers violating his property with their sinful ways' and that 'enough was enough and he was damned if he was going to stand back and allow such practices to continue under his own nose.'

He delivered a lecture to Finlay on the values of honour and abstinence and ended up by telling the two that if they wanted to continue indulging in such carnal lusts the only decent thing for them to do was to get married and the sooner the better as far as he was concerned.

'Really, Mr Sutherland? Do you really mean that?' Maudie sat up, bits of hay falling from her hair, her breasts springing out full and free from the open bodice of her blouse.

Ramsay's eyes popped. For fully thirty seconds he stared at the wondrous sight before turning away to make his exit, growling as he went, 'Don't you dare question me, my girl, I always mean what I say, so just you two get out o' my shed before I throw you out – and start making plans for your future.'

Finlay and Maudie looked joyously at one another. They laughed. They kissed. Coyly Maudie tucked her breasts back into her blouse. 'Best to wait till we're married, Finlay, in that way you'll appreciate me all the more and your father will have no reason to think bad of us.'

'Oh, no!' Finlay ran a hand through his sandy red hair and flopped back in the hay. 'I can't wait, Maudie, I'm about bursting at the seams as it is. Father won't know anything about it if we do it quick.'

'No, but I will, Finlay.' Maudie stood up. 'I'd best get back now and see to supper . . .' Her dimples flashed. 'And of course, I must tell Rita and Aidan the good news.'

Finlay groaned. He fastened his trouser buttons. A realisation came to him. Maudie wasn't really as soft as butter. That was just an impression she gave. She could wind people round her little finger with just a flash of her dimples and a wiggle of her bum. She had managed do do it with Ramsay and Finlay admired her for that. In Finlay's experience no one had ever got round his father the way Maudie had – and in such a short space of time too!

Finlay did up his shirt buttons and thought about the intimate confidences Maudie had shared with him. She had more or less hinted that she had never yet lain properly with a man. His eyes gleamed. If she really meant what she said she might still be a virgin. It would be good that, to go to bed on his wedding night with a girl who was as pure as the driven snow for all her flirting and fleering and carrying on. Finlay followed Maudie out into the starlit night and linked his arm through hers. Toby came running to welcome them, arching his back and purring, weaving himself in and out of their legs as they made their way across the yard to the cosy lights shining from the windows of Vale o' Dreip.

All enmity forgotten, Maudie rushed down to Keeper's Row to

give her delighted aunt the glad tidings about the forthcoming wedding. She then made her way to No. 6 of the Row to burst in on Hannah and say breathlessly, 'We're to be sisters-in-law! Finlay and I are to be married! I wanted you to be one o' the first to know! Auntie was right, I had to spread my wings and make a life for myself. And it's going to be wonderful, I just know we'll all be one big happy family.'

Hannah was taken aback to say the least and was unable to utter one single comment in those first few startled moments. Maudie however had enough to say for both of them. She was in a complete and utter daze of happiness and Hannah took her by the arm and made her sit down while she went to put the kettle on. But nothing could stop Maudie's excited flow of chatter, not even the large mug of tea and the plateful of freshly baked ginger snaps that Hannah set down at her elbow.

'Oh, I'm that looking forward to meeting my future brother-in-law,' Maudie went on, gazing at the biscuits without really seeing them. 'If he's anything like Finlay he'll be all right and it would be lovely if we could have the wedding while he's home on leave.'

Hannah didn't say anything to this. Rob and his brother hadn't always seen eye to eye and Hannah wasn't all that keen on her brother-in-law either. But perhaps he would change now that Maudie had come into his life; she certainly seemed to have captivated everyone at Vale o' Dreip and even Ramsay, that paragon of virtue, appeared to have accepted her into the bosom of the family without question . . . except . . . A thought struck Hannah.

'Where will you get married, Maudie? Ramsay's very keen on the Free Church, he won't like it if you and his son take your wedding vows elsewhere.'

'Ach, no one need bother their heads about that.' Maudie had calmed down enough to cram a whole ginger snap into her mouth, washed down with a noisy gulp of tea. 'We aren't being married in a church at all. Mammy suggested holding it in Vale o' Dreip's very own kitchen, attended by the same minister who presided over her and Daddy's wedding twenty years ago. Ramsay didn't like it when I told him that but it's too late now for him to do anything about it and everyone else is as pleased as punch. Oh, it will be a grand day, all my family there, my brothers and sisters, aunties, uncles, and cousins, my granny on my father's side who brews her own beer and wears funny big hats and bosses everyone about all the time.'

The implications of having Maudie in the family struck Hannah with force. Her list of relatives seemed endless, and the granny with the big hats and the beer didn't bear thinking about. 'When is all this going to be, Maudie?' she heard herself asking faintly.

'Well, Finlay and me can't keep our hands off one another,' Maudie imparted with perfect candour, 'so it will be as soon as possible, March probably, when the daffodils are out and the wee lambs are gambolling and skipping in the fields.'

'March is going to be a busy month then. I'm due to have a baby in March.'

'I know, Rita told me, everything is going to happen at once. Dolly Law and Mollie Gillespie are having their babies then as well and Connie is going to marry John from Bougan Villa.'

Maudie had begun to run out of steam. She sat back in her chair and fanned her face and then she leaned forward again to put her hand over Hannah's.

'I hope you'll let Vaila be a flower girl at my wedding. She's such a bonny wee lass and a credit to you. Finlay told me all about Morna and how you took Vaila in after her mother died. It was a lovely thing to do and I think you're a very good person, Hannah Sutherland. I'm proud that soon I'll be a part o' your family and I just know we're going to get on well together.'

Hannah was overwhelmed by this. Tears spurted to her eyes.

'Och, there.' Maudie put her arms round her future sister-in-law and gave her a big comforting hug. Hannah had never known anyone like Maudie before, and though her head was spinning by the time that young lady took her leave, she also felt an odd sensation of contentment washing over her.

She sat back and thought about it. Could it be that Maudie saw something in people that more sophisticated mortals didn't? Could it be that she was really some sort of superhuman who had come to Kinvara in the guise of an artless and innocent young girl? One who made good things happen to those around her. A saint, perhaps – or an angel . . .

Hannah checked herself and laughed. She had been reading far too many books – and Rob was coming home tomorrow! She still had the house to clean and clothes to iron for the children, her hair to wash and her white blouse to starch, because pregnant or no she had to try and make herself look as presentable as she could – in the circumstances.

The men had come off the relief boat and were on their way homewards, Moggy John MacPhee, Big Jock Morgan, and Robert Sutherland. All of them were jubilant as they made their way to Keeper's Row, each of them had reason to be glad that their leave from lighthouse duty had arrived at last.

Moggy John went happily into No. 3 to be smothered in affection by his wife and six children; 'Morgan the Magnificent' roared with delight when he entered No. 5 and saw a tiny girl dressed in white waiting for him under the Christmas tree, his first introduction to golden-haired little Bonny Barr who clapped her hands when she saw him and shyly spoke his name.

Rob Sutherland paused for a moment outside the door of No. 6 before turning the handle to go inside. He was immediately surrounded by Breck and the children, all clamouring for his attention, all trying to speak at once. When the fuss was over with he lifted his dark head and gazed at his wife. Hannah had never looked better, her hair was shining, her skin glowing, her hazel eyes sparkling and filled with all the love and longing she had held for him these past long uncertain months.

'Hannah.' He spoke her name softly. 'You look wonderful.'

She moved into the warm waiting circle of his arms and everything that was sweet and dear and wonderful belonged to her in those first precious moments of their reunion.

Christmas Day brought Harriet Houston and Charlie Campbell to No. 6 of the Row, holding their heads up well in the midst of all the speculation and talk about their living together at Butterburn Croft, however innocuously. Harriet had received Hannah's invitation with some reservations. That it included Charlie made her wonder at her daughter's motives. Would there be an atmosphere, she wondered? A modicum of disapproval, perhaps? Hints and innuendoes that echoed the general mood of the neighbourhood at large?

But Hannah displayed none of these disagreeable tendencies. She was in fact in jubilant and festive mood and seemed more concerned that Johnny Lonely hadn't turned up at the house by twelve of the clock and hoped that he hadn't taken cold feet at the last moment.

'Go and see if he's coming, Vaila,' she instructed her stepdaughter when another half-hour had ticked by with no sign of the hermit. 'He's maybe out there, too shy to come in. If you see him just grab him by the hand and make him follow you.'

Andy went with Vaila and sure enough there was Johnny, hanging about in the endrigs of the cornfield, cold and miserable-looking with his hands dug deep in his pockets and his hat pulled over his ears.

'Johnny!' Vaila ran forward, 'You've to take my hand. Hannah was worried about you but I'll tell her you were just coming along.'

It was a wise remark for such a small girl. Johnny grimaced. He braced himself. Andy was waiting to take his other hand. With a child propping him up on either side he was persuaded indoors, looking as if he was being led to the hangman's rope. The blessed warmth of a cosy hearth awaited him. Charlie was there to make him feel at ease with his talk of the sea and ships. Rob soon joined in. The womenfolk were too busy at the stove to be bothered with much else. Breck's head was on his knee watching his every move. The children sat at his feet and listened in fascination as he chatted.

He relaxed. He ate a hearty dinner and joined in the festive toasts. The presents were handed out, nobody was missed, the children laughed and exclaimed and covered Johnny's embarrassment when he received the woollen gloves and scarf that Hannah had asked Cousin Kathy to make for him.

Afterwards, everyone danced to the strains of music coming from the gramophone that Rob had given Hannah for her Christmas present. Andy and Vaila jigged round the room; Harriet danced with Charlie and tried not to look into his eyes; Rob waltzed with Hannah and smiled when her 'bump' made contact with his belly. 'Don't worry, it will take more than that to keep us apart,' he whispered into her ear and she giggled and looked like the Hannah he had known when first he had met her.

Johnny Lonely had positioned himself near the gramophone as 'winder upper' but the womenfolk were having none of that. Harriet and Hannah danced with him in turn, then Vaila, her young face serious as she concentrated on the movements of his feet which were surprisingly light and rhythmic for a man who spent so much of his time scrambling over the rocks on the seashore.

Afterwards it was just Rob and Hannah, sitting together by the fire, the clocks ticking, Breck snoring, the holly boughs shining in the lamplight, everything peaceful and quiet around them.

'It's been a perfect day.' Hannah lay back against her husband, 'You here, Mother strangely quiet and not bossing anyone around, the children so pleased with everything, Johnny, for once, not looking as if he would like to up and run away. I can't remember when I've been so happy.'

'There will be lots of days like this, Hannah.' He nuzzled her ear as he spoke. 'And every one of them will be special as long as we go on caring for one another as we do now.'

KINVARA

January to March 1927

Chapter Twenty-Six

Soon after the New Year a letter arrived at the Morgans' house requesting that Bonny be returned to the orphanage as her mother was now fit enough to look after her child and wanted to take her home as soon as possible.

'No!' Janet's hand shook as she stared at the message. 'I won't do it! Bonny belongs here now! She's as much mine as anybody's and she wouldn't be happy going back to a home and a family that she's more or less forgotten.'

'Janet, oh, Janet,' Jock said huskily as he put his arms round his wife and held her close. 'I was afraid o' this, all along I was afraid and hoped it would never happen. But Bonny's place isn't really here with us and never has been and I think in your heart you know that for yourself. Giving her back won't be easy, God knows we love the bairn and would do anything to keep her, but it isn't meant to be, Janet, it just isn't meant to be.'

She clung to him and cried and when Joss came in from school and heard the news he cried too for the 'wee sister' he had protected and cherished and who was soon to be taken away from him as if she had never been.

For Bonny's sake the family put on a brave front. Janet cried herself to sleep at night but forced herself to be bright and cheerful in the daytime so that little Bonny Barr never knew of the heartache that surrounded her as she toddled about outside in the sunshine and played happily with Andy in his cart and had donkey rides on Joss's strong young shoulders.

Janet had tried to explain to her that she was soon going back to her own 'mamma' and the little girl had nodded and repeated the name before wrapping her arms round Janet to coorie into her neck and say, 'Stay here with Janet,' in a small bleak voice that made Janet's heartache all the harder to bear.

On the appointed day she got the child ready for the trip to the orphanage, wrapping her in the warm coat she had bought for her along with the bright woollen mittens and scarf that Cousin Kathy had knitted.

Jock brought the trap round to the front door. Bonny looked at it; she gazed back at the house; at the last minute she seemed to grasp what was happening. Tears spilled from her eyes, her lip trembled, she held on to Janet's hand and sobbed, 'No, don't want to go, stay here with you and Joss and Jock.'

Her voice was small and frightened and Janet's courage almost failed her. Her breath caught in her throat, ragged and sore. She bit her lip to keep back the tears. Bonny was watching her, gazing beseechingly up into her face. Such a tiny girl, her fair ringlets falling about her pixie-like face, that little rosebud of a mouth – and those eyes – so blue and big and trusting . . .

Jock came to the rescue then, lifting Bonny up in his strong arms, placing her in the trap, sitting beside her and talking to her in a quiet reassuring voice. Janet composed herself. She climbed up beside the little girl; Jock wrapped a rug round their knees and took up the reins.

The people of Keeper's Row came out to watch and wave as the trap went by, sad for Janet, sad too for the child who had touched all of them with her determination of spirit and her eagerness to enjoy life in spite of all the odds. Joss wasn't there. He had opted to go to school as usual, simply because he couldn't bear to say goodbye to the little being he had come to regard as the baby sister he'd never had nor ever would.

* * *

Bonny's mother was a thin anxious-looking young woman with haunted eyes and a nervous smile. When she saw her daughter she fell down on her knees and held out her arms and Janet let Bonny go, watching wordlessly as the child's fragile legs took her across the room to her mother.

'Bonny.' The young woman's eyes lit up as her daughter approached but at the last minute Bonny shook her head vehemently and went back to Janet to cling to her skirts and hide her face in the familiar folds.

'Bonny.' Janet knelt down beside the little girl. 'It's time for you to go home now. Your mother is here and she loves you very much and is really happy to see you again.' She took the child by the hand and led her back across the room. 'Perhaps if I could visit now and then it might help.' Janet tried to keep her voice steady as she made the suggestion but the other woman shook her head. 'No, it's better to say goodbye now, it's going to take her long enough to settle down with her own family as it is.' Seizing Janet's hand she squeezed it and said sincerely, 'Thank you for everything you've done for my daughter. I know how attached you've become to her and how hard it must be for you to part with her but I've missed my wee lass and always knew I'd come back for her some day.'

Janet nodded. Briefly she laid her hand on Bonny's head and then she turned and walked away, out of the door, knowing Bonny's eyes were on her, watching her go, wondering why she was being left like this and never knowing how Janet's heart was aching with the hurt of the parting and that she could hardly see where she was going for tears.

'Oh, Jock,' she sobbed when she drew close to him. 'How am I going to be able to bear this? In my heart I think always knew that she was going to be taken from me but not like this, never to see her again, cut off from her as if she had never been in my life.'

'She'll always be in your heart, lass,' Jock said, near to tears himself, 'but there are plenty more like Bonny in the orphanage, just waiting for someone like you to come along and give them a good home.'

'No, there will never be another Bonny. She was different and she was special and I'll never get over losing her like this.'

She climbed into the seat beside him and put her head on his shoulder and they drove home to a house that was empty and silent without the presence of the child who had brought such joy into it. Janet stood in the lobby and found herself listening and all at once she seemed to be surrounded by echoes – a small voice calling her name – unsteady little feet pattering their way through the rooms – a song that came to her from a long long distance away . . .

Oh little Bonny Barr went flying far.
Yes, little Bonny Barr went flying far.
Well she landed on a star
Because she had travelled far.
Yes, Bonny Barr had landed on a star.

Janet put her face into her hands and cried, for herself, for Bonny, for the sadness of life, and she prayed that the child would one day fly as high as she could go and perhaps discover the star that she so richly deserved to find.

Some weeks later another child came to No. 5 Keeper's Row, a little boy this time, unable to speak, walk, or smile. The Morgans soon changed all that. Before long the house was ringing with the sounds of busy feet and happy laughter and there was never a moment to sit still and mope. But none of the family ever forgot Bonny; they would always remember a tiny eager girl with big blue eyes and golden curls and hoped that she would remember them too and come back someday to visit them in Kinvara.

Hannah had been a great support to Janet during all her upsets and the two young women had become firm friends as well as good neighbours. But as the weeks progressed Hannah had more than enough of her own affairs to occupy her. The arrangement between Charlie and Harriet had not worked. They had become more and more attracted to one another and soon realised they could not go on living together under the same roof on the pretence of a mere platonic partnership.

Marriage was the only possible solution to their feelings and this intention Harriet conveyed to her daughter at the first available opportunity. A stunned silence followed her announcement. 'But, Mother,' Hannah eventually gasped. 'You can't really be serious. It isn't even a year since Father died and he would surely turn in his grave altogether if he found out about this.'

At this Harriet shouted with laughter. 'Perhaps he has done so already, Hannah, he was never a body to see the romantic side o' anything and I don't mean that disrespectfully. Oh, come on, lassie, give me a chance, why should I make myself miserable just for the sake of appearances? Charlie and I have found something in each other that your father and I never had in all the years we were together. Happiness is what counts in this life, Hannah, and I intend to grab mine with both hands in spite of what people might have to say about me.'

A week later she and Charlie went to Inverness to be married in the registrar's office, attended by Hannah and Rob, Janet and Jock, and a few other friends and acquaintances.

The tongues of Kinvara wagged. Jessie MacDonald lamented Charlie's lost freedom like the passing of a dearly beloved, weeping and wailing and making verbal mincemeat of Harriet, accusing her of every evil under the sun, saying that she was a temptress and a hussy and that she had deliberately gone to live at Butterburn Croft with the sole intention of 'hooking a poor weak man like Charlie who didn't know any better'.

'Well, at least he's made an honest woman of her,' Mattie

pointed out with a certain amount of gleeful enjoyment. 'You said yourself they were living in sin so what better way to remedy that than a wedding ring?'

'Honest! She's a thief! She stole Charlie from under my nose and I will never get over that fact as long as I live.'

'He was never yours for her to steal,' Effie pointed out reasonably. 'Charlie was never the sort o' man to give himself wholly to anybody and Harriet must be some woman for him to have lost his head the way he did. She has proved that all things are possible where men are concerned and should get a medal for that fact alone.'

'Ay, and I know where I'd like to pin it!' Jessie cried mournfully and was not at all pleased when the others hooted with laughter and told her she should be glad she had escaped a Campbell's clutches after all the evil deeds the clan had committed 'way back in the dour dark mists of time'.

Charlie only smiled to himself when snippets of all this filtered to his ears. He felt no regrets for what he had done. Harriet was his kind of woman, strong, intelligent, able to talk to him on a level footing, domineering in some respects but soon withdrawing her horns when she saw that he was having none of that and was very much a man with a mind of his own.

In many respects their relationship went on as before. She was quite amenable to him going off on his fishing trips since she was a woman who had seldom wearied of her own company and was never happier than when she was mucking about the croft, feeding and tending to the animals. But there was one big difference in both their lives now; he no longer returned to a cold house and an empty bed, no more did she lie awake visualising a future bereft of human companionship with nothing to look forward to except more lonely days and nights.

Charlie was always there on her horizons. When he went away she knew he would come back and that they would care for one another all the more for having been separated. All in all the new arrangement suited them both admirably and Jessie

MacDonald could have talked herself blue in the face for all the impression it made on one very contented member of the Clan Campbell.

Chapter Twenty-Seven

The new babies were arriving thick and fast in Kinvara. Mollie Gillespie gave birth to another beautiful girl who, much to the young mother's relief, bore a strong resemblance to Donnie, 'right down to the quiff and the hiccup' as Effie so neatly put it, thinking to herself that anything would have been acceptable to Mollie as long as it didn't have black hair and a beard.

After a rough ride in Shug's cart over a stony cliff road to 'get the wee bugger moving' Dolly delivered a small but healthy boy with 'lungs on it like an elephant' and an appetite like a navvy only at its tender age it drank milk instead of ale.

Hannah's time was also fast approaching. Doctor MacAlistair had assured her that Andy's condition wasn't hereditary and that there was no reason in the world why she shouldn't have a normal healthy child. Even so, she counted the days with a mixture of anticipation and dread and was most alarmed when her new daughter arrived on the thirteenth of March, taking it as a bad omen for her baby's future.

'Och, don't be silly, Hannah,' Effie scoffed with a laugh. 'Just look at your daughter, she's the most perfect little girl anyone could wish for and no one could ask for a better birth sign. On my wall I have a star chart with the dates of all the babies I've ever delivered and it's uncanny how accurate it is.'

Absently she patted the head of her mongrel dog Runt

who went everywhere with her and had attended as many confinements as Effie herself. 'Take my Queen Victoria now, she's a typical Gemini, sweet-natured one minute, cantankerous the next, her split personality coming through as sure as fate.'

Hannah, dazed by the trauma of birth, was in no fit state to fully appreciate Effie's philosophies. 'Queen Victoria? Your pig? With a birth sign?'

'Oh, ay, pigs are very like us, you know, and have as much right to a place in the astrological system as any o' us.'

'I'll take your word for it,' Hannah said faintly, feeling most relieved when Effie took herself off to 'make a nice hot cuppy' thus leaving the way clear for Rob to enter the room and view the new arrival. The baby was lying on Hannah's breast, a tiny mite with flaxen silky hair and dark blue eyes and little pink fists that came out from the woollen depths of her shawl to box energetically at the air.

Rob fell down beside his wife and new daughter. He kissed them both, he laughed, his eyes were misty. It was the moment he had so anxiously awaited but now that it was here he could find nothing to say.

Hannah laid her hand on his dark head. 'Shh,' she said gently, 'everything is fine, we have a beautiful daughter. I thought her birth date was unlucky but Effie said no, she is destined to take her place among the stars alongside Effie's pig and other such important personages.'

They both shouted with laughter, relieved that all the tensions were over with and they could relax now for a while. Hannah had already decided on the baby's name. 'I'd like to call her Essie,' she told her husband, 'I saw it on a gravestone once and thought how nice it would be for a girl.'

'A gravestone!' His laughter sprang afresh. 'You really are the limit, Hannah, but all right, Essie it is, and if I could have a choice for a second name I'd like Hannah, Essie Hannah Sutherland, a grand name for a fine wee lass.'

Vaila and Andy came in to see their tiny sister. They were each allowed to hold her for a few moments and in the excitement Andy quickly forgot his disappointment at not having a brother while Vaila was enchanted just to have a baby of any sort in the family and could hardly tear her gaze away from it.

'We're five o' a family now,' Hannah said in some wonderment. 'How we've grown these past few years, first Andy, then Vaila, and now Essie.'

'No regrets?' He looked at her and she saw a hundred unspoken questions in the dark depths of his eyes.

'No regrets,' she said decidedly as she gathered Andy and Vaila in closer to her and at the last minute Breck who wasn't going to be left out in the cold, new baby or no.

When Rob had a minute to himself he went outside and gazed towards Oir na Cuan lying still and empty at the edge of the ocean. He remembered how it had once been when Morna was alive, filled with light and love, happiness and laughter, sadness too in the knowing that they could never fully belong to one another. Yet they had shared so much, had known so many wonderful experiences – had talked and talked as if there were no tomorrows.

The hurt in him was still raw and deep and he knew he would never fully relinquish her sweet memory. To ease his pain he often spoke to her and now he whispered. 'Another babe has been born, Morna, a wee sister for Vaila, they will be company for each other as they grow up and Hannah is really pleased to have had a daughter. Vaila still talks about you. She will never forget her mother, but Hannah has been truly good to her and treats her like her own child. Life goes on, Morna, but sometimes I'm so lonely without you I feel as if only half of me walks and talks and lives . . .'

He couldn't go on. He took one long last lingering look at Oir na Cuan while the cool breezes washed over him and the sigh of empty places was all around him, then he retraced his steps homewards to go back inside and softly close the door.

* * *

Ramsay came down to No. 6 of the Row to see his new granddaughter. He held her in his arms and studied her in detail and only when his scrutiny had been satisfied did he proclaim his delight at her perfection of form. With him he brought a bottle of best malt whisky to 'wet the baby's head', making it plain to everyone that he was not a drinking man as a rule but that there were some occasions when even he had to bend to tradition and this was one of them.

The glasses chinked, the toasts were made; over Ramsay's head Hannah caught Rob's eye and she knew that he was thinking the same things as her but was going along with everything for the sake of peace.

'At last I've done something to please him,' Hannah told her husband when her father-in-law had departed. 'When Andy was born he didn't see fit to come near the place. Now there's Essie, a child worthy of the Sutherland name and Andy might well not exist for all he cares.'

Rob put his arm round her and gave her a little shake. 'That's Father all over, afraid for his reputation, pig-headed and narrow. Don't let it spoil what we have. Bitterness never did anyone any good, we've had enough o' that in the past and must count every one o' the blessings that belong to us now.'

She nodded. 'You're right, Rob, I know you're right. Deep down I'll never really forgive him for shutting me out but it isn't so important now, in the end he's the one who deserves the pity – so – to hell with the rules and up with tradition!'

She held aloft the glass that she had barely touched in her father-in-law's restrictive presence. Rob poured himself another from the bottle that his father had left and sat himself down beside his wife to enjoy with her a few quiet moments as Essie Hannah Sutherland slept the sleep of the untroubled newborn.

* * *

'I want you to make my cake, Auntie,' Maudie said when she was in visiting one day.

'Me?' Bette shook her head. 'No, I could never do that. Why don't you make it yourself?'

'It wouldn't be right, Auntie, besides . . .' A sprite of mischief danced in her eyes. 'I want to give you a chance to prove yourself.'

'You cheeky . . .' Bette began then halted. 'All right,' she promised rashly. 'One way or another I *will* prove myself to you and let you see you aren't the only one in this family wi' brains. You shall have your cake or my name isn't Elizabeth Ann MacGill.'

The day of Maudie's marriage to Finlay dawned sunny and bright and really quite warm for the time of year. Maudie's relatives arrived in force to storm the portals of Vale o' Dreip and fill the rooms with their chatter and excitement as they prepared themselves for the wedding.

Maudie's reunion with her mammy and daddy and brothers and sisters had been tearful as well as noisy, as had been Bette's with her sisters. Mungo had been granted special leave for the occasion and the house was bulging at the seams as everyone chattered and laughed and chinked their glasses as they partook of the pre-wedding drams.

Ramsay had no say in anything and was forced to take a back seat while Rita did her best to cope and was thankful that Hannah had arrived to help get everything into some semblance of order.

But at last all was ready; a respectful silence reigned as the visiting minister took his place and gave a discreet little cough to signal that the ceremony was about to begin. Maudie was radiant that day with her rosy cheeks and her dimples and wearing a pale green suit that showed off her shining chestnut hair to advantage. She was also somehow slimmer, a fact which did not totally owe itself to the 'wee starvation diet' she had recently undergone.

Tillie and Tottie Murchison had been only too eager to supply the figure-enhancing corsets for both Bette and her niece, stressing the difference a good uplift would make to their appearance and that their 'wee secret' would never go any further than the draper's shop since they prided themselves on being 'the souls of discretion' on matters that were private and personal.

The minister began to speak. Maudie forgot her corsets, she forgot everything in the joy of the moment. She was delighted to take Finlay as her lawful wedded husband, while he in his turn received her gladly into his keeping and blessed the day she had rumbled up to Vale o' Dreip in Mungo's trap.

After that the bride and groom placed themselves at the table and the cake was cut. Maudie couldn't resist the first taste. Beamingly she turned to her aunt. The praises showered upon Bette's somewhat red ears. Behind her back she crossed her fingers and gave silent thanks to the part that Wee Fay had played in making a cake that was perfection in every way.

Wee Fay had been sworn to secrecy, and Bette knew that she would never break her promise. Even so, now that the moment of truth had arrived, Bette squirmed a bit and grew hot under the collar and felt as if she was going to burst out of her stays at any moment. And these feelings remained with her for many a long day to come – whenever she thought about Maudie and the cake and remembered how that young lady had winked at her over her plate when she thought no one else was watching.

When the more formal proceedings were over with everybody swarmed outside. The flower girls forgot to be sedate and ran about in the sunshine; the aunts and the uncles, the brothers, the sisters and the cousins, made up for lost time and talked as if they would never stop; the granny who drank whisky as well as beer lost her big hat to a gust of wind and everybody pointed as it went sailing merrily away till it was just a dot in the distance.

'Och, well.' Its erstwhile owner shrugged her shoulders

and looked philosophical. 'I never liked it much anyway and there are plenty more where that came from.'

In the midst of all her excitement Maudie didn't forget Johnny Lonely, a man who was supposed to be dour and unapproachable yet had been so unstinting with his patience when he had spoken to her about the glories of the countryside, making her feel less worried by all the empty space around her and more appreciative instead. For Johnny she cut an extra-large piece of cake and entrusted it into the care of Dougie the Post, who was Mungo's cousin twice removed and who had been quick to remind Mungo of that status when the wedding invitations were being issued.

A dance was held in the barn that evening. Everyone made merry, including Ramsay himself who mingled agreeably with his new relatives through marriage and even managed to summon up enough goodwill to speak affably to the visiting minister who had travelled far and was very much looking forward to a stay at the Manse with the Reverend Thomas MacIntosh and his good wife, Kerry.

In the midst of the celebrations, Maudie and Finlay slipped away to spend a honeymoon on the isle of Mull where the Sutherlands had blood connections.

Bette shed a tear or two as she watched then going off. Who would have thought it? Her niece, marrying a Sutherland? One of the best families in the district with plenty of means to their name. Maudie would live with her new husband in one of the estate houses and she would never want for anything. Most importantly of all she had love. Finlay had his faults to be sure but he wasn't a bad lad when all was said and done and Maudie seemed to have him well and truly under her thumb – as was the right and proper place for any man to be . . .

Her peaceful musings didn't last long. The trap had been hung with tin cans and old boots and made a terrible racket as it clattered away down the stony track. In seconds a crowd gathered, cheering, laughing, shouting out good wishes, ribbons and confetti invaded the air, Maudie's hand came up, then Finlay's. That was the last anyone saw of them for two whole weeks, just enough time for Vale o' Dreip to return to a semblance of normality and for Ramsay to sit back and try to figure out just how much the wedding had cost him and how a guileless girl like Maudie had managed to wreak such changes in all of their lives in the first place.

Connie's marriage to John was a sober affair compared to Maudie's but the preparations leading up to it had been no less busy. Granny Margaret and Prudence Taylor-Young had become reasonably close to each other in their mutual quest to give their respective offspring a good start in married life.

The restoration of Bougan Villa had been their main concern and Harry Hutchinson, the builder, had worked his fingers to the bone to get everything ready on schedule, no easy task with so many women ordering him about and sometimes never a cup of tea to wet his whistle when the dust from the rotting rafters got into his lungs.

But somehow he completed the job in time for the wedding and Prudence was so pleased with him she gave him a bottle of whisky by way of thanks and told him he was a big improvement on his father before him who hadn't known a slate from a brick.

Granny Margaret snorted at this and muttered about the bad job he had made of *her* roof and how it was pure daylight robbery actually to charge people for doing what he did. Harry trundled away in his cart. He sought a quiet spot on the shore. There he sniffed in the clear air. He supped his whisky and went to sleep only to dream that Granny Margaret and Prudence were chasing him with giant chisels and enormous rusty nails, and even in his dream Harry knew he could never escape the rigours and hardships of life as a builder as long as people like Granny Margaret and Prudence Taylor-Young existed.

If Harry could have seen Connie going up the aisle to meet

her John he would have said it had all been worthwhile. She made a beautiful bride in her white satin dress with flowers braided into her red hair and her green eyes sparkling. The three Simpson sisters each had husbands now but Connie didn't forget to spare a word for Bram MacIntosh as she was leaving the church. 'I'm sorry I couldn't wait for you, Bram,' she told him with a twinkle. 'But it was lovely of you to ask me anyway.'

Bram grinned. 'Don't worry, I'll get somebody else. I told you all the girls at school were after me and I suppose I'll have to marry one of them someday – if I'm not too busy that is.'

When all the fuss was over, Kerry strolled with her husband in the Manse gardens. 'I have a confession to make,' the minister said suddenly and rather sheepishly. 'You know that vase Mother gave us as a wedding gift – the one on the hall table? Well, I knocked it over with my sleeve when I was getting ready for today's ceremony.'

Kerry looked at him sharply. 'Oh, Thomas, you never did! Can it be mended?'

'No, it smashed into a thousand pieces, I had to put it in the dustbin.'

Kerry's eyes positively sparkled. Linking her arm through his she said soothingly, 'Oh, well, accidents can happen to the best of us – and to be truthful, I never liked it anyway.'

'Nor me.' His voice was light with relief. 'I always thought how ugly it was and how self-conscious it looked sitting on that table in the hall.' A frown creased his brow. 'Do you think it will bring bad luck? Breaking it like that?'

Laughter spurted from her lips. 'I shouldn't think so, look what it did for Connie.'

'What?'

'Oh, nothing. At least, I'll tell you about it someday – meanwhile let's just enjoy this respite from all the hustle and bustle and hope Bram and the others aren't getting up to any mischief behind our backs.'

He smiled into her eyes. Together they walked arm in arm in the sunshine while all around them the daffodils were bursting into bloom and the birds were singing in the bright and beautiful land that was Kinvara in springtime.